AMAZING
FAITH

Fiction

Three Day Pass
Show Me the Way
The Bed She Made
Phoenix Island
The Banker
Will the Real Toulouse-Lautrec
    Please Stand Up?
Overdrive
The Family
New Sound
A Change in the Wind
The American
Number One
The Coast of Fear
The Swiss Account
Trocadero
The Brave and the Free
Blood and Dreams
Gameplan
Embassy

Nonfiction

The Swiss Bank Connection
The Mob: The Story of
    Organized Crime in America
Dog Day Afternoon
Hide in Plain Sight

Leslie Waller

AMAZING FAITH

McGraw-Hill Book Company

New York St. Louis San Francisco Bogotá Hamburg Madrid
Mexico Milan Montreal Panama Paris São Paulo Tokyo Toronto

1 2 3 4 5 6 7 8 9 D O C D O C 8 9 2 1 0 9 8

ISBN 0-07-067932-0

LIBRARY OF CONGRESS CATALOGING-IN-PUBLICATION DATA

Waller, Leslie, 1923–
  Amazing Faith : a novel by Leslie Waller
    p.   cm.
  ISBN 0–07–067932–0
  I. Title.
  PS3545.A565A82 1988
813′.54—dc19   87–31045

Book design by Kathryn Parise

PART
ONE

· 1 ·

In the half-light just before dawn, the French coast to the west—Menton, Monaco, Beaulieu—still slumbered in darkness. Here in San Sebastian, this tiny principality nestling within Italy, the first light gave everything an unreal look, mist-bound, nacreous, slimy.

The fishermen, returned from a night's trawling, looked up as the tall ship ghosted into the harbor. She was a grave, somber vessel, painted black, and some of the men recognized her as the *Finisterre*, chartered out of Nice. On this visit she flew a U.S. ensign.

Indigo sails hung slack from her two masts, wrinkled as bats' wings in the airless dawn. The black ship moved with stealth, or so it seemed to the fishermen. Odd, the effect she had.

The absence of human life could be explained. Passengers would still be asleep this early. The crew could be, oh, anywhere. The sinister darkness of the hull? Well, after all, not every craft can be sparkling white. But those indigo sails. What had been the idea, a sort of mock-fashionable blue denim?

One fisherman shook his head cynically. The follies of the rich failed to interest him. But his partner, an older man, hastily crossed himself. A raven, he thought, the omen of evil.

"Gesù, Giuseppe e Maria, proteggetemi," he breathed.

But then the forward motion of the *Finisterre* ceased. As the ship stood motionless its illusion of evil began to fade. Crewmen appeared, sprang ashore and began warping inch-thick hawsers around bollards. The reluctant sun rose an extra millimeter and glistened brightly in the ketch's stainless-steel rigging and spars, her extensive array of Monel-Metal radio antennas.

Instead of a sepulchral wraith out of the sea's black night, a deluxe sailer of forty feet, Bermuda rig, had produced a silent, no-nonsense landing among the dozens of other luxury ships. Nothing more. Yet another well-heeled arrival at this tiny principality devoted equally to gambling and tax evasion.

So it appeared to the fishermen, all but the older one who had crossed himself. He had not shaken off that sense of dread, that feeling that the black ship brought with her death and chaos...chaos and death.

But, of course, fishermen were always so superstitious.

· 2 ·

In the wooded hills above the harbor and town, dawn can be cold even in summer. These heights belong to Italy. At first they loom chillingly while the sky fires up bright flarepaths of orange and cerise to the east over Genoa. A cold, seeking wind, the *tramontana*, blows south across the Alps into Italy and the small, independent principality at the water's edge called San Sebastian.

By 6 A.M., however, about the same time as the *Finisterre* had moored, at least one of San Sebastian's ruling family was already awake in the cold dawn. Here, in the Italian heights, stood Prince Florian's ancestral hunting lodge. His wife, Her Serene Highness Princess Faith, had already showered and was grooming herself for another round of doing whatever it was a ruler did.

A ruler, Faith reminded herself, quoting a family joke her son had first voiced when he was six years old, makes sure everything is straight and properly measured. She smiled softly, remembering. Other than that, she thought, being up, washed and dressed at 6 A.M. wasn't any different from an early call on a Hollywood studio set.

The only difference was that, instead of acting before a camera, she would spend the day making sure everything was straight and properly measured.

She and her daughter, Paola, called Polly, often slept up here in the heat of summer. Her husband, Florian, and their son, Michele, called Mike, usually slept below in the air-conditioned palace that overlooked the harbor. But air-conditioning bothered Faith's sinuses. She preferred the piney ambience of the hunting lodge. It kept her head clear.

This morning, standing before her full-length cheval glass, she adjusted the mauve chiffon scarf around her long, elegant neck while completing her usual merciless inspection. Black patent pumps, gleaming; pale ecru stockings smooth over long calves; brilliant white linen dress cinched by a thin mauve belt around a waist almost as narrow as when she'd been Polly's age, seventeen; face made up not to look made up, as always by her own hand, never by a maid or her secretary, Jill.

She could no longer remember looking any other way, a lifetime image San Sebastian revered, yet still Hollywood's slim, leggy black-haired beauty with the trick Billy Ritz had first noticed of combining flame and ice. That smoldering look of magically banked fires ready to erupt: of course a trick, one she had been born with and had had the cleverness to maintain over the years.

She examined her waistline closely, turning this way and that. Nothing gives a trick away faster than losing its chief ingredient. But no, the magic still held.

In the early days they had wanted her to do sultry Latins, fiery gypsies. Nonsense, of course: Billy wouldn't hear of it, nor would she. Once they typed you as Carmencita your career was locked into self-parody.

No, she was what she was, fine-grained Black Irish with a spine of vanadium steel that never quite showed. It intrigued people. In a Hollywood world of stereotypes, it kept them guessing.

Faith stared at her reflection. In the same mirror she saw Polly, behind her, step into a pair of cute black patents with small Cuban heels, her first shoes that weren't flats. As a girl in Chicago, Faith had called them Mary Janes. With a high heel they'd be Ruby Keeler's dancing shoes. But Polly wouldn't be allowed high heels until next year. Faith knew that girls Polly's age had been wearing heels for years. But none of them were serene highnesses.

Jill Tremont gave Faith her bag, in which Jilly had put only two things: a folded handkerchief and a small gold-bound appointment diary. Under her arm the secretary carried a thick leather portfolio that accompanied her everywhere.

In a carrying stage voice Faith now called: *"Siamo pronti!"*

The words bounded down the echoing halls of the hunting lodge until a man called back:

"Vengo immediatemente!"

Sweating, though the day had dawned cool, the chauffeur arrived with two extremely large packages. *"Altezza,* these come with us?"

"Stai attento, Emilio," the Princess cautioned him. "They're beyond price, Waterford from my Grandmother O'Connell. Jill and Polly spent an hour last night packing them *come uova."*

She paused, aware that everyone was waiting for further direction. It was true: they all took their clues from her, not because she was their employer or their mother. It was because she was their ruler.

In her life, Faith told herself, she had had two rulers, her domineering father and her even more domineering mentor and director, Billy Ritz. Both had loved and tried to rule her. But she had escaped them both, simply by becoming a ruler in her own right.

Gazing at the faces of her daughter, of Jill, her secretary and lady-in-waiting, of Emilio the chauffeur, she realized all over again why she liked being a ruler. Why she enjoyed giving them their instructions, their cues, their chalkmarks, their moves, their camera angles, even their expressions.

On their own, so many people got it so badly wrong that they knew they needed direction. On their own, they spoke and thought so slovenly and made so many serious mistakes with their thinking and their emotions, that without guidance they were doomed.

Often the guidance turned out to be an evil domination that

doomed them even more deeply to disaster. Faith had seen it too often to relax her guard. Feckless people without goals ended up serving masters like political dictators, or organized criminals like the Mafia.

That was why, if you knew what was right for them, you ruled fairly and productively. They appreciated it and so did you. Glancing around her, she clapped her hands twice.

"Emilio, we are wasting time. Here's the plan. You take Jill and the crystal in the limo. We'll lead off in the Jag. Come on, Polly."

"*Momentino, Altezza.*" The chauffeur stood his ground. "I must precede you."

Faith glanced at Jill. "What's the problem?"

"New security regulations." Jill's voice was small, perfectly inflected, British and diffident. "It's a bore, but you and Florian must always be preceded by an escort."

"Such makework nonsense."

Faith's gray-green eyes swept the room as if testing for the odd lurking anarchist bomb-thrower, beard and all. There had never been a breath of political dissent in San Sebastian. Terrorists, even imports from Italy, were unknown here. Still, a regulation was a regulation.

"Right, Emilio. *Tu vai prima. Andiamo!*"

The procession made its way out into the cool light of dawn. Carefully Faith and her daughter stowed the wrapped crystal around Jill in the rear of the long Mercedes 600. She embraced the bundles as if they were babies. Emilio touched his cap and cautiously edged the heavy limousine forward at hearse pace.

Faith got behind the wheel of the squat, sky-blue Jaguar XKE. Sitting beside her on the front seat, Polly took her mother's bag from her. Faith started the engine, listened to its roar smooth almost to inaudibility. She lowered her front window and gestured to Polly to lower hers.

The *tramontana* whipped in and fluttered Faith's mauve scarf. Being an American, she left the window wide open. Polly, raised as a European, had only partly opened hers. She now quickly closed it against the lethal draft of air.

"Seat belt," Faith said.

They both buckled in. Faith shifted into low, tapped the accelerator and the powerful car surged up a slight rise and down a tree-lined lane toward the public road.

There the limo waited like a nervous chaperone. The lodge's gatekeeper had opened the great iron portals topped by gilded spearpoints. He and a uniformed *maresciallo* of the carabinieri from the nearby village were holding up several cars and trucks to give the limo and the Jaguar open access to the road that winds down through Italy to San Sebastian and the sea. As the Jag came into view one driver of a halted car sat up excitedly and began blowing kisses.

On the downward run Emilio kept the limo at a cortege speed. Eager to overtake, the Jag's tires squealed softly on curves. The road had been well engineered as the direct route from Turin in the north to such coast towns as San Remo and Savona. For that reason, the highway would soon clog up with traffic.

Faith dropped the Jag back a bit and held the powerful car to the inside of each curve. The air blew crisp and cool in her face. Very soon the *tramontana* would fade away and one of the hot winds of summer would smother them. The worst was the dry *scirocco*, bearing the brick-red dust of the Sahara as it roared in across the great sea like a marauding Saracen horde, covering everything with a fine film of powder.

On the curves, tires squealed, Faith downshifted for a sickening series of hairpin twists. She wondered how Jill was getting along with her precious burden of Waterford. "Yech," Polly said, holding her stomach.

"Language." It was an automatic response, copied from one Faith's father, Eamon Brennan, had used to bully, cozen and command his brood of eight children.

"What language?" Polly asked with fake innocence, something no Brennan had ever dared ask Eamon.

No Brennan but me, Faith reminded herself with a sideways glance at her daughter. She *was* a chip off the old block, even to her hair, jet black with blue highlights like an Indian squaw. Their faces were subtly alike without being identical. The camera loved Polly's face as it did her mother's.

The camera loves you, Faith thought as she drove.

8

So many photographers had said this to Faith in the old days, so many advertising men when she modeled, so many film directors. Would they still say it now, decades later?

The mirror, she reminded herself, is not the camera. She could fool herself with the mirror into thinking that at her age she still had a teenage body and her full Hollywood starburst of face power. As you move before the mirror, she thought, you consciously better your position, correct your pose. But the camera, when it is no longer your friend, never lets you get away with tricks. Was it still in love with her face? This was the one thing about Faith Brennan on which everyone used to agree.

Otherwise, she remembered, there were differences of opinion. Her fans, of course, remained loyal. The clubs still did a brisk business trading photos and other trivia. But what did it mean, after all, this business of the camera loving her?

What did it signify that a bit of glass and metal never failed to produce superb likenesses of her face? One critic—who loathed her films—had put it in words she always remembered, not because they were cruel, which they were, but because they were an insight that veiled more than they disclosed.

"It is the business of the camera to reduce three dimensions to two," he had written. "This flat likeness only hints at what in real life has depth, thrust, reflective shadow. Faith Brennan is thus the supreme camera actress: she already lacks one dimension, that of depth."

A faint, wry smile twisted Faith's mouth as she recalled one of the few really poor notices the press had given her. She had always been what the film industry wanted: a strong personality type, consistent, much like a crisp, well-salted box of popcorn. Movies were not an art form for Hollywood studios of that era, they were a product. The ingredients, including the actors, were simply parts of a product package.

The wry grin widened slightly. She had packaged herself quite deliberately as Serene Highness of San Sebastian. Still, she supposed a few critics would go on panning the performance.

But one thing it no longer lacked was depth.

She was well aware of how devastatingly accurate that critic had been who called her two-dimensional. And perhaps, she thought

9

now, he had even been right that her lack of depth had made her the perfect camera actress. What neither he, nor anyone else, realized was that by becoming a ruler, she had created the possibility of profound depth.

In Hollywood she had been ruled by well-meaning geniuses like Billy Ritz. Here she ruled herself and, over the years, pretty much everything else, too.

After more than two decades of marriage to Florian, she still saw him as well-meaning and lovable in a noble, anachronistic way. But certainly he had never ruled San Sebastian. Not before her and very little since. There had been a power vacuum. She had filled it.

In so doing, the job itself had given her the depth she had lacked. With each passing year of the two decades, she had added to herself, making the decisions people wanted made, giving the direction Florian silently begged for, providing the backbone needed.

The road took a sharp left. Faith toed the brake to avoid banging into the limo's rear bumper. She said nothing about Emilio's old-maid tactics but Polly already knew that when she was not being chaperoned her mother liked to take this morning drive at a brisker pace.

In any event, they would soon cross the lightly guarded border from Italy into San Sebastian. Along the way more people would salute them. As a bride, Faith found the custom was for men to doff their hats in a low bow while women curtsied. This both thrilled and offended the recent American arrival.

She had managed to convey this mixed reaction to her subjects, who grew confused as to how to convey their loyalty. Some improviser, having watched American films, started the fashion of waving, as to a friend. An even bolder innovator began throwing kisses. These forms of salute were now common when Princess Faith was alone. To Prince Florian, however, the men still gravely bowed and the women curtsied.

"Fish out the diary and read today's schedule, please?"

Polly opened the small gold-cornered book. "Fashion breakfast, eight-thirty A.M."

"God," her mother groaned.

"Language," Polly mimicked, deadpan.

"Go on."

"Ten A.M., new obstetrics wing, Eamon Brennan Memorial Clinic. Noon, garden party for top-seeded tennis people. Two-thirty P.M., African Violet Delegation. What's that? Four o'clock, open Waterford exhibition. Seven P.M., cocktails, dinner, Oakhurst and Faircloth. Is that a new rock group? Do I have to be there?"

"Two very nice American couples. Bankers."

"Do I?" the girl persisted.

"All right, then. Just for drinks."

The Jaguar's tires stuttered along cobbled streets as Emilio led the crawl through the medieval heart of San Sebastian. In doorways shopkeepers rattled up their metal storefronts and blew loyal kisses. The atmosphere seemed thick with love.

· 3 ·

Flanked by male escorts who might have been doctors but were, in fact, security men, Princess Faith moved briskly through the new obstetrics wing of the hospital founded by her father.

The security people eased her into a Mercedes 600, which purred quietly through narrow San Sebastian streets, preceded by a similar long, black automobile and followed by yet another.

At the far end of the harbor, where the poor fishermen kept their boats, a film company was shooting exteriors. The producer had pleaded with Faith to visit them today, before they left for interiors in Rome. She had no desire to watch anybody filming anything. But she hadn't seen the star in over a year, so...

"Marvelous to see you," he exclaimed, showing her a set of teeth as dazzling as modern dentistry could make them. He had once been considered tall, decades ago when he first became a film star. Now other male actors towered over him. Or had he shrunk, Faith kept wondering.

His aquiline face, with the same sharp-edged finish as hers, seemed no longer fresh-minted. The publicity photographer for the film kept up a steady stream of soft, *shush-clack-whirr* that a motor-ized 35-mm camera makes when being pushed fast. In a moment a TV man joined them, his on-the-shoulder video camera silently zooming in, out, in like a mantis inspecting prey. And running across the pebbled beach came the society photographer of the lo-cal newspaper who also serviced Rome and Nice papers, his Hassel-blads banging against each other.

"...looking absolutely the same, my old darling," the star was murmuring in his trademarked drawl. An instant aura of easy com-plicity surrounded them both.

Clack-whirr. The beach, casually roped off with a length of or-ange plastic tape on stilts, was now further protected by men from the Gold Berets, Faith's own security force. Altogether, her desire to see the star again was requiring the service of some fifty-odd spe-cialists, not including the photographers or film crew.

"Must say, me darlin'," the star remarked, "you do mobilize a right mob of frighteners." *Whirr-shush-clack.*

There had been a time, early in her reign as Princess, when this extra expense would have worried her. Now there was something extremely comforting in knowing, first, that one was watched over and, second, that the cost of it was totally unimportant.

Bystanders were collecting, young ones with nothing else to do, tourists with cameras and autograph books, elderly strollers. "What hurts," the star was complaining in mock chagrin, "is that none of these geeks bothered to show up till you arrived."

"Were you married once to royalty?" she asked. "One gets used to it."

"Not royalty, ducks, just a multibillionairess. "S'quite another thing." *Clack-whirr.*

"My dear, it sure as hell is," she agreed, sending them into care-fully modulated chuckles. Like most players past a certain age, they knew that excesses of joy or grief did lasting things to one's face.

"Can I get you to dinner tonight?" Faith asked. "Some boring American bankers."

"Never have I turned down such an enticing invitation with such regret," the star said soothingly. "You alone, instantly. You and Florian, superb. But you and bankers, well, um, no." *Whirr-shush.*

"Garden-party lunch with the tennis people today?" *Clack.*

His dark eyes glinted with malice. "Oh, yummers, tasty young tennis studs basted in sweat. With my rep the scandal mags'd be full of nothing else. You remember that Australian fellow with the sexy serve?"

"I do indeed. Was there anything to it?"

"Is there ever?"

"Anyway," Faith went on, "we do require our tennis studs to shower before mingling so there's really nothing in it for you, darling." She stopped and seemed lost in thought for a moment. Then, more in politeness than interest, she asked: "What's this epic you're doing?"

"Usual switch on a Doris Day besieged-virgin comedy. Only I'm the virgin." They both chuckled again, carefully. Then: "Miss the old days, luv?" *Shush-clack-whirr-shush.*

"Not anymore. I've got this place pretty much shaped up, something I could never have done with MGM, let's say."

For a long time he said nothing, his dark glance flicking back and forth over her face. "That's important to you, control. It is to me, too. This flick is the third I've produced with my own money."

They glanced around them and saw that the controlled pandemonium was threatening to break loose if he didn't go back to work. Without the need to keep quiet while cameras were rolling, the crowd had begun to hoot and giggle and shout rude remarks.

"I'm afraid my gorillas are trained to bust heads," Faith said, getting to her feet. "Before that happens..." They hugged briefly and kissed the air on either side of their clean-cut, famous faces.

What one wears for a hospital ceremony is not what one wears for a tennis lunch. In her own suite of palace rooms, the Princess stood at one window while Jill Tremont paged slowly through the contents of her sports wardrobe. In the distance, the black ship seemed to be basking like a sleeping cat. Faith watched it for a moment and then shifted her glance far beyond to the old port where the film crew was still fussing with its reflectors and floods.

As he got older, she thought, he seemed in much better control

1 3

of the faggy note. Or else, she corrected herself, we've all become so accustomed that we no longer recognize the gay grace notes. Or he was currently back in a hetero mode again.

"Simple white cotton tennis skirt," Jill asked, "with that delicious mauve cotton pullover? Boat neck? Super on you."

"I'm lunching with them, Jilly, not playing a set."

"Just trying to express your innate sportif flair."

Faith turned from the window to Concetta, her personal maid, and held her arms above her head. Deftly the maid stripped her down to bra and slip. Later, Concetta and Jill would go over them very carefully and decide if they required ironing or spotting or cleaning.

"Is there a mauve or a peach skirt in cotton?" Faith asked.

"This one. Sort of nectarine, would you say?"

Faith smiled crookedly. "Apricot?"

"And a white cotton pull," Jill finished. "Absolutely smashing!"

She held them against Faith as they stood in front of a tall mirror with side panels. "Ye-es," the Princess said at last. "It'll have to do. White pumps. Medium heel."

Jill and Concetta, working together, dressed Faith in a few moments and, on their knees, hitched the skirt half an inch sideways. "There."

The Princess swung this way and that, pivoted on one toe, staring critically at herself. She stood straighter, swung sideways, slumped seductively, stood with arms akimbo, then outspread. "Nope."

"What?"

"Too much bust. Let's reverse the colors."

Up went her arms. Off came the clothes. On went a simple white skirt and a cotton pullover of a color called Cornflower Blue. "Nope."

"Dear God, what now?" Jill muttered.

"Apricot, ye of little taste."

"That's a stunning blue."

"Not with my eyes. There. That melon one."

"You mean the Smoked Salmon?"

"I mean," Faith said in a crushing tone, "the muskmelon, cassaba, spanked-Siamese-baby one."

Both of them began giggling until Concetta, who could not truly follow the conversation, began to giggle helplessly herself. Her cousin, Valeria, who served as number two maid, was summoned to find a pair of medium-heeled pumps of matching hue in the footwear wardrobe next door.

Garbed at last, Faith did a much longer version of her model's strut, scrutinizing the swing of the skirt and the way the pullover bloused. Finally: "We're out of time, team. This'll have to do."

She sat down at her long dressing table, laden not with perfume or cosmetics but with framed snapshots. "What do you think, Jilly" Simple gold chain and matching earrings? Scarf?"

"Too hot for scarves. Simpler and thinner the better. Have you seen the way the lady champs dress? Or the wives of the men? It's stripped-for-action stuff."

"Other than my tremendous middle-aged beauty," Faith told her, "there has to be another way of telling lady tennis player from Princess. So bring me that yummy Old Rose scarf David sent."

She draped and adjusted it around but not quite in the neckline of the melon pullover, then made a face and converted it to a belt, carelessly knotted to one side. "Nope."

"You are now," Jill Tremont announced, making a production of consulting her wristwatch, "precisely eleven minutes late."

"White Hermès with that pale brick figure in it."

She knotted it as a sash and did an abbreviated tryout before the mirror. "Let's vamoose, pardner," she announced.

At four o'clock, when she opened the Waterford exhibition held in the downtown bank that sponsored the show, Princess Faith wore a pale silk blouse, a summer-weight dark blue suit and navy pumps, high-heeled, with no jewelry worth mentioning and a large bouquet of flowers clasped to her breast during most of the ceremony.

The press and TV coverage concentrated mostly on the group of glass she had loaned to the show, family gifts from a grandmother in Ireland. Because the bank was a large international one, there were rather more press than usual and a much grander selection of what are called invited guests, those who come to openings in that first half hour before the general public is allowed in.

Former kings, the royalty of failed monarchies, one very ancient Russian grand duke, plus a large group of businessmen's wives whose husbands were major commercial clients of the bank, and a contingent from the arts...these made up most of the guest list.

The arts people were painters, actors, singers, even a conductor, all of whom had shows opening, all of them requiring that added fillip of publicity that a photo with the Princess could certainly promise.

One would have thought, Faith noted, that after all these years a certain staleness would have developed about palace-linked publicity, but it hadn't happened yet.

Even twenty years on, the press and TV still gobbled up such material. She wasn't sure why, except that in a world grown ever more brutish and nasty, she and Florian managed to maintain the light, relaxed note. It didn't sell newspapers, but it certainly offered some relief from the daily ration of massacre and catastrophe.

Despite its nonserious purpose, the Waterford exhibition had been mounted with the kind of overblown gravity that a bank thinks befits it. This, together with the many people who sought a personal introduction to the Princess, turned the event into a rather formal one in which she had only Jill to channel and introduce those prominent enough to be presented.

"The Mesdames Honoria and Hermione Balfour-Fitzgibbons Smythe."

"Mr. and Mrs. Abdel Hasmanyi, Eurasian Credit Trust."

"F. Carter Spinwright III, U.S. Consul General."

"Mr. David Niven."

Shush-click-whirr-shush.

"David, I nearly wore that absolutely edible scarf you sent me. Thank you for coming to this, well, rather starchy little do."

"But I thought you knew. I, too, have an Irish grandmother."

"Did you get down to the beach to visit Himself?"

"My dear, not on your life. It's all right for a world beauty like you to pose with him. But when he and I are in the same frame you only see him."

"Her Highness the Royal Princess Muamaronia of Byblos."

"Colonel and Madame Fawzi bir Keckhmet."

"Lord Hugh Utmost and Lady Utmost."

"So pleased you could come, Lord Utmost. Is this to be considered a formal representation from the British Consulate?"

"Just keepin' an eye on the glassware, m'dear."

Laughter. *Click-whirr.*

"Dottore e Signora Attilio Fatto. La Signorina Fortunata Fatto."

"Chuck Berns."

"Baby!" Kiss. Kiss. *Click-whirr.* "Would I like ten percent of this? How ya doin, honeybunch? Still knocking 'em dead, I see."

"And without an agent, either."

"Is this possible? I ask you."

"Noble Farnsworth Poindexter, U.S. Consulate."

The tub was seven feet long and made of Carrara marble, pale white with striations of a green that matched Faith's eyes. She had wondered whether the tub had always been somewhere in the palace but found that Florian himself had picked it out just before the wedding, rejecting dozens until he found the right color.

This was to be her only moment of rest today. The bankers' dinner would begin soon with cocktails. She could be late to this because Florian had already agreed to be on time. But this gave her only an extra half hour at the most. She lifted her right foot and flexed the ankle, inspecting her toenail varnish, then the left.

Something bothered her, something left over, like the memory of an old love affair. The star on the beach? She had appeared in films with him and yet he still had the power to make her uneasy, while Niven, with whom she had never worked, remained a true pal.

She soaped her elbows a second time, using the rougher loofah to keep them smooth. Now she remembered. It was her own insight into the way the star could play straight or gay just as he could play jewel thief or banker. The ultimate in insincerity, but so convincing. Whereas, having made her decision more than twenty years ago, she had played one and only one role ever after.

Well, most people did, didn't they? It was, after all, only actors who had the chance to switch character the way she had changed sports clothes before lunch.

She sat up straight. The perfumed bathwater held a faint floral note, pale and hesitant, like baby's breath. She soaped her breasts slowly, using the rough loofah again because it stimulated her nipples deliciously. It was too bad Florian was, even now, joining the bankers. Otherwise she would have gotten him to loofah her properly.

She dropped the sponge and lay back in the water until only her face and hair remained visible. It had been the right decision, two decades back. No doubt about it. She had chosen precisely the right role.

The make-believe ones were fun and games. This one, being real, was more suited to a long run. Not a film, nor a play, but a life. Moreover, responsibility and, with it, power. How many acting roles gave you that?

Come to think of it, how many lives gave you that? She was lucky. She stared at the ceiling twenty feet over her head, the intricate mosaic work, sixteenth century, surely. Cosmati brothers. She'd seen their work in cathedrals.

She sighed deeply and tried to feel one last moment of bliss. Her body, only slightly distorted by the water, stretched out before her, slim and sensuous. A faint fluff of bath foam had caught on her dark mound of pubic hair, like a sailboat anchoring on a wooded islet.

Then it bleached out in a white flare of memory. Flash! A scene of naked flesh came back to her. Long legs, wound in sinuous ecstasy. Two naked bodies clutching foully at each other in torment and stench.

She stumbled out of the tub and wound a great towel around her, not waiting for Concetta to help her dry herself. She covered her entire body from toes to neck, hiding her nakedness, keeping her glance from meeting her reflection in any of the great mirrored walls.

Desperately, she stood with her back to the mirrors and stared blankly at the closed door. If only she didn't have to open it to the ugly real world.

This was the trouble with roles you played for life, she thought. You are reprieved from them only by death.

· 4 ·

It was the height of the summer social season. Private parties filled deluxe hotels and yachts with a pleasant sensual vibration. In villas and high-rise duplex apartments, elegant people gathered to look each other over. Scandal reporters lost sleep. There was a party of the week, a party of the day and often, it seemed, a party of the hour at which one had to be seen. And if that were not enough, the principality itself scheduled social events the invitations to which were considered beyond price.

Even so, and with flashbulbs popping all over town, as the day progressed and word got around of the simple palace dinner for two banker couples, everyone felt that pang of chagrin that the truly social feel at not being invited to what was obviously The Party.

What made it so special was the fact that it was being held in the palace. Many grand parties were staged there, elaborate banquets, memorable balls, but rarely a small, intimate palace dinner for two pairs of outsiders who may have been socially acceptable in, say, Manhattan—well, after all, who wasn't, if they had the loot?—but were total, unknown parvenus in San Sebastian.

In the early days of Faith's reign, when San Sebastian was still struggling financially to hold its own, she had carefully put into effect the kind of economies that would never have occurred to a Mediterranean ruler of Florian's ancestry, one for whom the *bella figura* appearance of things was all-important, hang the expense. In pursuit of appearance, his principality had been on the verge of bankruptcy.

Now sleek with prosperity, San Sebastian had the powerful attraction of the rich for the rich. There was much more to this magnetic pull than met the eye, and Faith knew it.

Yes, there was the knowledge that one was utterly safe, including one's jewels, mingling with the other guests, the streets guarded by a thoroughly reliable security force. And if it was also true that a lot of the rich were terribly new to it, what of it? Lacking a traditional hierarchy, San Sebastian still had a strong social structure.

Ruled by Faith. Let the rich arrange their own lines of encounter with each other, she alone decreed the ranking of those arrangements. She alone conferred status on an encounter.

They might fret and fall prey to envy, but the rich took it. They had to. Where else in the pleasure circuit, the financial milieu, the marriage mill or the adultery round, could one find such guaranteed social value?

Certainly not in the big political democracies nearby, where the rulers at the top changed at the whim of voters and every form of terrorism, from simple boycott and blackmail to open assassination, determined who went where to do what.

All these things Faith knew well, after ruling this principality for more than two decades. And once she and Florian had control of a treasury fat with gambling profits there were no limits any longer to the degree of elegance they could show the world.

Each being that much older, they now appreciated the quality of their life even more than when young. And, after so much experience in the public eye, they also understood the tremendous value of being inwardly at peace with themselves and each other.

Love showed. It came across in public events, in televised appearances and most of all in polished hospitality performances, walkabouts, party chat, receiving-line banter.

Faith was now even more capable of a regal performance than Florian, yet one with a strong American aroma of democratic goodwill. The aroma, never the taste. But the heart of it all was their relationship to each other. Love made everything else real.

It *had* been a love match, even the cynics agreed. Yes, the hard-pressed Florian had assumed she was a millionairess, which she was. Yes, Faith had seen the principality as a way of becoming her own ruler. We all have motives. But none of it would have worked if the two of them hadn't been in love. They still were.

The eyrie from which they ruled, the palace, dominated San Sebastian physically, as Faith dominated it socially. Its presence loomed above everything. Originally a fortress, the immense pile rose high on its outcrop of volcanic rock, with a terrace that gave unhindered views of the entire principality. It was from the terrace level, in the old days, that archers loosed their envenomed arrows while boiling oil seared down over invaders and miscreants were bagged alive before being cast a thousand feet into the sea.

It was now the turn of the two American bankers. They and their wives gazed upon Princess Faith with a hungry, yearning intensity that only an American adolescence spent in darkened theaters could induce.

Watching their reactions, the movie director Billy Ritz tried not to smile. He and another guest of the evening, the singer Maggie Rose, had been included in the dinner, he knew, as a kind of high-class makeweight. And he also served as an extra man because the young Prince Michele had at the last minute perversely refused to join them.

It was doubtful if either of the American couples knew what a powerful name Billy Ritz had once been or how, even today, his works were constantly studied in college film classes. The bankers and their wives probably wouldn't have realized that it was men like Billy who were responsible for their having wasted their adolescence in darkened theaters watching stars like Faith Brennan.

As far as the world remembered, Faith had sprung full-blown, like Athena from the brow of Zeus. This was quite true if one considered him in his usual mythic role as All-Powerful Father, Hurler of Lightning Bolts and General Disturber of the Peace.

In this incarnation he was called Eamon Brennan, Brennan Bank and Trust Company of Chicago. He sired eight children by his wife, Mary, sending her in the process to an early grave.

"I know Mama died happy," Faith once told Billy. "Even though I was only six when she passed on. I remember the whole thing, with Cardinal Mundelein celebrating the funeral mass. The open coffin. That smile on her lips. Almost... triumphant."

"She made good her escape," Billy replied. "No wonder she was happy."

By then, secure in her film career, Faith understood how emancipation from Eamon Brennan could produce joy even in death. Like a lot of fathers, he required physical nearness, touching. As the children grew older, he settled grudgingly for telephone calls, day and night. By way of a cloud-born chariot, this Zeus had his long, low-slung ivory Cord roadster with the coffin nose. He'd think nothing of motoring off to see Jim, in Madison, Wisconsin, or surprising Caroline in St. Louis. Zeus was everywhere.

He had each of their lives plotted far into the future. And no one said no. No one but Faith. Alone among the eight, she defied Zeus. Instead of grinding her down to fit his heel to her throat, Eamon Brennan had fallen on his knees before his fifth child. The god worshiped at her shrine.

Later, when Faith was busy with her own children, she often remembered how she had checked her father's will to meddle and reshape his offspring.

"Standing up to him is the only thing a bully understands," she confided once to Billy Ritz. "Not just one time and then back off. The boys tried that. But over and over again until I broke him of the habit."

"Don't act the queen with me," Eamon used to complain. Any true antagonist of his could only be thought of as regal but still, far into her teens, someone he could cuddle on his lap.

"It's disgusting," Caroline had burst out once. "Who is she, visiting royalty?"

"A royal pain in the ass," Jim suggested, getting to his feet in case Eamon threw a punch at him.

"Language," Eamon said in a mild tone.

He guided this queenly child most carefully, especially when it came to her grooming. "God, if only your mama was here to explain the details. Grooming and bearing."

"Dad, how can an American girl be Queen? This isn't England."

"Faith, that degenerate bunch of German slobs on the Brit throne? They can't touch you. There's a natural royalty and you got it. I mean, it...it's like..." He would shake his head at the inadequacy of his language to describe how servile was his worship of the one child who stood up to him and slugged it out.

The idea that in America royalty was found in front of Hollywood's cameras did not dawn on Eamon or Faith until the middle of the war, 1943, when Faith had just turned seventeen. It arrived in the form of Billy Ritz.

He had come to Hollywood just ahead of Hitler's *Anschluss* of Austria and was now in the Signal Corps making training films. Transiting from the Coast to shoot a gonorrhea short in Long Island, he had changed trains in Chicago and was spending an evening watching a revival of *Death Takes a Holiday* at the Goodman Theater, a showcase connected with the Art Institute.

A dated play, even then, it nevertheless had some good parts, particularly the ingenue, Rhoda Fenton. The willowy girl with Comanche-black hair and ice-green eyes was something Billy would never forget. In uniform, and with his Hapsburg air of authority, he got himself backstage to the dressing room Faith shared with three other women.

Billy was jockey size and jockey thin. If he'd had the tormented matinee idol face of a Joseph Schildkraut or Francis Lederer, he might have deployed his Viennese charm to greater success. As it was, with a troll's funny face, he was making no impression on the raven-haired goddess.

He fumbled in his wallet for a card that gave his pre-army studio affiliation. On the back he scribbled "Sol, remember who sent her to you." He handed the card to Faith.

"Sol Pantages, MGM. By now Paramount, I heard. Give him this card and the rest is automatic."

"Casting couch, the works?"

Billy tried to look innocently hurt. "Sol is like my father. He knows real talent when he sees it, Miss Fenton."

"Brennan." The look she flashed added a few silent epithets.

"Sorry. You played your character so well," Billy recovered, "that for me you became her. Where have you worked before?"

"Class plays. Academy of the Sacred Heart in St. Louis."

"Only amateur experience?" Billy pursued. "Then how did you get this part with the Goodman?"

So far Faith had given him nothing but the kind of deadpan reactions one gives a pest. "I got the part," she said, "because my father is the biggest contributor to the Goodman's budget. Is there some other way?"

Faith told Billy, years later, that it wasn't until his face fell apart and he began to guffaw that she had warmed to him for the first time. But it wasn't until 1945 that she finally went to Hollywood, exhibiting a caution that characterized her whole life. Beneath that gypsy facade of smoldering fire lay something quite icy.

Even Sol Pantages noticed. "Billy," he complained as he pawed through contracts and budgets, "what gives with this Brennan girl you wished on me? You got a thing for her?"

Billy looked hurt. At that moment married to wife number three, he was playing the wedded-bliss part most faithfully. This was long before wives four and five, or the many Oscars he was destined to win. If only Sol had noticed, maybe his secret was safe.

They both came from the same suburb of Vienna, where the *heuriger* wine froths. The mark of their total assimilation was that neither spoke the mother tongue to each other, even in private. "You got a letch, Billy?" Sol persisted.

"What makes you say that?"

"Some nobody ingenue from the sticks and already she's repped by the Morris office? And asking five bills a week? Mishugah."

Billy ticked off his points, finger by finger. "One, Chicago is not the sticks. Two, already you made a small mint on her loan-out to Republic. Three, so cough up five big ones and stop kvetching."

"I knew it. You got for her the hots."

"A paternal thing, all right."

The producer's face broke into horizontal lines of mirth. "Tasty stuff, huh?"

Billy looked shocked. "Sol, the girl is cherry."

Pantages' small blue eyes looked round with wonder behind his Ben Franklin reading glasses. "So much effort up front and not one taste of nooky?"

The little director shook his head. "Emmis, Sol. There is something about this girl...." He almost gave up, much as Eamon had so many times before.

"It's something regal," he began again.

"Regal, schmeagle. Something like an ice cube with a hole in it," the producer snapped peevishly.

"Sol," Billy Ritz said, laying his hand on his heart, "she's like a queen."

Pantages eyed him sourly and for a long time. Then he shrugged and scratched his nose. "I have seen guys turn inside out for a broad who was sensational in the sack. But an Ice Queen?" He smiled. "What the hell, maybe we got a novelty here. Let's give her a whirl."

"I'm sorry, Your Excellency, uh, Your Highness," one of the bankers was fumbling, "but I didn't get that."

"Just that we can now take yachts of up to seventy feet in our harbor," Faith repeated, smiling softly.

Her glance went to Prince Florian, only a glance, nothing more, but it brought him to his feet. With a bow he deftly escorted the nonbanking guests out onto the terrace. "We'll be along in a moment," Faith called after him.

Then she turned to the banker nearest her and delivered a smile of such high voltage that it made all previous ones that evening resemble mere pursings of the lips.

"Let's linger just a bit. I can't tell you lovely people," she murmured in a tone that was meant to seem unheard from the terrace, "what a tremendous treat it is for me to chat awhile with real down-home Americans."

· 5 ·

Like any queen, she had ladies-in-waiting.

Both were on the terrace now, with Prince Florian and Billy Ritz, while Princess Faith continued to charm her compatriot visitors outrageously beyond the limits of ordinary hospitality.

There was a reason. With Faith there was always a reason.

To continue attracting high-rolling gamblers and major-league money managers, San Sebastian had to provide the amenities these birds of passage required in their often temporary roosts. The harbor, for example, needed sufficient size to accommodate increasingly more lavish ships, whose length and girth swelled yearly to advertise their owners' burgeoning affluence.

But to enlarge harbors requires immense sums of money. In San Sebastian's case, nearly a billion U.S. dollars was the estimate. This sum would not only serve visitors' demands but would for the next five years provide jobs for every able-bodied citizen of San Sebastian who cared to lift a spade, hammer or wrench.

Tonight Eamon Brennan's daughter was flicking bait in front of American fish. If they bit—and clearly they already had—tomorrow Florian would yank up on the line and fix the hook firmly. Like a good fisherman, Faith had baited her line with irresistible goodies and something that also dazzled the eye.

In this case it struck the eye a blow from which the bankers' wives were still quite dazed. She wore the Gulda emerald.

During their many visits over the years, neither Billie nor Maggie Rose had ever actually seen the emerald before tonight, except in photographs. It was an understatement to refer to this gold breastplate simply by its major stone, an emerald fully an inch across, bezel-cut and winking with cold, galactic power at every breath the Princess took. Like its wearer, it seemed to have come from some interspatial lair beyond our ken.

According to the booklet Jill Tremont mailed to those who asked for information, the solid gold setting, shaped like stylized hawk wings, was originally Scythian, of sixth-century provenance.

The booklet was coy about how the breastplate came into Gulda hands, but it was generally admitted that the bandit Guldas had looted it around the year 1250 from a merchantman bound west from Izmir to Barcelona. Even then it could hardly have been for sale, this barbaric blaze of hot yellow and ice green. Most scholars guessed it had been meant as a gift from a Byzantine monarch to the Moorish sultan who ruled Spain.

It was a family superstition, to which Florian adhered, never to have it appraised. Virtually uninsurable, it never left the palace. But in Faith's capable hands it could still command awe, as tonight. For those of more vulgar taste, there was also the lady-in-waiting, Maggie Rose, her great breasts and even greater voice, a naggingly nasal instrument of intimidating power.

No one knew what had originally brought Faith and Maggie together. But it was, in fact, the rowdy cultural life of Chicago that had done the trick.

The city had its celebrated symphony orchestra, of course. But its chief theatrical attraction had always been the loony Olsen and

Johnson *Hellzapoppin* extravaganzas. Over the years this gala used up hordes of attractive young women with lithe legs. Other than their underpinnings, and their Catholic origins, the two graduates of Olsen and Johnson on hand at tonight's dinner were studies in contrast.

The contrasts began above the long legs, where Maggie's rather blocky torso supported firm, immense breasts and a face dominated by the curved scimitar of a nose that some Sicilians inherit from Saracen ancestors.

It was popularly assumed that Maggie's razorlike muezzin tone on a high note was created by being filtered through this monumental nasal enhancement. She refused to have it bobbed and made its exacerbating tone part of her charisma, hard earned by dogged work, dramatic gall and half a dozen psychoanalysts.

It was drama, in fact, that set her style and the way she handled a song, however banal the words. Critics used words like *portamento* about a girl from an Italian ghetto near Hackensack who couldn't read music till she was already a star.

Out on the terrace she had just reminded Florian of this. "No, honestly?" he asked. "But this is some kind of brag, is it not? You Americans love to seem such savages."

"Flo," Maggie said in her nasal baritone, "when you gonna learn we *are* savages? Sure, we knocked off the Apaches, but what we've still got out there is a jungle."

Her huge, heavily made-up eyes swept across the view of San Sebastian below them, but managed to include Billy Ritz's face as well as that of Jill Tremont. Nonsurvivors, the pitying look said.

The small Viennese director concentrated on lighting an even smaller cigar. He might be past his prime and not too bankable in Hollywood circles, but a survivor he was. And so, too, was Jill.

Her technique had been that of the smallish bird or insect, camouflage. Over the years she had turned herself from a very attractive young actress to one of those colorless, mousy maiden aunts back in Cheshire for whom she had been named. Good works. Long walks in all weathers. Well, after all, only two weathers in England and if one waited for sun one never did get one's walkies.

The irony of Jill surviving as a replica of her maiden aunt, refined, of a *good* family with a spotless Norman name but retiringly
self-effacing, lay in the fact that she had left England for the States
to further her career as an actress. This was on the strength of a
vague promise an American film agent had made one night in
London at a party.

"Lots of work for your type," he assured her. "The refined but
sexy type." Wink. Business card.

Ironies within ironies. What he hadn't explained to Jill was there
might be a demand for refined sexiness, but it had just been filled
by a Chicago girl named Faith Brennan.

None of this dawned on Jill until, not having her green card,
she had been put through the full treatment, everything, the most
demeaning, soul-rotting survival course Hollywood can devise for
young hopefuls.

No, Billy reminded himself—*everything:* not merely the casting
couch, but blowing a Universal producer on her knees under his
desk, picking oranges one autumn to pay her rent, party girl in West
L.A., dime-store demonstrator of a mechanical onion-chopping giz-
mo in Wilshire, walk-on in a Silver Lake little-theater production
for no pay, handing out sample packets of a new cigarette on street
corners in Century City, B-girl in poker bar in Gardenia, private-
eye setup for divorce photos, temp dress-department model at I.
Magnin, on and off unemployment compensation so many times
she had lost track.... Survival?

She had gotten an invitation to a cast party from a friend of hers
who had a bit part in the new Faith Brennan flick. It was Billy who
spotted the similarity.

"You're her height," he had told Jill, "and coloring. What's your
name?"

"Jill Tremont."

His pug nose wrinkled. "Couldn't they come up with a better handle? Jill...St. James? Nah, even phonier. But dump the Tremont."

She tried for a funny grin. "It's really my name."

"Under any name I have you for a steady job."

"What?"

"Faith needs a stand-in."

They did only one picture together before she made Jill her sec-

retary. "No typing," she explained. "The studio handles correspon-
dence. Just the daily grind. Appointments, shopping, guest lists,
arrange my bills in some kind of order, pay them. You get the picture." That had been about eighteen months before Faith met Florian for the first time, a quarter of a century ago, Billy remembered.

Slowly, at first, but steadily Jill had turned herself into the invisible woman. She had pruned away all her options in dress, hair-
style and makeup until what she had left was this startling imitation
of Aunt Gillian. No one had suggested she frump herself into invisibility. She had done this to herself.

On state occasions like this, Jill would put on a pretty gown and
let Faith herself handle the makeup. Miss Jill Tremont could still
knock their eyes out, as Bob Henniger had said.

That had been quite a romance until Florian learned Bob was
CIA. It was Florian who had to reprimand Jill for her disastrous
judgment in men. Faith had never held her responsible for this near
lapse in palace security. Faith would never do that. She was the
most generous person in the world to a friend. So American.

She had always been typically American. It was not what had
first attracted Billy Ritz to her, nor what had made her a star. But it
was what had kept her a star, even now, when she had been off-
camera for twenty years.

To borrow a line from a men's magazine that had once done a
rather too frank profile of her, in the nicest possible way Faith Brennan had balls.

There was that strain in American women, so the magazine reflected ponderously, that sort of pioneer strain that helped to preserve human values while American men ran rampant as pigs in
shit, slaughtering the Indians, fouling the rivers, poisoning the sky
and murdering each other.

The magazine had been too macho to follow its line of thought
any further when it came to the image of the two American sexes.
The men couldn't be trusted with anything, certainly not guns. And
the women picked up the pieces and tried to make a civilization
out of a howling desert. This was the aura Faith had always projected.

In every Hollywood generation there is always this cool, char-
ismatic leading lady the audience knows did not fuck anybody to

achieve stardom. They can't cuddle up to her like a daughter, but they can respect the hell out of her.

She is Bette Davis or Katharine Hepburn or Faith Brennan, a woman above all of *high standards.* That was what the land had required to tame and conserve and replenish all that raw male energy that hacked a nation out of a wilderness.

In the informal dining room that adjoined the terrace, Princess Faith now rose and led the other guests out into the open air. Behind Florian and the women and Billy Ritz, an awesome spread of kilowatts turned San Sebastian's night into day. It formed an entirely suitable background for a rich girl who had gotten even richer.

From the harbor—even without its future billion-dollar refurbishment—long strands of glitzy lights were casually strewn like diamanté necklaces from the masts of oceangoing yachts. Even at this distance it was possible to see that some ships were so grand that in place of dinghy tenders they had small helicopters. What banker wouldn't hasten to finance the further convenience of such people who so obviously knew how to live? It was, after all, what banks existed for, to lend to those not in need.

Beyond, masked by a jungle of high-rise buildings, lay the sports areas where San Sebastian played host to the most prestigious international events in tennis, auto racing and soccer.

"You can hear it. Listen," Florian commanded in a hushed voice. "The sound of it."

Maggie Rose grinned maliciously. "I hear it. Roulette wheel purr and the death rattle of collapsing wallets."

Florian laughed, his face lighted from underneath by the lights of his native land. "All of it delights me so. And I have only two people to thank for it."

"Faith," Billy Ritz suggested.

"Above all, Faith," the Prince agreed. "Without her this would still be a shambles. But also you, Billy, for bringing Faith into my life."

"*Liebe Fürst,*" the little Viennese murmured.

As Faith and the guests moved nearer to the railing, Maggie Rose smiled nicely at Billy. "You do have Florian snowed," she said in a voice like the freshly cut top of a tin can.

"Will you look at that view!" one of the bankers enthused. "My God, it's worth money."

· 6 ·

In a congeries of rooms as diverse and endless as the palace, all sorts of things went on more or less side by side without any overlap. It was probably this potential for infinite diversity that led earlier Guldas to such elaborate construction. In Mike's case, it provided complete insulation from the high-voltage display being acted out on the terrace.

If the banker guests had missed the company of the present financial adviser and future ruler of the principality, they never once alluded to it.

It might well have crossed their minds. The young man known formally as His Serene Highness Prince Michele Lanzarote-Portago Gulda had trained first at Wharton School of Economics, then at Harvard's Graduate School of Business Administration and, finally, with Brennan Bank and Trust Company of Chicago. It was he who had drawn up the harbor-expansion loan agreement the bankers were being asked to consider. Thanks to the palace's multiplicity of rooms, Mike was holed up in his own suite listening to Ella Fitzgerald records.

"No," he had told his father earlier in the evening, "I will not sit down to eat with that prime pair of assholes."

Florian's handsome, unlined face went dark with suffused blood. "You will not use such words, do you understand?"

"That first clown, Charley Oakhurst, wouldn't know a front-loaded convertible debenture if it jumped up and pissed in his ear," Mike continued, unfazed.

"Michele!"

"And the other has to take off his shoes to count past ten. It's an insult to San Sebastian, buttering up that pair for development funding."

Florian stared at him for a long time, during which the anger receded from his face. "If they're stupid," he said then, "so much the better tomorrow, when we talk business. You're not too refined, are you, to be at that meeting?"

"Never fear, Pop. I'll be there."

"Bene." Florian roughed up Mike's thatch of thick blond hair. "You're the hotshot banker, eh? Just like your Grandfather Eamon, eh?"

"Is that supposed to be a compliment?"

While Faith's father had been alive, Mike had had a bellyful of the Brennan family. It was of the Gulda side of his heritage that he stood in some ignorance. At his communion, his parents had given him a leather-bound book purporting to be the Gulda history. But it turned out to be a publicity confection whipped up to secure certain Vatican privileges. It fell to Mike to winkle the truth out of old books, Uncle Billy Ritz and the back files of sensational Sunday supplements.

The original clan of *banditi* had been pirates, preying on rich Mediterranean shipping during the Renaissance. Over the centuries the Guldas could have died out, like the Medici, the Sforza, the Visconti, but for the fact that in each succeeding generation Guldas produced increasingly more cruel and successful pirate chieftains, a good enough recipe for success.

What maintained their grip on this tiny promontory of the Italian Riviera in the modern era was the extreme good business sense of the last of the pirates, Umberto, who ruled as a prince from the 1890s to 1930.

Longevity, in the end, was better than mere intelligence but Umberto had both. Then a series of political moves started to erode both his principality and his control of it. The latest threat, in 1922, was this ridiculous strutting journalist called Mussolini.

It was, as most things are in Italy, a matter of money. Mussolini had not yet won the full support of the old-time industrialist families and large landowners. His hold on the government was enforced by a small army of thugs in black shirts. Unless he could fund the cost of expansion, Il Duce feared the Savoia clan would edge him out, not because he was evil, but because he could, and therefore *should*, be toppled. A strong man must be *perceived* to be strong. The illusion costs money.

Some say it cost Umberto Gulda a billion lire, in times when the lira was worth more than it is now, to outfit, arm and expand the Blackshirts into the supreme terrorist army they became. This guess is based on the fact that most of the money went for uniforms. In Italy, first things come first.

In return, Umberto got all of San Sebastian, its castle, its palazzos and its extensive harbor, politically separated from Italy.

The treaty made him answerable to the Vatican. But Umberto could now coin his own money, collect his own taxes, issue his own bonds and stamps and do almost anything he pleased except wage war on Italy. Historians who have dug deeper into the Gulda-Mussolini pact assume it was Il Duce's way of throwing the Vatican a bone during the touchy decades of standoff before he signed a concordat with the Pope.

During the reign of Umberto, especially around the turn of the century, San Sebastian had been preeminently *the* place to see and be seen in. Archdukes drank toasts from their mistresses' slippers. Crown princes fought duels at dawn behind the *gran terrazza* of the casino. Portly German industrialists blew their brains out after losing the ownership of their vast steelworks. Bolshevik exiles nursed a sidewalk caffè espresso all morning, arguing over how to topple Mother Russia while eagerly trading the latest St. Petersburg gossip. Sopranos enchanted dukes. Princesses enslaved colonels. The music never stopped.

Umberto's son, Pippo, who came to power at his father's death in 1930, was the one most beloved by the Sunday supplements. He gave value, too. Holed up in his fortress-nation through the long years of world economic depression followed by World War II, Pippo spent nearly all his time in nonstop orgies, contracting one social disease after another until there were no new microbes or courtesans left to conquer.

Under Pippo, who might well have profited from watching some of the films Major Billy Ritz was then producing for the U.S. Army, San Sebastian grew seedy. Cannes, Monte Carlo and Beaulieu were creaming off the royalty and nobility. San Sebastian was getting the dregs. Well, why not? Some of its hotels had only just barely been electrified. Hot water was still a doubtful commodity. The flush of gay notoriety that once had been San Sebastian now faded to those hectic spots of rouge applied to the cheeks of a corpse.

Up to that point in the Gulda family history, Mike had been able to follow by research. But when paresis carried off Pippo and the 20-year-old Prince Florian acceded to the ancestral throne, reliable information grew scarce in library files. Seedy San Sebastian no longer had any hold on the world's imagination, nor did Florian project an image that might attract the corrupt interest of the Sunday supplements.

The young Florian had been the product of Swiss and British schools. According to what his mother had told Mike, his father had in those days spoken in an absolutely music-hall parody of an upper-class Brit twit accent. It had taken Princess Faith and Jill Tremont several years to weed out the "I say, old chap" from Florian's style.

"First of all," Billy Ritz told Mike, "you have to understand that your average San Sebastiano is a cruel sonuvabitch at best. They gave your father no support. He was too young, too tall, too British, too blond, too this, too that. Too unmarried. An unmarried prince, till he marries and produces a male heir, is a danger to the nation."

Mike knew that with no male heir, the whole principality would be subsumed back into Italy again and the San Sebastiani would lose their taxless status.

"Second," Billy continued, "there was this problem of the casino contract." He paused and grinned softly, his little gnome's face thoughtful for a long moment. "Your father had inherited the contract from Pippo and it was a pip."

Mike knew about the contract, too. His Grandpa Eamon had dinned it into him over the years as an illustration of how a carelessly written legal instrument can bring down vast pleasure palaces.

"I mean," Billy explained, "here was this grungy casino, where nostalgia freaks like me showed up to gamble. I mean the nightly take was still respectable. Then your Grandpa Pippo signed a contract with a syndicate based in Nevada and Athens. He held fifty percent of the casino shares, and got fifty percent of the net take."

Mike frowned. "Who let him sign anything that stupid?"

"Right. You know how the boys work it, don't you? There is no net. They're scamming millions and your father is walking around in rusty gold braid, like a dress extra in a Republic costume meller."

The little Viennese paused. "That was when I met him. He was just a little older than you are now. Melancholy. His credit was good only at the casino, where the boys made sure he could tank up on cognac. Kept him passive. It was sad to see." Billy sighed. "Even sadder because not one of the local people would take the time to help him out of it."

"You'd think," the male heir of the principality said, "they'd realize they had to support him or the whole joint would be gobbled up by the Italians."

"Altruism," Billy Ritz intoned, "is not a San Sebastiano trait."

It was obvious to Mike why his father had never alluded to this part of the family history. Too painful to recollect. In this his father misjudged his son. Mike had his Grandpa Eamon's stomach for spiky, hard-to-digest chunks of truth. As a trained financial man, he respected what could with confidence be fed into a computer as hard fact. That and Ella Fitzgerald singing an old Gershwin tune called "I Am Just a Little Girl Who's Looking for a Little Boy Who's Looking for a Girl to Love."

At midnight, when he judged the dinner party to be ending, Mike leaned out his window for a breath of air. Below waited the long black Mercedes 600. The chauffeur, an old friend, caught sight of him and waved discreetly.

Mike cupped his hands around his lips and whispered: "Good hunting." It was an odd thing to tell a chauffeur, but everyone already knew the heir to be somewhat, er, eccentric.

· 7 ·

In the rather limited world of luxury limousines, the Mercedes 600 offers quiet distinction well above the blatant heft of Cadillacs, Daimlers and Zils.

When it comes to chauffeurs of limousines, however, few proprietors anywhere in the world could boast of a driver more talented, skilled and discreet than Eugenio Magari.

He was the son of the man who had kept all the palace cars in condition for the past forty years. Slight of figure, with pale olive skin and shocking black eyes of an intimidating steadiness, Geni had not won the chauffeur's job because of his automotive connections.

Oddly enough, he had the job on merit. Now in his mid-thirties, Geni had shown remarkable promise during his school days, with such high marks that he had been sent at principality expense to the intelligence schools run by the French Sûreté near Paris and United States Army Intelligence at Langley, Virginia.

For chauffeuring was only one of Geni Magari's talents. Officially, he carried the rank of *colonnello* in the Gold Berets, whose talented marching band gave every public occasion a sparkle and dash. It was popularly assumed that this touristic service was the Gold Berets' only assignment.

But, just as it requires only a smallish air conditioner to cool an automobile, so a small principality does not require a huge, ungainly intelligence service to keep order, or in the words of its charter "to promote tourism, commerce and industry."

In short, the Gold Berets were secret police.

Standing outside the Mercedes now, Geni heard its radio crackle. He got into the limousine and picked up the hand mike. *"Si? Mi dica."*

Over a walkie-talkie somewhere in the palace one of the waiters cleared his throat and said: *"Finito."*

Geni Magari switched off the radio and switched on the air-conditioning. In only a moment the interior of the long auto was sweetly cool, just as the Oakhursts and Faircloths appeared at the top of the stairs.

On the short drive to the harbor, none of the Americans said anything. It was, Geni noted, as if they already knew his tape recorders were turning. Smart people, bankers, especially this particular pair.

At the night-hued *Finisterre*, Magari smoothly braked to a halt, got out and opened the door for his passengers. "Can I be of any further assistance?" he asked in his American-accented English.

Charley Oakhurst, the senior of the two bankers, was a tall, spare man with a jutting jaw. "No, thank you. Good night."

Geni piloted the Mercedes around several corners and parked it out of sight next to a small gray Renault 5-TS. As he steered the Renault back toward the ketch, he activated its battery of electronics hidden in the trunk. Two miles away, at the farthest end of the soon-to-be-enlarged harbor, another Gold Beret, Arturo Giacobbe, activated the instruments in his gray Renault 5-TS.

Between them they could triangulate and position a radio signal down to an accuracy of five centimeters.

The night sky began to darken now in earnest as much of San Sebastian's street lighting dimmed or disappeared. Stars could now be seen. Even a thin crescent of moon appeared as the principality prepared for sleep. An untroubled slumber, Geni Magari thought.

Borders patrolled. Hotels monitored. Casinos policed. Streets under surveillance. *Tutto in ordine*, everything in order like what he imagined Italy had been under Mussolini: regulated, predictable.

It was wrong to call San Sebastian a police state, as the young leftists did. Here, Geni told himself, one had complete freedom as long as nothing disturbed tourism, commerce and industry. Most San Sebastiani, and all the foreign tax exiles, knew what a good deal they had. It had not always been that way in this tiny land, nor in others.

As a teenager Geni had spent many hours in the dark of San Sebastian's old movie house where German crime films of the Weimar years like *M* and *Dr. Mabuse* competed with ancient Warners and Paramount gangster films. Lawless lands, these films portrayed, where the gun was all, the police corrupt or incompetent and the lone detective risked his life to make some form of justice prevail, if only for the sake of a happy ending.

The radar sweep produced a faint blip beyond the twelve-mile limit. *"Guarda,"* Giacobbe murmured over his radio. Geni slowly swept through the radio frequencies. At about 21 megahertz he picked up the transmission from the *Finisterre*. Morse code. He didn't bother to translate, knowing it would be done later from his tape recording.

He picked up his hand mike and called in Helicopter Control, gave precise map coordinates and asked for a visual ID.

"Too dark," the pilot complained.

"Nevertheless," the *colonnello* of the Gold Berets commanded, "try infrared."

*   *   *

By 2 A.M. the bridge and deck of the *Finisterre* were deserted except for Charley Oakhurst, who couldn't sleep. Well, who could, under the circumstances, he asked himself. This close to this big a deal? Impossible to stay calm.

And it was the biggest, make no mistake. Oakhurst picked up his night glasses, powerful binoculars whose wide front lenses were hooded to mask a telltale flash of light. The gray Renaults were gone, he noted. A characteristic of pip-squeak operations, buying a fleet of the same make of car.

Charley Oakhurst was one of those bankers who knew nothing about lending rates, business cycles and the like. Charley was a social banker. Through him, powerful friends could reach out and touch the untouchable profit. A social banker is worth a dozen wizards of economics or math.

He had calmly watched them bugging his radio transmissions to the offshore ship, which by now, they had surely identified as the *Spiritu Sanctu,* owned and operated by the I.U.D. Having satisfied itself as to the source of the offer Oakhurst would make tomorrow, the principality would be sure to view it with much more respect as coming from the investment arm of the Vatican itself.

Or so Charley devoutly hoped. He put away his night glasses and came down the hatch to the forward cabin. His wife, Connie, looked up from her paperback as he changed into pajamas. "Neither of us can sleep, huh?" she asked. "You want a book of your own?"

Instead of replying, he asked: "What did you really think of Her Nibs?"

"That's the third time you've asked." Connie put her book down. "I told you, Charley. She's one helluva gal. Very impressive. Very natural. Very smooth."

"Woman of iron?"

"What makes you say that?"

Oakhurst groaned softly as he laid his bones in bed beside his wife. There was a limit beyond which he could not pursue this discussion with her, or anyone else, for that matter. "My guess is the Princess runs the joint, lock, stock and barrel. Am I right?"

"Any complaints?"

"Me? None. But the people I work for...and how."

"Which people?"

"G'night, dear."

There was no way he could discuss with Connie the decades of Faith Brennan maneuvering that had not only freed the casinos of outside "help" but kept them free. With her father's guidance, she had outsmarted the boys at every turn.

Not that they hadn't tried winning back the principality. The deals they'd offered! Dozens, each one curtly refused. And now this new one Charley was fronting for, complete with tasty Vatican dressing, had been custom-designed to distract her attention long enough for her to say yes. How could she complain? No gangsters, no hoods, just good solid Catholic clergy.

Lying beside Connie in the dark, Charley grinned. His long New England jaw turned the movement into something that could scare a shark. It was, after all, an angling contest, he thought. She'd baited her hook with show-biz dazzle. He with the odor of sanctity.

He could feel his banker's heart beat faster. Slowly he edged over on his right side to ease the feeling. But, God, the deal was enough to stir anyone's blood. The loan would give the boys a foothold again. And the world knew how expert they were in converting a foothold to a stranglehold.

What possible right did Faith Brennan have to stand in the way of it? Who did she think she was, delaying progress? This time Charley's grin was so thoroughly frightening that it was well it occurred in darkness.

Prince Florian's suite had always been his, as a bachelor and after the marriage. He had caused to be remodeled out of other rooms a suite of equal size for the Princess. A hallway connected them and it was usually at Faith's end of this passage, both of them having readied themselves for bed, that they would embrace and retire, each to his own suite.

It was along this corridor at nearly 2 A.M. that Florian now moved slowly in his dressing gown and slippers. He paused at the door of her chambers. Over the years they had developed similar patterns in which they had no trouble falling asleep but often awoke in the small hours.

He turned the knob of her door and padded quietly into her dressing room. From its doorway he could look into her huge corner sleeping chamber, both windows wide open.

He smiled softly in the darkness. This American passion for fresh air kept them from sleeping in the same bed every night, that and a certain sense of protocol. And Florian's sure knowledge that he could never have bedded the woman he loved in his own bachelor quarters where so many other women had slept in the years before he'd married.

Tonight it wasn't the need for a woman that had brought him here so much as the need to talk to someone he loved and trusted, moreover someone he knew to be far brighter and stronger than he when it came to the affairs of San Sebastian. He listened to the quality of her breathing now, hoping to find her awake.

"No, fast asleep," Faith said suddenly. "Are you my friendly neighborhood prowler?"

He sat down on the edge of her bed. "Your fellow insomniac."

She reached out and drew him down against her. They embraced lightly on this summer night. With a sudden sideways movement, Florian shrugged off his dressing gown and slid in beside her under the light sheet that covered her.

"Decided to take the plunge after all?"

He grunted. "You American women are sexually aggressive. It is your most endearing feature."

"Just lucky, I guess."

He wrestled himself around a second time and took her in his arms. He hadn't come for this, he reminded himself. It was just—

"You're naked!"

His voice sounded so shocked that he began to chuckle at his own surprise. "My dear, don't you realize, with all this damned cross-ventilation..."

"I know. I know. That's how girls get pregnant."

"It is?" he wondered lazily, kissing her again. "Is it?"

*   *   *

It requires an agent of at least the rank of *colonnello* to awaken Prince Florian at two-thirty in the morning. Geni still in chauffeur's uniform, Florian hastily regarbed in a dark blue velours dressing gown. He extended a small ceremonial glass of bitters. "Here, Geni," he urged. He had known the Gold Beret since Geni was a boy. Florian had been taught to drive a car by Geni's father.

The bitters was compounded of thirty herbs into a drink of which no one would ever want more than one sip. The men touched glasses. "Oakhurst," Geni said then. "He has authorization, if something called 'Clause B' is part of the loan agreement."

Florian's forehead furrowed. "This mystery ship...?"

"It's the I.U.D.'s normal headquarters vessel, the *Spiritu Sanctu* out of Gaeta near the U.S. Sixth Fleet."

The Prince smiled slightly. "Are you aware that in some quarters I.U.D. refers to an intrauterine contraceptive device?"

Geni frowned so massively that it was almost a rebuke. *"Internazionale Uffizi Devozione,"* he intoned. "My guess is that Clause B hypothecates a share of casino profits as collateral for the loan."

"So. Not just churchmen. Not just bankers. But now gamblers, like us." He sighed heavily. "I hardly need tell you how the Princess will view this when I tell her."

"Will you have t—?" The question died on Geni's lips.

The two men seemed to notice their bitters for the first time. Each took a ceremonial sip and put the glass down almost untouched. The Prince stood up. "So much for the harbor project, with its thousands of jobs. I am keeping you too long, Geni. You were right to bring this to me before tomorrow's negotiations. Today's, that is."

Driving away in the gray Renault 5-TS, Geni played the scene back and forth in his mind. The clue to what would happen was that remark about the Princess. The moment *il Principe* told her the true identify of Oakhurst's backers, using Vatican camouflage to gain control of casino funds, she would smell the discreet spoor of the Mafia. It was absolutely certain.

Tonight's surveillance had been carried off perfectly, but its results would only sabotage the negotiations with Oakhurst. He would be politely refused.

Geni Magari parked the car in a government garage and walked home under a sky reeling with stars, even a faint wheel-like edge of the Milky Way. He sighed over the thousands of lost jobs. He frowned about Mafia control. Finally, he laughed.

There was nothing much else to do about it.

· 8 ·

One end of the great terrace, the part that faced the sea, had been shielded by trellises. Over these cascaded sheaves of thick bougainvillea in clotted grapey purple and a tangerine-like orange. This effectively hid from public view the first family of San Sebastian as they ate an open-air breakfast in peace and quiet.

The morning after the dinner with the Oakhursts and the Faircloths turned out otherwise. Faith arrived at the table to find Billy Ritz huddled over a cup of black coffee. They eyed each other, but said nothing. She scanned the horizon of the Mediterranean with what Billy had always called a faintly proprietary air. Only a bit of it was hers, the part fronting on her principality, but she had made it into an extremely important and lucrative bit.

As she stood at the masonry edge of the terrace, shielding her eyes against the slanting morning sun that came in over the polluted skies of Genoa, an early morning *tramontana* fluttered her thin batiste dressing gown, flattening it against her slim body for a moment. Give or take a few pounds, Billy thought, wasn't this still the same girl he had first discovered? Didn't her tar-black hair still have a certain gypsy drama about it? Although nowadays it needed help to remain pure black. Her face...

"Lights," Billy croaked in an early morning voice. "Camera. Action." He seemed to fold his small body around the cup of coffee cradled in his hands, making it his new heart, the organ that pumped caffeine through his veins after a troubled night of fitful sleep.

"Ah haive awlwuz duhpinded," Faith drawled slowly, "awn th' kahndniss uv strainguz." She giggled suddenly and brought her hand up under chin, as if patting loose flesh in place.

"Leave it alone," the Viennese counseled in a low, raspy voice. "Don't call attention to what doesn't show. Cut. Print."

"Is that all you're having?" she asked, sitting beside him.

"For now." He pushed the cup away. "I don't get hungry much anymore. It's a symptom of old age."

She kissed his plump, gnome's cheek. "Old age indeed."

"Whereas you, my dear, remain ageless."

"There is a two-syllable word Mike occasionally uses," she told him. "It would go well right here."

"Bullshit? To your oldest admirer you can't say a simple word like bullshit? Of course you can't because it ain't bullshit. It's the truth. You don't age, kiddo."

She stared into his small, sleepy eyes for a moment, an agonized look, searching for truth and not wanting to find it. Then she turned away. "Love is blind," she murmured. "Poor Billy." She poured herself some coffee and, although she added nothing to it, sat for a long time stirring it.

Billy Ritz watched her sharp-cut profile, incised on his vision like a die-cut image on a coin. She had been fretting about aging for some time now, he knew, especially in front of the mirror. It was bad enough to do it there, where, after all, it was what one did before a mirror. But lately she had been having these doubts everywhere, anywhere, here on the terrace, last night at the dinner table.

To see ourselves as others see us. Billy's mouth flattened grimly. Those bankers and their wives had devoured her face. It was a greed people their age suffered, having been raised on a diet of Faith Brennan. How had she stood up to such a cruel test?

Now he saw her lift one hand again so that the back of it came up under her pointed chin, still without sag or wrinkle. Billy knew the rumors: face-lifts by the score, my dear, silicone injections, the works. But Faith's face was still entirely her own. Science had yet to intervene.

She got up and leaned over the parapets, her cool gray-green eyes swinging slowly across the watery panorama. Early-morning fishing boats, having trolled all night, were returning to shore. A smallish yacht nosed its way out of the harbor. Across the business district, toward the sports areas, a crew was clipping and watering lawn tennis courts. One of them spotted her. With a great *Commedia dell'Arte* gesture, he doffed his cap and bowed low over an extended leg. She waved to him and sat down again at the table, out of sight to anyone but Billy.

Florian now arrived, the pink *Financial Times* of London under his arm. He bent over her shining black hair and kissed her ear, casually patted Billy's shoulders, and sat down opposite them at the large wrought-iron table, topped by a circle of thick plate glass. Billy could see that the Prince had slept badly too.

"One of those spy conferences in the wee small hours?" Faith asked.

He nodded and held his glass of juice out to her. *"Salute, amore."*

"Cin-cin."

She let him finish his juice before reopening the topic. "What did Geni Magari have for you this time?" she asked. "The pillow talk of the Oakhursts?"

Florian grinned amiably. "Something like that. I'd tell you now, but I want Mike to hear too."

A faint vertical ridge formed between Faith's pale, intense eyes. "I don't want the children involved in this kind of business, Florian. You know that."

Teresa, the cook's assistant, brought platters of eggs and bacon. The three people sat in silence until she had left the terrace. "But Mike is already involved," his father explained to Faith. "I rely on his judgment, *cara*. Now that your father is no longer with us, I have his closest associate as my counselor."

She made a face. "Mike as a clone of Dad. It's a fate worse than death."

Billy was well aware that every part of San Sebastian's business or financial life during Faith's reign had been personally vetted by Eamon Brennan until his death.

"Mike's too young still for that kind of responsibility," she said at last.

"Twenty-two?" Florian sipped his coffee. "At twenty-two I was already saddled with this job." He turned to Billy. "Remember what a kid I was? Mike's qualifications are a hundred times better than mine were. His mind...his training..." He shrugged. "And since he must one day reign, why delay?"

She made the same face again, a kind of wrinkling of the flawless nose, as if sniffing something faintly rancid. The *tramontana* gently turned a short wisp of her hair over one eye, like a questioningly upraised eyebrow.

"I know I'm old-fashioned." Faith sighed unhappily. "I just hate the idea of my children having the whole heavy, dirty load of adult living. Thank God, Polly's still a long way off."

A door opened and shut. Noisy slippered footsteps crossed a parquet floor. Mike shambled into the sunlight, blinking and squinting. Ella Fitzgerald takes a heavy toll if you listen to her half the night.

"Morning, all," Mike said in a fair caricature of a London bobby's tone. He bent down and kissed both parents' cheeks in turn, patted Billy's bald head and finished off a glass of orange juice in one swallow before pouring a second glass.

"What sort of dirt did Geni dish up?" he asked them.

His father frowned. "Palace internal security must be at an all-time low."

"I hadn't gone to sleep yet. Nobody else has the ball—" He stopped himself and hastily amended his statement. "Nobody else has the nerve to wake you at that hour. It had to be Geni."

"He brought me unusual, but not unwelcome, news."

"About those two clowns you were feeding last night?"

"About Signore Oakhurst's principals."

"He ain't got no principles," Mike cackled.

Florian's frown deepened. "It's too bad," he told Faith. "I was wrong about this one. He's a very young twenty-two."

"You mean," Mike asked, "the rumors that he fronts for the Pope? Oakhurst has been discreetly leaking that one for some time. Which doesn't automatically make it true."

"Geni intercepted code transmissions to an I.U.D. headquarters ship. That makes it a bit more than a rumor, Michele."

A silence fell between them. To Billy Ritz they both seemed to be avoiding looking at Princess Faith. Mike loaded several spoons of sugar into his coffee. He stirred it a long time, stalling. Then he rubbed his hands with Uriah Heep unction. "So. If we okay the deal, we're using Vatican money. How righteous can we get? Manna from heaven."

"So it would seem." Florian glanced almost surreptitiously at Faith, who seemed to concentrate all her attention on pouring a thin stream of cream into her coffee. Not a word of all this seemed to be getting through to her but her husband, her son and Billy all knew differently.

"We will be presented today," the Prince went on slowly, almost unwillingly, "with a condition no one spoke of last night. Magari feels they will attach a percentage of casino take as collateral."

At no time did Florian's glance return to his wife's face, but the lines of force radiating back and forth between them had suddenly grown almost intense enough to be felt. Faith sipped her coffee and slowly buttered a bit of toast. Then: "The Vatican in the gambling business?"

Mike snorted. "You should know some of the businesses the I.U.D. invests in."

"I find nothing reprehensible about the gambling business," she corrected him, "for lay people like us. If you were a true saint, you might call it socially evil to put temptation in the way of weak people. But if you followed that line of thought, you would have to close every bar and restaurant,"—she smiled slightly—"and half the hotels in Christendom."

Florian's troubled face cleared for a moment as he grinned back at her. "Then in principle you're not against the Church participating in our casinos?"

Faith's slender neck seemed to grow longer suddenly, like that of a swan preening itself. Her face went entirely deadpan. "Florian," she said, "you know I don't approve of this conversation in front of the children."

"What children?" Mike asked mildly.

His mother gave him an exasperated look. "It's no great adventure, being an adult." She reached across and patted his hand. "It will happen to you anyway, Mike. Why rush to meet it? Enjoy yourself now."

But Mike had other matters on his mind. He turned to his father. "Oakhurst has other clients besides the Pope. His bank fronts for three families back in the States, the Gambinos, the Trafficantes and the Alessios out west."

"Way, goombar," Maggie Rose called, appearing in the doorway in a puce dressing gown whose design was based on shapes seen in a delirium. "You calling the roll of my relatives?"

"*Ecco*," Mike said, jumping to his feet and escorting her to her chair. "There is always room at our table for the Godmother herself."

Maggie Rose's morning cheeriness began to thicken like a cumulus thunderhead. "You no like," she said in a fake Italian accent, "Cousin Luigi break-a you arm."

"But remember one thing," Mike added, pointing a finger toward heaven.

"Right," Maggie agreed, raising her own finger. Together they chorused, "Mafia? They ain't no Mafia," and broke up giggling.

An icy silence radiated outward in gelid waves from the side of the table where Faith sat, as if someone had left open the door of a frozen food locker, a big one.

"Uh-oh," Maggie Rose said in an undertone. "ixnay on the okesjay."

Polly arrived in her usual neat, no-fuss way, already dressed for the day while the rest lounged about in robes. "Who died?" she asked, gulping her orange juice.

Her brother's eyes flicked sideways to their mother, but he said nothing. "Someone said a bad word?" Polly surmised in a too-innocent tone.

"I don't find the subject of the Mafia appetizing at breakfast. And it seems—" Faith checked herself, then surged forward again, despite her distaste for the matter. "It seems we were entertaining last night a—" She signed with exasperation. "A bag man, I think the term is, for some American mafiosi, who also represents the Vatican. *Damn* it!"

Her outburst galvanized them. "I'm sorry, my dear," Florian began apologizing.

"Not bag man," Billy said, "Front man. Cutout. Beard. *Cuscinetto*. Not bag man."

"Breakfast's in ruins," the Princess told them. "The idea that such filth ends up on our plates for us to swallow each morning—"

She whirled on her son. "You remember what Zola said? About having to swallow a toad every morning? In my household, I simply will not have that."

Mike held both hands palms-up in front of him, protectively. "Hey, Mom, I'm sorry. But Charley Oakhurst exists. And you want the loan."

"No."

"What?" This from everyone but Polly.

"No." Faith took a long, steadying breath. "Forget the loan."

"Baby," Maggie Rose moaned, "you're upset. I don't blame you. But look at this thing objectively. I mean, money is money. It has no morality."

"But it does," Faith objected. "Charley Oakhurst can pretend it's Church money, but if it's Mafia money it has blood on it."

"Oh, come on," her friend said.

"It was extorted by loan sharks. It was scammed by swindlers. It was taken in fives and tens from miserable spaced-out junkies who stole and murdered to feed their habit. It came from prostitutes and..." Faith's voice gave out.

"And gamblers," Maggie Rose reminded her. "Let's not forget the profession San Sebastian shares with Nevada and Atlantic City. I mean, while we're casting stones, that is," she added in her nasal voice.

The former Faith Brennan got to her feet, a bit shakily. She looked at each of them in turn. "I find this entirely disgusting," she announced in a voice that might have turned scrambled eggs to concrete. "Good morning."

And left.

The long silence at the table was broken only by the sound of Polly's knife and fork as she polished off her bacon and eggs. Then she got to her feet in a pretty fair imitation and stated, "I am going to console *Maman*."

And left.

Maggie Rose finished her black, unsweetened coffee. "I guess I put my foot in it that time," she told the men. "But you know Faith has this, this *thing* about the boys. I mean it's an obsession. If she knew a few—"

"Or had 'em as cousins," Mike added maliciously.

"Family is family. When I needed them, they were there for me. Not friends," the singer emphasized. "Family. *La famiglia è tutto* and you fucking well know it."

And left.

Father and son sat without looking at each other. Billy poured another cup of coffee. Then Mike said, "The start of another perfect day. What're you going to tell Oakhurst?"

"The same thing we told that consortium last year," his father replied. "And that syndicate three years ago. No part of casino take is up for sale. If Oakhurst wants to make the loan anyway, fine."

"You know he won't. This is about the sixth time Mom has scotched such an offer. I mean, you have to hand it to her. She's consistent."

Prince Florian was silent for the longest time. Then he shifted in his chair so that he was facing his son and Billy more directly. "She," he began, "has the strength. Ask Billy. If it was up to me, I suppose I'd have this place in hock again, the way my father did. I'm good for the day-to-day operation of San Sebastian. But someone has to have the moral fiber for the big long-range things. That's your mother. Right, Billy? I don't ever forget it. Mike shouldn't, either."

No one spoke again. There was nothing to say.

· 9 ·

The views in this palace, Maggie Rose told herself, were sets either for an MGM musical with twenty-eight principals and a cast of smiling thousands or else *The Slime that Ate Pasadena* starring fifty-one special-effects men and eighteen gallons of reconstituted chicken blood.

The corridor, along which she was now industriously lurking, led to the front entrance, where her limo was waiting. But this shortcut also passed the unmarked door where, each morning at half-past eight, the bunch that ran the joint held their daily meeting. Florian, she knew, would arrive at a quarter to nine and everyone would be off by nine.

More than this Maggie knew not, neither the name of the *con-*

siglio d'amministrazione nor who belonged to it. Nor the peculiar relationship these rich and powerful men had with their Prince. She
only knew that she had to waylay Florian this morning before he
met with his council and then went into the meeting with the bankers of last night.

Hearing footsteps behind her, she quickly stooped as if to ad-
just the strap of her sandal. Florian came striding along with his
valet tagging behind, flicking a whisk at invisible motes.

"Buon giorno. Altezzo." Maggie turned her posture into a curtsy.

"Bun di, Gummare," he intoned in the local dialect. "Enough,"
he told the valet, dismissing him. "What brings you out so early,
Maggie?"

She watched the valet retreat out of earshot. "Flo, the two people in the whole world who love Faith the best are standing right
here. Tell me I'm wrong?"

"Well, there's Michele and Paola and—"

"No jokes. This is a matter of life and death," she cut in. "Can
I guess what you and the council will be discussing? Before you go
into the meeting with Oakhurst?"

"There's nothing to discuss, Maggie." They started along the
corridor. "I'm telling Oakhurst no."

"Because he's fronting for the boys," Maggie added as if it were
part of his sentence. "What if he isn't? What then? What if he is?
Do you realize, my darling Prince, that up till now the boys have
been handling this with kid gloves? Does it take a genius to see
that if you say no again they may throw away the kid gloves?"

"Possibly."

"Probably," she corrected him. "And if they do, you and I lose
the one person we love most, Florian. I kid you not."

He stopped and wheeled on her. "Is this some kind of message?"

"It's a cry for help."

His face had gone quite gray, she saw. Without another word
he swung open the meeting-room door and disappeared inside.
Maggie stood there for another moment, trying to gauge if she had
made a dent or not.

*   *   *

Like any convincing work of art, the governing of the principality had to appear seamless and inevitable, as if it functioned by supernatural fiat. Largely this was carried off by Faith and Florian but much of it depended on an efficient palace bureaucracy, of which Geni Magari was a good example, dedicated, efficient and thoroughly ruthless.

This morning, however, Faith was unable to speak to anyone, friend or foe, until her anger cooled.

Only it doesn't cool quickly, she told herself. What Irishwoman enjoyed the luxury of a rage that could conveniently burn itself out?

Silently, Jill laid a variety of garments before her. The scene went on for three minutes before Jill tried to break the ice. "You see, this first appointment is somewhat odd. That's why I can't make the decision."

Faith read her typed schedule. At nine she was slated to open an international conference of nuclear scientists who had decided that their life-or-death decisions were best worked out in a tax-free milieu of roulette and blackjack. At ten she presided over the first of the tennis matches in which unknowns had the chance to ambush champions. At eleven-fifteen the San Sebastian chapter of the Girl Scouts was making merit awards to its members, the top three to be presented as always by Her Serene Highness. An hour later she was due to welcome a fact-finding subcommittee of the United States House of Representatives charged with preparing a report on the impact of international terrorism on the vacation and business travel abroad of American citizens. Like the atomic scientists, but with slightly more reason, the subcommittee found the San Sebastian ambience, um, useful to its labors. If she could elude lunch with the congressmen, the Princess had a spare thirty minutes before touring a newly built teaching facility for hotel and restaurant personnel. Here future waiters, chambermaids, bartenders, chefs, security men and managers were given some fluency in several languages and minimal experience in their chosen craft as well as special instructions in exercising discretion. At three-thirty, down at the harbor, Faith was expected to stand in an odor of sanctity as the bishop blessed the new fishing fleet. Promptly at 4 P.M. a location unit of CBS television, reporters and crew, were to begin filming a six-part documentary, *Royal Resort*, with a guided tour of the palace featuring the one ruler who knew what to do in front of cameras. Six in the evening was the scheduled start of eleven different cocktail parties at various luxury hotels, the hosts of which all expected an appearance by Her Serene Highness and would not, in fact, close down their merrymaking until that manifestation had been made or definitely canceled by force of outside necessity. Most of the hosts anticipated a formal cancellation, which was considered as socially useful to them as an appearance. In practice this meant that Faith had to be escorted on foot from one party to the other, motorized transport being impossible during the evening traffic, or else that a series of artful and credible excuses be concocted, the falseness of which could not immediately be checked out. By seven-thirty she and Florian would head dual reception lines prior to a state dinner in honor of the foreign ministers of San Sebastian's great and good neighbors, Italy and France, assuming Italy had a foreign minister at the moment and could prove it. This dinner, including speeches and a ball afterward, would be expected to endure until well past one in the morning.

She looked up from the typed schedule to find Jill watching her with wary intensity. She tossed the typed sheet on the bed, saying:

"Awfully thin schedule, isn't it?"

"Practically a day off," Jilly murmured hollowly.

"Will you tell me something? You're a British subject. You have a monarch of your own."

"Indeed."

"Tell me, whatever happened to the prerogative we used to have of pointing a finger and shouting 'Off with his head!'? Tell me that."

"Whose?"

Faith frowned at her. "Does it matter? Whose idea was it to saddle me with these nuclear people? What am I supposed to say to eggheads who have brought the world to the brink of extinction?"

Jill blushed. The compiling of the schedule was her duty, although the choice of events was made by the *consiglio* of palace bureaucrats. "The Prince was to have met with the scientists," she murmured apologetically, "but he's closeted all morning with those bankers."

Faith continued to stare at her. "How long will it take him to say no? Ten minutes?"

Jill sighed unhappily. "In the world of finance, nothing takes ten minutes."

As she dressed for her first appointment, Faith found that the only way she could master her anger was by concentrating on something else. If she'd been Sicilian, she told herself, this something else would be revenge, the plotting and savoring of it. But, given the spot she was in, the best alternative was thinking about the most important event of the day.

This was certainly not the dinner and ball for the French and Italians, nor the world-class tennis tournament. The press would concentrate heavily on these affairs, as well they should, but the ruler of this bothersome and frustrating principality had to be more cold-blooded in focusing her attention.

Beyond question, she had to devote most of her thinking to the CBS documentary. It would be seen everywhere. It would tell the world what to think about San Sebastian for the next few years, or until another film was made. And the world, used to letting TV arrange its thinking for it, would comply.

As propaganda for the principality, it was worth hundreds and hundreds of tiresome interviews with journalists. For the past week, therefore, Faith had been conferring with some of the *consiglio* about what the world should be told to think.

As always with committee thought, their advice was contradictory. San Sebastian certainly didn't need the kind of publicity that stimulated endless busloads of slob tourists in baseball caps and Instamatics. It also had enough millionaires and more than enough brokers and financial managers waiting to fleece the millionaires. The principality's art galleries and jewelers, its furriers and antiquarians were at present hard-pressed to find enough products to flog to the idle rich.

For the past decade San Sebastian had had nowhere to go but up, building immense jungles of high-rise buildings. Now every square centimeter of downtown space was crowded beyond belief.

Only the lovely old houses that looked down on the town from almost unscalable heights were left to the developers. In what the locals called "Old" San Sebastian, the medieval heart of the principality, there was space for expansion, if the old stuff could be torn down.

Friends of Florian, many of them financial men, some holding jobs within the bureaucracy, kept urging him to raze the old quarter and replace it with a kind of Disneyland "Old" San Sebastian without the smell of drains. Friends of Faith, mostly foreigners from England and the States, kept urging her to preserve this priceless artifact of history.

On one thing everyone agreed: the six-part TV documentary would be an ideal way to restate the public image of the principality in one mold or the other: true history or fake theme park.

All she had to do was decide which.

At precisely nine o'clock, the *consiglio* session ended and the various members waited for the Prince to rise to his feet, releasing them. Florian glanced around the table. He had a quorum, but not the full council in attendance. It was here, he knew, that any democracy might be found in this principality.

Most of the counselors were elderly and rich, with the exception of *Colonnello* Eugenio Magari, head of Gold Beret Intelligence, and *Dottoressa* Ilde Pincio, director of Women's Affairs, an appointee of Princess Faith.

The rest, with few exceptions, had bought their way to power, including his chief of staff, Admiral Licio de Gongaza, the presiding officer of the Senate, Briguglio Belpaese, and the director of Sports and Leisure Activities, *Avvocato* Hans Graf, who, in a previous Olympics, had actually won a bronze for San Sebastian in the men's downhill slalom. To a man they had counseled agreeing to the harbor-funding scheme.

The format of every council meeting was simple. Counselors proposed certain measures for the Prince's approval. If he rejected a proposal, they waited awhile and resubmitted it in a watered-down version. Eventually, Florian agreed, even to something he had originally not wanted. This took years, sometimes, but was on the whole a far more democratic procedure than the principality had ever enjoyed before.

In the case of the harbor improvement loan, the counselors knew that he would go against their advice and reject the offer. Democracy worked only in one direction. There was nothing they could do to force him to reverse his decision.

Nor would they ever, in some blind access of united rage, gang together to topple him. The running of the principality was too compartmented for that kind of crisis to erupt. It was understood—from time immemorial—that the Gulda clan profited from the casinos and only from the casinos while everyone else profited from the rest.

In poor times this didn't mean much. But in the past twenty years, with control of the casinos back in Gulda hands and San Sebastian rising to new levels of affluence, money was everywhere to be made. Or, to put it a cruder way, by marrying Faith, Florian had made them all rich.

Property speculation was the primary source of profit for these men of the *consiglio*. (*La Dottoressa* Pincio was the double exception: female and poor. But in the past two years, acting on information discussed in these meetings, she had invested her meager savings in a tattered old building which, upon being razed, brought the good lady enough profit to keep her handsomely in her old age.)

Like most big cities of world class in finance and the arts, San Sebastian had enjoyed property-value increases of obscene profitability. If for no other reason than this, the *consiglio* would remain forever in accord with the Gulda clan.

Florian rose. So did the rest. He glanced sideways at Geni Magari to detain him. Moments later they were alone. "I am in receipt of a very strange message," Florian began, and related the encounter with Maggie Rose.

"Not strange, sir," Magari responded. "I'm sure she's acting out of friendship. They will soon drop any pretense of legal action if we continue to frustrate them."

"Wh-wh-"—Florian moistened his lips—"what can we expect from them?"

"Just what she said, an attack on Her Serene Highness."

Florian's face fell. Then his lips tightened very visibly. "What sort of attack?" he whispered.

"Sir?"

"What sort of attack?" he asked more loudly.

Geni thought for a moment. "This is an age of specialists, sir. The international Mafia will first use local people, San Sebastiano small fry who take illegal bets or sell drugs. These will set up a situation. Then a specialist will step in. What the Mafia doesn't already have on retainer it can lease from a terrorist group."

"What specialists?" Florian's voice rasped hoarsely.

Again the secret policeman paused. He glanced apprehensively at his ruler. Everyone knew how much in love with the Princess her husband was. In a Mediterranean community of some sophistication it was a subject of amused surprise. "You will be unhappy if I tell you, sir."

"I am usually unhappy at whatever you tell me, Geni." Florian tried a small smile and failed. "You don't imagine your news of half-past two this morning was a joy for me to hear? I haven't had a moment's peace since then."

"Sorry, sir." Geni took a long, tentative breath. "Specialists. First the, er, marksmen. Snipers who can put a bullet in the throat of a President of the United States while his Cadillac is in motion. Then we have the chemists, who can produce an outbreak of food poisoning at a banquet. They don't stop at killing half a dozen people to make one assassination look plausible. Of course we have the demolition experts, who can make anything explode with lethal effect, on demand. Another kind of specialist deals in vehicular homicide, auto accidents that look very real and a particular kind of sideswipe with a heavy truck that leaves the target car crushed with everyone in it. Finally, if one studies one's recent history, one realizes that there is yet another type of specialist, the dedicated assassin who goes right up to his victim and with a knife or handgun murders him at close range because—a—he has hopes of escaping or—b—he is a dedicated fanatic or—c—he is a dupe of others who have psyched him up to this moment. To this type we can add the..."

Long before Magari had cut short his catalog of death, Florian had sunk back down in his chair again. He was staring in misery at the polished mahogany table before him, where a lined pad, a pen and an unopened bottle of mineral water stood in reproachful silence. "My God, Geni!" he burst out.

"Sir?"

"How in the name of God can we protect her against such a... an encyclopedia of threats?"

"We are doing so," the policeman assured him. "We have protected the entire family with some success and we will continue to do so. At the same time..."

The silence between them began to shimmer with evil like the wet trail of a slug across grass. "Say it, Geni. Say there is always a first time."

Magari nodded mutely. The silence in the room began to condense around the two men like a deadly dew.

"...these Corinthian columns are decorated at the top by hand-carved wreaths of acanthus and fig leaves as well as bunches of grapes and pears." Princess Faith's voice sang out clearly across the mighty expanse of the grand ballroom, now set up for tonight's state dinner with rows of round tables, each surrounded by eight chairs.

"Cut. There's an echo back there," the director called. "You hear it, Izzy?"

"I can filter it later," the sound man promised.

"Okay. Your Highness, we'll insert a C.U. of the column here and you just go on. Sound?"

"Sound rolling."

"Action."

"*Royal Resort*, Take seventy-nine." *Clap!*

"The murals at the head of the table are by Bramante," the former Faith Brennan told the world. "In fact, all over the principality, if one looks, one can spot little gems of decoration by..."

Moving slowly toward her, three cameramen carrying shoulder-braced minicams zoomed and panned, recording endless videotape of the walls, ceiling, doors and furnishings. They moved ahead inexorably like large-eyed warrior ants decimating the enemy, until they clustered at Faith's feet as she stood on the dais, still narrating.

"...typical of medieval and Renaissance art treasures to be found throughout the principality. It is no exaggeration to say that alongside our famous high-rise towers we are also trying hard to conserve and protect our cultural heritage from the past. In this regard..."

They were circling her now, getting tight close-ups and medium shots of her famous face and figure, the inky gleam of her black hair and the precisely minted contours of her profile. The lenses seemed to caress her, as they always had, like lovers freshly hypnotized with love.

"...inlaid with seven kinds of wood native to San Sebastian. Here the white birch, here the walnut, surrounded by a framework of...

"...overhead oak bracing is early seventeenth century, handcut, drilled and doweled. This ceiling alone took Donatello and several dozen assistants and apprentices nearly four years to finish. Some baked terra-cotta bas-reliefs in the exterior walls of the old quarter are also attributed to him, although it's unlikely he did more than approve an assistant's design. The old quarter, by the way, is one of our most precious...

"...through this window previous rulers of San Sebastian would gaze at length for a glimpse of a trading armada that was long overdue from the eastern sea. Such merchantmen carried spices and dyes, medicines and fabrics and the most amazing..."

The caravan of cameramen, sound men and the rest of the crew moved forward as she swept ahead, delving into side chapels rich with gilded mosaics and great chandeliers, pausing before another view of the sea, moving down long corridors thick with framed engravings and maps, all the while the crew, the reporters, the director, everyone hypnotized as were the cameras by an upgushing torrent of love.

If the camera loved her face, as it always had, so did the people behind the camera. If her troubled husband had been there to see this outpouring of love, he would have forgotten his dark fears of the morning and commanded Geni to relax his vigilance.

How could anyone even dream of harming her?

· 10 ·

Billy Ritz had told everyone he was leaving soon for Yugoslavia to look into development money for a new film. This was a lie, but perhaps a white one. He was in fact stealing home to California to snooze by his pool and let his nerves simmer down. The truth he confided only to Prince Florian.

"I love visiting you guys," Billy explained, "but I'm getting too old for all the behind-the-scenes melodrama."

Florian was on his way to tender formal greetings to an international gathering of cardiologists. Their work sessions would crowd several of the huge high-rise hotels, but the opening session was being held rather dramatically in the auditorium of the Eamon Brennan Memorial Clinic.

More than a clinic, the place housed a medical school of modest pretensions, a public wing of well-appointed wards, a private section for high-paying patients and a lot of the latest electronic apparatus used in diagnosing heart and brain problems. It had been established by Faith's father merely as a clinic to provide free service to the people of San Sebastian, but after Eamon Brennan's death and his bequest of an immense wad of money to the foundation, things had gotten a bit out of hand. The original purpose of the place began to swell out of all proportions to its founding concept.

Architects and designers had taken over. Extensive gardens had been landscaped, complete with pools, sculpture and a small area where esteemed guests could use the facilities of a rather posh little bar.

It was here, in perhaps the most exclusive spot in all San Sebastian, lolling in privacy with tiny cups of espresso, that Billy and the Prince conversed in extremely prudent tones as they waited for the courier who would come to lead Florian to the dais of the auditorium for his brief speech of welcome. His Serene Highness, amid this luxury, looked strangely sad.

He gazed fondly upon the small Viennese director, but beneath the outer gentility Florian's face had gone quite grave. He glanced around, as if for eavesdroppers, knowing that the only person who could overhear was, in a certain sense, licensed to eavesdrop, the Gold Beret intelligence agent who served as barman here.

"Faith will be destroyed."

His lips didn't move, so quietly did he say the words. Surrounded by greenery and the splashing sound of fountains, his startling statement seemed to shudder in the air for only a moment before being totally erased.

Billy Ritz blinked as if slapped, so lethal was the idea. *"Mein Gott,"* he muttered, "You surely don't th...?"

"She loves having you around," Florian went on, to Billy's instant relief. "She'll be unhappy that you have to leave." He paused and eyed the director with sudden alertness. "Did you think I meant...?"

Neither man spoke. Then Florian went on in a more somber tone, "After this morning's meeting with Oakhurst, I suppose anything could happen. The look on his face when I had to turn down his loan proposal!"

He stared into his tiny coffee cup. "You would have thought I had pronounced his death sentence," the Prince continued. "I suppose that means Mikey is right and Oakhurst is nothing but a Mafia go-between." He set the cup down so hard it made Billy blink.

"God, Billy, this world is so...so ugly!" He hunched over now in silence and the little Viennese judged that for any affairs of state remaining on today's agenda, the Prince would not have much heart.

He was supposed to lunch with a group of sheiks from oil-producing countries. To review the new squadron of helicopters added this week to the Gold Berets. To have cocktails with five separate and distinct sets of VIPs who were to officiate at the tennis tournament.

It is a mark of the difference between nobility and common folk that he would do all these things in his usual grave, diffident manner, seemingly interested but never involved, a perfect Prince Florian performance. At heart, Billy knew, he was sick.

What bothered Florian was that on this one point he could simply not speak his mind to Faith, because the subject of his heart-sickness was Faith herself.

In his Mediterranean heart he simply did not agree with her. Sharing the casino take with the boys who did gambling best was the point of difference. No one of the Gulda blood could seriously take a holier-than-thou attitude about modern-day pirates, could they?

And yet, even in his Gulda heart, Florian knew she was right, he was wrong and it was impossible to be candid about it with her. More remained unspoken in his heart: the danger she was in.

It is in the nature of progress that immovable obstacles will always be pulverized by irresistible forces. Only movable barriers can exist anymore in this new world, Billy told himself. And a movable barrier is, of course, no barrier at all.

It was not as if she had never made compromises before. No one got to be anything in this world without compromise. Billy Ritz had long ago told Florian of the several years of dickering between himself and Eamon Brennan before Faith had been allowed to go to Hollywood.

It was a basket of eels, as far as Florian was concerned. Billy had to donate half his own gross percentage of Faith Brennan films to one of Eamon's nonprofit charitable tax-avoidance foundations. In return Billy got an override on any Faith Brennan production. Everybody had a bit of everyone else.

The thought of it had revolted Florian, that whole compromising give-and-take world of business. And Faith knew it even better than he. Perhaps that was why she didn't want it talked of in front of the children. Perhaps that was why she had a special loathing for the Mafia part of the business community, that high-risk, high-profit sector in which death and the threat of death played such a key part in any negotiation.

Billy knew she especially resented Maggie Rose's ties with the underworld establishment. But being in show business brought one into contact with the many mob bankers, brokers and bookers who controlled clubs, record companies, jukebox outlets and the like.

That was the thing about Faith that had attracted Florian that first time, her high standards. She had been making her second film for Billy in the Cinecittà studios in Rome. Florian had been summoned to the Vatican to make a tedious report. He was thirty years old. Faith was twenty. She looked even younger under the arc lights and reflectors, even more seductive in her dark, forceful way.

Billy had taken them both to dinner in an elderly restaurant near the Piazza di Spagna, a place called Ranieri's, where one entire room had been cleared of other diners to afford His Serene Highness privacy.

That evening, every facet of it, like the Gulda emerald, glittering with history, was as bright as new in Billy's memory. Florian had been broke. Totally, pockets-inside-out broke. He had his return railroad car to San Sebastian but he literally couldn't have tipped the attendants. Billy decided the Prince needed a lush evening in Rome before he plunged back into the stupid poverty of his existence.

Florian had begun, naturally enough, by lying to Faith, trusting Billy not to give him away. He had described his life in San Sebastian so glowingly that the words almost choked him. "...stable of ponies, really rather good polo mounts, 'pon my word," he was burbling away.

There had been a longish pause while Faith digested this. Then: "You're adorable," she said, "when you lie like that."

"Ma'am?"

"Please," she insisted, "We're friends. Friends tell each other the truth."

Billy had felt it necessary to intervene. "Faith, you have to understand the nobility. As with actors, illusion is important to them. And Florian doesn't have a helluva lot more than illusion to sustain him."

All of a sudden Florian felt the sobs well up in his chest and the tears pour down his cheeks. It felt as if someone had punched him hard in the gut and it stopped very quickly, but it had never happened before in a public place in front of a lovely girl of impeccably high standards who would now consider him beyond the pale.

Instead she passed him her handkerchief. It smelled of Chanel. Florian pocketed it. He still had it, to this day, tucked in the dinner jacket he had worn that night. That night he found it impossible to meet her glance.

"That bad, is it?" she asked at last. "Are things so poor you can't have company?"

"Beg pardon, ma'am?"

"I mean, can I pay a visit to San Sebastian someday?"

But shooting schedules intervened. Two years passed. Then Billy phoned to say that Faith and her father and he were visiting friends in Villefranche. Could they take a spin over to San Sebastian that afternoon?

In two years—and three more films—Faith Brennan had already reached the lofty position she would hold in the film world. What lay between Florian and Faith came into being that one hot, hurried afternoon.

He had gone overboard on getting one of the private salons in the casino swept out, dusted and furnished as a pleasant sitting room with a view of the harbor where he could offer his guests tea.

"Christ," Eamon Brennan responded with his normal tact. "Anything stronger than that?"

Billy and Eamon finished the bottle of good cognac—Florian's ration for the week—while Faith and he drank tea, first hot, then iced. He took her for a walk in the casino gardens, perhaps the only place in the principality that was kept to any degree of neatness. He showed her the picturesque fishing boats drawn up on the stingy shingle beach. She watched the menders of nets as they bowed to their sovereign and to her.

The sun hammered down on them until they were both lightheaded. In that condition, he let Eamon Brennan pry from his lips the story he had told Billy many years before, of the casino contract he had inherited which gave the Greek and Nevada outsiders everything while he had nothing. He wondered why anyone of Eamon Brennan's stature would be interested in such a desperate tale told by such a loser.

Shooting schedules intervened once more. They met more than a year later in the Brennan enclave, ten secluded acres on the north shore of Lake Michigan above Evanston. Florian had been asked— he had no idea who inspired the invitation—to address Chicago's Downtown Chamber of Commerce on the topic of European investment opportunities. Naturally, he came as Eamon Brennan's guest. It was a short stay but a memorable one, strolling the parklike paths and glades of the Brennan estate with Faith, who had interrupted location shooting in New Mexico for a weekend visit.

They came to the shore of Lake Michigan and a huge old boat-house of the McKinley era which so reminded Florian of one his grandfather had built in the Victorian era on the shores of the Mediterranean. The two bodies of water seemed alike too.

"Don't you think so?" he asked Faith as they sat on a log bench and watched the water. "I say, you know, almost no surf, not like a real ocean, wot?"

"I'm not a great traveler," she responded. "About the best I can do on location is visit the local museum."

"If you came to San Sebastian again," he began, "for a longer visit, that is, I could show you some terribly exciting things. I could..." He paused, overcome with an idea, a big one.

"Yes?"

"I could..." It stuck there again, too big to come out.

She watched him quite openly. "You're really not a twentieth-century man," she said at last. "You're really out of the nineteenth. I absolutely adore you for it."

"Will you marry me?"

The courier came hurrying into the private garden of the Eamon Brennan Memorial Clinic. The moment Florian spotted him he rose to his feet. "Cardiology calls," he told Billy in an undertone. "Have a pleasant trip and come back soon, Billy."

The little Viennese watched the Prince stride toward the con-ference that he would now officially open in the auditorium. As al-ways, Florian looked strong, supple, lithe, a quasi-military figure of a man. But underneath, Billy recalled, that line of Faith's told another story: Florian wasn't really meant for the mean streets of the twentieth century.

Yet he had the responsibility of guiding her along some of its dangerous back alleys. Why couldn't he turn to his wife of more than two decades and say, very plainly:

"Look here, my darling. If you stand in the middle of the road, they will run you down."

The warning seemed to rattle around in Billy Ritz's mind as he watched Florian disappear inside the hospital. Why not let the mob have a nibble again? This time it wouldn't be the choking contract it once was, but only a taste, enough to slake their thirst, so to speak. Surely Faith could give them that, if it meant saving her own life.

Sadly, he got to his feet and let the chauffeured limo return him to the palace, where he finished his packing. Florian was a fool, he decided. There were times when a strong woman had to be restrained and this was one of them. Oakhurst would be around for a few more days. Let Florian make some sort of deal, over Faith's head. That kind of sellout was man's work anyway.

Because this was surely the end of the line for the businessmen whom Oakhurst represented. They had tried one legitimate ploy after another. This last, with the Vatican carrying the can, would be their final legal attempt. From now on they would revert to type. It would take time and patience to make it look like something other than a murder. But they had both.

He found Mike in the library. "Is your mother back?"

"She and Maggie were due to meet David Niven for coffee."

"And I'm off to the airport. Please tell her good-bye for me, will you?"

"Can't you stay awhile?"

"The great money hunt," Billy explained, a partial version of the truth.

"Tell me about it," Mike said, meaning please don't. "I'm about to chase up cash for this harbor project."

"The difference is, you'll find your money and I won't. How'd you like to be my producer, wunderkind?"

"You have to promise me two starlets a day."

"Crazy kid, there are no starlets anymore. Don't you know that? There are only very serious, dedicated actresses looking for meaningful parts that speak to the core problems of modern existence."

"You sure know how to turn a guy on."

A limo was waiting for Billy as one of the valets carried his bags downstairs. Billy settled in the back of the long Mercedes 600 and watched the back of Geni Magari's head as he steered the heavy vehicle through San Sebastian's cobbled streets. *"Colonnello."* Billy called. *"Tutto va bene?"*

He could see Geni's lips moving and he knew that the secret policeman was saying something ordinary like *"Tutto in ordine, Commendatore,"* or something reassuring like that.

But through a trick of stress or fatigue or, Billy wasn't sure, clairvoyance, what the little director seemed to hear was Florian's grave voice saying:

"Faith will be destroyed."

PART
TWO

· 11 ·

Sometimes he read documents and press clippings. Sometimes he sat in the palace library and thought about San Sebastian and his parents and his future.

On the surface his parents had always seemed to enjoy a very simple relationship, so open that it was hardly worth talking about. Both his mother and father were of a piece, consistent with their own histories, not given to deviation from a straightforward norm.

But Mike was beginning—despite years of college—to pick up the rudiments of wisdom. Thanks to his Grandpa Eamon, he had seen through the delusions of such pseudo-sciences as economics. Now, at last, he was also beginning to realize that nothing, not even the marriage of his parents, was entirely what it seemed.

The storybook air of fantasy about it that had fueled hundreds of pages of pap in fan magazines and those extremely slim periodicals that came with Sunday newspapers no longer covered the principality with a shimmering layer of moonbeams.

At the same time, however, it had become abundantly clear that San Sebastian had made a sensational comeback once it added the Brennan colors to those of the Guldas.

Mike occasionally ran across a passing mention of this entirely business miracle in the pages of financial journals. Lacking the inside information to flesh out the San Sebastian story, most editors

Leslie   Waller

let it pass as part of the Faith Brennan charisma that attracted new and much classier people to the tiny enclave.

But Mike knew better. In fact, there was a hell of a good story behind the rebirth of San Sebastian as a fashionable resort. It was a story his faculty adviser at Harvard Graduate School of Business Administration had once suggested should be told.

A seductive idea, that one. Mike had completed all his credits for an MBA but lacked a subject for his thesis. Why not dig up all the facts about the resurgence of the principality and make them the basis for his final paper?

One day somebody would do exactly that, wouldn't they? And why, then, shouldn't it be an insider who had the good name of San Sebastian at heart? Better Mike than some stranger, right? Easy to say, impossible actually to do because a Gulda did not spill family secrets.

However, a Brennan might.

The back door to the library opened and Jill Tremont entered, without seeing Mike. Clad in a long dressing gown and high-heeled, flimsy slippers, she carried under her arm the badge of her office, the large morocco leather folder. Still unaware that she was being watched, she sat at a corner desk she kept as her office.

Mike watched the half-moon reading glasses slip slowly down Jill's pretty nose until they hung precariously at the end of their fine gold chain tether. He had to hand it to her, Mike thought. She managed somehow to turn good looks into total dowdiness.

"Che c'è?" he whispered loudly.

She let out a small scream, whirled in her seat, eyes wide with terror, and then relaxed on seeing Mike. "You devil."

"Boy, were you lost in thought."

She held up a small slip of tan paper in one hand and a larger sheet of pale blue in the other. "The schedule gets more intricate every day. What are you doing in here?"

"Research."

Mike had learned that this word, signifying nothing but hard work, turned off most inquiries. "Research," Jill echoed. She frowned in a way Mike could only describe as librarianly.

70

"You're one of the few primary sources I have for this project. Have you got time to answer questions?"

Her face went pink. "Questions?" She began making churning motions, as if fending off a swarm of mosquitoes.

"Nothing personal," he assured her. "I'm researching the original deal put through about the time I was born. The one that got Georgiadis off our backs. I've got some material from Grandpa Eamon and a lot from Uncle Billy. But it's just facts, no nuances. That's where you come in."

Jill looked vague. "Let me finish this first." She turned back to her work and Mike continued watching her lovely profile.

It was entirely unlike his mother's. He knew Jill had originally been her stand-in. But a stand-in wasn't a double, he reminded himself. Jill's profile was soft, with a small, neat nose and extremely well-formed, smooth lips, a chin that failed to come out quite as far as her lower lip. It gave her a very vulnerable quality.

His mother's profile, by now incised on the San Sebastian 1,000-lire coin, was everything a mint required: precise, sharply defined, with a crisp edge to each feature and a strong chin. Jill's was the profile for a candy-box top, hinting at luxurious, even fattening, pleasures.

As to what Jill might remember of the matter he was researching, Mike had his doubts. But in outline he had already put together what had happened, the historic emancipation of San Sebastian's casinos from foreign (read Mafia) control.

It was the wellspring of his parents' power, the power he could see and smell but never quite get his hands on.

Historic was the word. Not only because the deal placed the tiny nation on a firm financial footing. Not simply because it represented Eamon Brennan's first and most far-reaching meddling in San Sebastian's life. But historic because it had become an article of his mother's faith. She lived by the independence of the casinos. It was her sine qua non. If anything ever came between his parents, it would be this one historic fact.

Mike turned away from Jill and paged slowly through his notes. They should begin, Mike had decided, with a simple exposition of how low San Sebastian had sunk, economically, under the tyranny of the group headed by Dimitrios Georgiadis of Athens and Little

Augie Pisano of Brooklyn, and later, Las Vegas. Since both men were dead, Georgiadis of living and Little Augie of gunshot wounds and suffocation in the trunk of an Oldsmobile Cutlass 88, Mike felt sure he could cut closer to the truth than if they were alive and litigious.

Under the terms of the contract Grandpa Pippo had signed with Georgiadis, the gambling syndicate and the principality had equal shares of casino net earnings, although casino expenses were met by the principality, not the syndicate.

In the period 1938 to 1948 the net had been maneuvered down from half a billion annually to something just over a million at the time Pippo passed on and Prince Florian was invested as the new ruler.

This million was shared equally by Georgiadis' syndicate (read Mafia) and the San Sebastian corporation known as Società Privata per il Turismo. Most of the Società's half went to pay gardeners, croupiers and others who kept the casino in order. What was left for His Serene Highness, Mike knew, was peanuts.

"When you came here," he called to Jill, "what year was it?"

She looked up slowly from her work. "I didn't get here till the wedding."

So the Eamon intervention hadn't begun until the mid-1960s. The old boy had to have sent in his spies and scouts and auditors. They would have combed through the principality and through Nevada and Athens as well. Finally, the old boy would have made his first move.

Mike had that move in front of him in the form of a packet of newspaper clippings reporting the results of a public inquiry called by Prince Florian and Princess Faith into the economic planning of their small nation.

The analysis made the obvious point: gambling and only gambling kept San Sebastian alive. The tax-haven offices, bearing the shingles of thousands of companies around the world incorporated in San Sebastian, brought some income but it was nothing compared to what the casinos *could* produce if they weren't being skimmed. If Georgiadis had been paying attention, instead of romancing a prima ballerina of the Ballet Russe, he would have seen that there was only one way San Sebastian could go.

He got word of it on his next visit to the principality. Holed up in the Hohenzollern Suite of the Gran Albergo Excelsior with Olga Tatianova, up to his navel in Dom Perignon and Malossol caviar, the Athenian was not very welcoming late one morning when the Prince arrived.

"I am empowered to buy your casino stock," Florian announced, once the ballerina had been bundled off into her bath.

"But I have no intention of selling, dear boy," Georgiadis parried.

He was a small, toadlike man rumored to have one of the largest penises in the world, but slowly dying of something those old VD films of Uncle Billy could have counseled him about.

"I am empowered to offer twenty dollars a share," Florian went on.

Mouth opening and closing, Georgiadis frowned in thought. Casino shares were selling at a bit less than the Prince was offering. The Greek had originally bought them from Prince Pippo for a dollar each. So twenty was not only a fair price but a profitable one.

"There is no reason I should sell at any price," he said then, remembering the billions he had looted from this tiny land and would continue to loot on the basis of his casino stock.

"There is one reason," Florian assured him.

It is a tribute to the stiffening power of having Eamon Brennan as a father-in-law that Florian was able to lure Georgiadis away from La Tatianova for a brisk walk to the San Sebastian mint, only two streets away from the hotel.

"Dear boy," the short Greek managed to puff as he scampered along beside Florian's long strides, "what on earth is so compelling about a visit to the mint? I have seen money being printed. It depresses me."

"We print other things at the mint," Florian assured him.

In the basement the tall, blond Prince and the squat financier stood watching a small letterpress machine stamping out ornate stock certificates. "What?" Georgiadis demanded. "You're printing more casino shares?"

"If you examine the charter of the casinos, you know there is a public and a private sector of ownership. You and I share the private one. The public shares have never been offered. I think it is high time we allow the public to share our success."

"But—"

"If you examine the charter, you also know the private shares are subordinated to the public in matters of management decision."

"You're watering down my equity in—"

"More than that, I am placing control of the casinos in the hands"—Florian's voice took on an ecclesiastical note he had learned from Eamon—"of the people."

"You tricky bastard!"

So it would have been back in the late 1960s, Mike had learned, that Dimitrios Georgiadis unloaded all his shares of casino stock at a profit that kept the other syndicate members from screaming with pain. For the first time in modern history a gambling enclave with the potential of San Sebastian was owned free and clear by a local entity unaffiliated with any foreign (read Mafia) principals.

Naturally, the five dozen certificates of public stock printed that morning at the mint for the personal discomfiture of Georgiadis were later burned. Control of the casinos was now firmly in the hands of the Società, meaning the Gulda family, meaning Brennan Bank and Trust Company of Chicago, the principality's chief creditor.

Jill came over to stand beside Mike at the long refectory table where he was working. "Did you ever talk much about this business to Mom or Dad?" he asked, showing her a newspaper photo of Prince Florian and other local dignitaries rededicating the Società to the greater good of the San Sebastian people.

Her wide-set, light gray eyes flicked back and forth over the photo. "The great day. I do remember how pleased Eamon and your mother were."

She sat down beside Mike and looked through some more clippings. "It seemed to tickle your grandfather," she said then. "I remember he and your mother talked of nothing else."

"That's hard to believe of Mom."

"She always stood up to him better than any of her brothers or sisters. But in the matter of chitchat she gave him his head."

"But this business. She'd have thought it was, uh, sordid?"

Jill's fine-textured English skin grew pinker suddenly. "The old man had a thing for me. I'm sure it didn't escape *your* eye, Sherlock. He could bully me when he couldn't touch her. So I was a favorite of his."

"The way a spider has his favorite fly?"

A surprising hoot of laughter escaped her and her cheeks grew red. She sat back, remembering. "As a matter of fact, it was in the same rooms at the Excelsior that Georgiadis had once used, that frumpy, fussy Hohenzollern Suite. The palace hadn't been renovated and all of us were camping out at the hotel."

"It's disgusting, Father," Faith said.

This was before Georgiadis had fallen into the trap and Eamon was wondering how high to price his buy offer. "There's a fine line between greed and expediency," he told his daughter.

"Disgusting."

"If so, then all of banking is disgusting." he snapped back.

"You may have something there," the former Faith Brennan coolly agreed. Turning to Jill, she went on, "In acting class, did you ever do Brecht?"

"Never. Did you?"

"The Madames of the Sacred Heart would never let us do Brecht's plays. But we did some poems and songs and a soliloquy or two. They are rather touching."

"Wasn't he a Communist?" Jill asked.

Faith gestured vaguely. "Now and then. I remember this one couplet. It's from..." She frowned. Her face underwent a change from personal conversation in a hotel sitting room to that of an actor onstage before an audience.

"What is robbing a bank?" she asked ringingly.

"Compared to owning a bank?"

Eamon's high cackle startled both women. "The Commie had the right idea."

"You agree with him?" Jill asked.

"You have to because he's on the button," the old man explained. "It's the same here, isn't it? What's being a Hollywood princess compared to owning your own little principality?"

· 12 ·

They met at a lunch party aboard the yacht *Bestseller*, which was moored at the far end of the harbor with no nearby neighbors. Its owner had rented the docking spaces around it to ensure privacy.

He was the author of novels designed around a combination of high-fashion bondage, flogging, humiliation and sadism. These basic ingredients were novelized amid lavishly rich settings for women readers who would never be caught dead buying porno.

It was not true that Charley Oakhurst was his personal banker, but he was Connie Oakhurst's favorite author. Whenever the Oakhursts visited the Riviera they were invited to a *Bestseller* lunch: booze, pot, coke, finger food and private cabins for afternoon sex.

Maggie Rose had been combing her way through the attractive young men and women, selecting and rejecting for her afternoon requirements, when Charley bore down on her in the aft deck area behind the bridge.

"*Carlos! Come vai?*"

Oakhurst's lantern jaw braced in a ferocious grin of anger. "Not so hot."

"I figured," Maggie responded. "She turned it down cold the other morning at breakfast. He had no choice. But personally, I think he—"

"Who the fuck cares what he thinks?" Oakhurst cut in savagely, his voice low as he glanced around him. "That woman thinks she's God."

"And he worships her."

"Do you have any idea...?" Hearing the strangled note of wrath in his voice, the banker made a visible effort to calm himself. He managed to look fakely relaxed against the railing.

"Tell me," he began again, "tell me how long you think it took me to get all the ingredients of this new offer in line? The money was the least of it. A billion is chicken feed. But the Vatican sponsorship. And the series of cutouts that keep anybody from tracking this back to the boys at home. Do you have any idea how long it's taken my people to assemble this offer?"

"A year?"

He looked chagrined. "Alex told you?"

"No, I just know it takes time."

"Fourteen months, my dear, fourteen months of expensive man-hours and, my sweet Christ, the costly buttering up of bishops and that candy-assed slob of a cardinal who sits on the I.U.D. Maggie, my Xerox costs alone are up over a hundred grand. And she turns me down."

"You make it sound like the end of the world. But I know the boys. They won't quit till they've got this little hunk of turf under their control again."

She sipped her daiquiri and found it too sweet. Sugar was Maggie Rose's prime enemy, right after any other form of carbohydrate. She pushed the drink out of sight behind a ventilator stack.

"You're talking to me like I was a quarterback whose end run didn't work. I'm disheartened, sure," Oakhurst said, "but you don't understand something, Maggie. This is no game."

"My goombars play for keeps."

"I don't need cheering up," he said through gritted teeth. "I need a life insurance policy with double indemnity in case I'm found in the trunk of a car with a wire around my neck and a canary in my mouth."

She burst out laughing at his lack of knowledge. "That's for an informer, Charley. The boys would never do such a thing to you. Auto accident, how's that? Or heart attack after a session in bed with me. Better?"

He calmed down visibly for the second time. "I spend a ton of dough on this—their dough—and I come up losers. Again. In their nose, I'm starting to stink."

Maggie's head shook slowly from side to side, but even in his disturbed state Oakhurst could see that she was carefully thinking through his problem and silently agreeing with him.

"How come they don't lean on you the way they lean on me?" he demanded. "How come Alex or Santos hasn't given you the contract on Her Serene Highness? You're in so tight with her."

"*Because* I'm in so tight."

"That doesn't make sense."

Leslie Waller

She paused, obviously wondering how much to tell him in the state he was in. Then, quickly: "The world knows we're close. Actually, that Viennese asshole, Billy Ritz, is closer. I just cultivate an old friendship because Alex wants me to. The other day I think I blew it. We were having coffee with Niven and I tried to rope him into helping me but he wouldn't budge. So I did my be-reasonable number as a solo. Let's say it lowered the temperature a lot. Alex will have a fit. I'm not supposed to play any role but Best Pal."

"What I suspect," the banker went on in a lower voice, "is that he and Santos will now stop playing Mr. Nice Guy. They've been patient as hell."

A frown of startling proportions began to develop around Maggie Rose's extensively made-up eyes. "Cool it, Charley," she said then. "The day you start handling strategy for the boys..."

"Yes?"

She left the lethal thought unfinished. Glancing forward, she saw that the sex part of the day was already starting. She was still stuck with this frightened man. Maggie Rose had been around in certain circles long enough to tell the difference between real anger and the kind that only camouflages fear. Charley Oakhurst exuded the sweat of cowardice.

It wasn't usually as obvious as Charley made it. Maggie could remember J.F.K. after he learned how the boys had reacted to his calling off the Bay of Pigs air cover. He'd been a lot braver than Charley Oakhurst.

Near the main hatchway that led below, a topless young actress was giving head to a paunchy French film producer whose belly overflopped his minibikini so far that it almost interfered with her work. Two even lovelier young women were coming her way now, closing in on Maggie Rose, whose dominant personality had given her the bisexual reputation that endeared her to all sorts of fans and especially homosexual ones.

She turned to the banker, wondering if he'd have the good sense to clear off, now that the action was under way. Get out of town, before it's too late, my dear. Take wifie-poo, too.

"Well, Charley, it's been great fun, but just one of those things."

7 8

"You wait," he snapped nastily. "It'll be your turn one of these days. Alex may be saving your ass, but he'll call it due."

"*Che será, será.*"

Definitely chicken, she thought. Jack Kennedy'd shown a lot more guts when he realized what he'd done. He could have been nasty, like Oakhurst, could have complained about the girls Maggie sent him, like the one who was also—private joke—balling Sam Giancana at the same time. But J.F.K. had class. This scared banker had shit in his blood.

"Smile, Charley," she called to him. "These are the beautiful people here today."

· 13 ·

La Principessa glanced at her wristwatch during the last game of the set that would decide who continued into the quarter finals of the women's tennis tournament.

The royal box, shadowed in the morning, had now come under its burning rays. Shielding her eyes with a program, Faith glanced through the crowd, making up her mind that she had spent enough time here and could leave.

The quarter-finalist candidates in the near court were boring baseline players in a contest of unforced errors. Now and then one of these muscular girls would, by a fraction of a millimeter's change in racket-head angle, accidentally send the ball either into the net or beyond the far baseline and a point would be scored.

Faith gave Jill a sideways glance, the equivalent of "Let's scram." As the Princess rose to her feet, she could see, across the harbor, the crowd aboard *Bestseller*. She managed not to frown disapprovingly, since this would be taken as a comment on the tennis, not the yacht and its guests.

Jill had to hurry to keep pace with Faith as she strode down the concrete walk to her waiting limousine. "We have to do something about that floating whorehouse," she muttered to her secretary.

"Now? He's been pulling that stuff for years."

They sat in the air-cooled limo, moving at a sedate pace through San Sebastian's narrow streets. As they passed, women blew kisses and men waved. This never failed to attract Faith, but today her mind was seething with other matters. She did not forget, however, to nod prettily to one and all.

"I also know that's the way he conducts himself at Villefranche and in Monaco." She was silent a moment. "We have to draw the line somewhere, Jill. Otherwise, we're just hypocrites."

Lately, Jill had noticed, a certain first-person-plural note had crept into the Princess' mode of expression. Being a long-time admirer of Queen Victoria, Jill didn't object to this usage.

"He buys a lot of booze locally," she murmured. "Hires catering staff. Pays the year-round rental fee on five mooring slips. And he's incorporated here, which I suppose makes him one of our own."

"That cuts two ways," Faith responded. "If he's legally domiciled in San Sebastian, we have something of a hold on him."

The Princess smiled. It had a shape that involuntarily mimicked her father's sneer of triumph. Jill noted the similarity, but said nothing.

"Oh, I know," Faith went on as if Jill had spoken, "San Sebastian is Freedom Hall. We're everybody's favorite tax haven. But being easy on taxes doesn't mean we have to flop on our backs, all four paws in the air, when anybody yells 'Roll over!' We have to draw a line and maintain it."

"I suppose we do," Jill agreed, but in a wistful tone, as if wishing it were otherwise. "They tell me that during the war it was incredibly lax around here."

Faith's face seemed to freeze. "But cheapo. Tacky. At least we've managed to upgrade the debauchery."

The limousine sidled smoothly in under the palace porte cochere. The two women descended, Faith consulting her watch again.

"Florian's with the Danish ambassador. I don't envy him."

"Those boys who were expelled last week?"

The Princess nodded as they walked to her suite. "It seems one of them is the son of a prominent Copenhagen industrialist. Papa is screaming that Sonny-Boy now has a drug bust on his police record." She sank down on a chaise longue upholstered in pale peach. She could see out the nearby windows but, instead, she closed her eyes. Neither woman spoke for a long moment.

"Will you do one thing, Jill? If Florian is attending that philatelic thing, get me out of it. Slight touch of sun at the tennis matches."

"Consider it done."

Faith opened her eyes. "Don't lay it on. I'm *not* ill."

"Right."

"I don't want anybody thinking I'm ill."

"Will do."

"And tell Maria I'm not to be disturbed. No servants, no calls."

She looked quite healthy, Jill saw, but suddenly very—what was the word?—conflicted? Faith Brennan conflicted? It was a rare sight indeed. As Jill left the room she closed the double arched doors behind her with a firm, muted click.

Faith lay back on the chaise and slipped off her patent-leather pumps. She hoped sleep would steal over her. The sun had been quite hot and the buffet lunch entirely disagreeable, awkwardly cut canapés, a kind of hideous super-Waldorf salad with not only nuts and apples, but, dear God, avocados and pineapple bits as well.

But sleep didn't come. After a few minutes she got up and began striding the immense anteroom, designed in peach and burnt orange for courtiers and ladies-in-waiting. She missed being able to talk to Billy Ritz. On stockinged feet, she strode from one wall of windows to another, glancing out each in turn, without really noting what she was seeing. She supposed it was the sight of the orgying idiots aboard *Bestseller* that had set her off, but she was now in the full throes of a crisis.

Either you have standards or you don't. Either you enforce them or you forget them. But you must be consistent.

In this vein she racked back and forth over the rejection of the harbor-development loan. Perhaps it could come from another bank? The proposition was a viable one; the treasury of San Sebastian stood behind it. Charley Oakhurst wasn't the only money man on earth.

But that wasn't really the point, was it? The point was maintaining standards. Drawing the line.

It began right in her own family. It began with allowing the children to eavesdrop on every squalid detail of modern life. With let-

81

ting Maggie Rose eat up vast quantities of her time with her dubious suggestions.

In the distance, thunder growled.

Faith stopped in mid-stride. Returning to the windows facing the sea, she stared challengingly at the darkening sky as if to say "I didn't order this, you fools."

In the harbor, yachts were beginning to bob and pull at their lines. There would be one of those loud, very wet Mediterranean cloudbursts, she could see. It would probably send more than a few of the *Bestseller's* guests to the rail. Seasickness, on top of booze and sex. That wicked smile appeared again on her lips.

She could see some of the smaller ships begin to buck at their lines as the wind freshened and sharp, short waves traveled the harbor's waters. A ketch she took to be the *Finisterre* had chosen this moment to up anchor and leave San Sebastian. Good riddance!

Here and there crews were resetting mooring lines to allow more slack. Whereas, she told herself, you are arranging in your mind to remove as much slack as possible. Two schools of thought on that, eh?

But running a principality was only superficially like running a yacht. Let one Danish industrialist's son off the hook and you soon were the focus of drugged youths from everywhere in Europe. Let one Vatican-fronted Mafia deal go through and you soon couldn't call your casinos your own.

She watched two people aboard the *Bestseller* stagger up on deck and barely make it to the railing before returning to Neptune their cargo of daiquiris and finger food. For the third time she smiled Eamon's sneer.

I am getting more and more like him, she warned herself. Even to having Maggie Rose under my feet all the time. It was his favorite expression, which he claimed was an old Irish saying:

"Keep your friends close. Keep your enemies closer."

It sounded more Sicilian to her. Revenge played a major role in his life as he regressed from the hale, active father of her youth to the querulous, nasty old man of the last few years before his death. And then, of course, that afternoon here in the palace when she had caught—

Her lips went pale. She could feel the color leave her face. It was as if a flashbulb had gone off.

She turned from the window and sat down abruptly at a small French Provincial table in cream-and-gold tracery and a tilting pier glass. She stared at her own face, half blinded by the flash of memory.

God, it still had the power to do that to her. After two years! Flash!

She tossed her head, touched her cheeks, as if willing them to grow vigorous with life again. Flash!

Why think of that afternoon? How to keep it from surfacing through the slime of memory? It had been the sight of the *Bestseller*. Have the ship banned from the harbor.

She frowned, thinking, and then was unhappy with the verticals she saw in her face. Do nothing obvious to the ship or the master would retaliate with some scabrous novel about them. Administrative error was best. Some idiot clerk in the Bureau of Harbor Registration would have assigned those spaces to other yachtsmen. When it came time for renewal in September, every berth would be full.

Would that stop her memory from flashing back to that afternoon here in the palace? It was a scene only three people knew about, and two of them had no idea she'd been a witness.

Were such occurrences common in the outside world, Faith wondered. But there ought to be a way of permanently disintegrating them until not an atom of memory was left. Didn't Buck Rogers have a ray gun that could do the trick? If not, he could get Dr. Huer to invent one. Her thoughts lurched wildly.

She stopped watching herself in the pier glass, cradled her head in her arms on the dressing-table top and closed her eyes. Only make believe, she sang in her head, I love you. Only make believe, that you love me.

In the distance, thunder rolled softly, then louder as lightning crashed out beyond the harbor. Exhausted as she slept, *la Principessa* heard neither peal. A high, leaden thunderhead began to build up over San Sebastian.

· 14 ·

One of the tiresome things about ruling a country was that, come hell or high water, the business of it went on with what was supposed to look from the outside like unruffled calm.

That evening, as lightning and thunder crashed across the harbor and rain pelted the cobblestoned streets of San Sebastian, the last touches were being made to the seventeenth annual ball given before the tennis finals.

If the ball had been delayed till after the finals, hardly a player of note would have been on hand for it. Most would have beelined to their next tournament, or to the clubs and sports centers they owned or managed. Although tennis had a social "side" to it, nowadays all was business.

In any event, the way the skies had opened up over this part of the coast, there would be no play tomorrow. The red-clay courts would need a day of drying off and careful raking.

With most of the big names still on hand, tonight's ball would have its usual sparkle, if the storm didn't drown them all. It had already begun to flood the streets of the municipality. In the harbor, yachts rocked wildly in winds of up to forty miles an hour that drove sheets of rain in hard horizontals seeping under hatchways and cabin doors.

Far out to sea, shipping was already feeling the storm's grip. Trawlers had hurried back to shore. Fishermen collected in portside bars to drink cheap grappa—that hideous brandy made from the fourth pressing of grape skins and branches—and curse the weather. The usual "I have sailed these seas for fifty years and not once do I remember a summer storm of such..." echoed in smoky dens.

One old fisherman recalled that this storm was the work of that devil ship, the *Finisterre.* He nursed the thought rather comfortingly. His dread of that black demon had been entirely correct. And now that it had left the harbor, it was wreaking its vengeance on poor old San Sebastian. Hadn't he predicted it?

It didn't occur to him, nor to anyone else at the time, that the *Finisterre* might well be making heavy weather of it out there in the storm of its own maleficent devising.

Geni Magari, who had marked its departure earlier in the day, was now on duty at the palace ballroom as a bartender. This was one of San Sebastian's brightest social events. Only the Christmas Ball got a larger chunk of the principality's budget, that and the auto-race party in spring.

He poured champagne into eight narrow tulip glasses and moved slowly with his tray through the Green Room. This was not the largest of the rooms that flanked the Grand Ballroom, but Geni knew that only those who came to be seen would linger in the overcrowded Gold and Scarlet rooms.

Those who came on private business that required discreet conversation invariably chose the Green Room. Mostly they were they Number Twos of the principality, those not powerful enough to be members of the *consiglio* but with enough clout to be invited to this prestigious tennis gala. Or well-to-do tourists and foreign businessmen.

Eavesdropping here, Geni had intercepted many a romantic intrigue, jewel heist, plot to loot a casino, all doomed to failure. But most of the private talk was business, usually the tiresome planning of Number Twos to become Number Ones.

Tonight, he decided, would not produce much in the way of illicit whispering. The storm's high humidity and the electrical tension in the air made people listless and feverish by turn. But none would be foolish enough to murmur confidential secrets while the CBS crews were here.

With minicams and lightweight sound recorders, four crews moved here and there among the guests, filming candid footage of people chatting, or displaying their finery or their famous and quasi-famous faces. The crews would stop here for two portly gentlemen, there for a fantastically revealing gown, a drop-dead piece of jewelry, moving always toward the core of the excitement, where the Prince and Princess stood.

The formal reception lines began in the Gold Room, where they led through a rather ornate archway into the ballroom itself. In an effort to speed up matters, the Prince received on one line and, across the archway, the Princess had a separate line. Geni noted that, as always, the Princess' line was twice as long as her husband's.

In Prince Florian's line were the dullards, business types who wanted a private word in his ear but were firmly hurried along by Mike, at his father's elbow. The attractive people, Geni thought, are all waiting to be presented to Her Serene Highness.

And she, too, had a major domo, only not like Prince Michele, who hustled visitors through. The guardian of her line was the singer Maggie Rose, who jumped the queue again and again to present some new friend.

Geni sighed, very softly. One day the association between Her Highness and the singer would produce something terribly awkward, if not dangerous. Despite the fact that she attracted Geni as a woman, and he would have been inclined to think leniently of her, Maggie Rose had a dossier in his files that went back thirty years, to her earliest days in New Jersey. Through what she was pleased to call her family—not so much a biological term but certainly a political one—she had attained unusual heights as an entertainer, regularly booked by Mafia-operated clubs and casinos, never at a loss for money to back her next album or picture, nor for Class A distribution. A protected species, Miss Rose.

The orchestra had begun to tune up. At these social events, which cut across many age groups and classes, the musicians were prepared for every sort of tune from Strauss waltz medleys through recycled Beatles tunes to nostalgic Cole Porter, Gershwin and heavily rhythmed disco.

Geni watched Maggie jump the Princess' line again to present a tall young man, spectacularly good-looking. Something about his face tickled Geni's memory. The boy had a narrow, small-featured face marked by thick black eyebrows and high, almost Arabic cheekbones under wide-set dark eyes.

Geni frowned very slightly. Princess Paola, beside her mother, smiled very broadly as the boy moved on. Then Geni remembered the boy's name. His frown deepened.

"Have you got a free box on your card, baby?" Aunt Maggie was asking Polly. "Etienne would love to have just one dance with you."

Polly frowned, examining her dance card. "I can always cancel Mike. I mean, I have him down twice in case I need to cancel."

"Smart cookie." The singer was silent for a moment, not wanting to press the matter too hard. Then: "The boy's a real dish, huh?"

Polly's cool demeanor hardly showed a crack. "But his backhand stinks. I mean, he was eliminated in Day Two."

"That what you're looking for in a young man? Tennis savvy?" Both of them giggled for a moment. Then Aunt Maggie continued, "Give me the number of the dance. I'll make sure he gets it."

"Who's Etienne Rousseau to you?" Polly asked.

"Just a dreamy dish I thought you'd like to sample."

Polly's voice remained blasé as always. "Does he know I'm San Quentin quail?"

"Polly!"

"Jailbait? Does he know I'm not yet eighteen?"

"Who teaches you this stuff, Mike?"

"You still didn't explain your connection with that dreamy dish of Frog."

"His mother's an old friend. Etienne's half American, like you."

"Okay, put him down for the third box." Polly paused for a beat and then, grinning wickedly: "I'll give him some pointers on his backhand."

"Try to be charming," Maggie Rose responded.

"Why? Is he rich?"

"No. Since when do you save your charm for the rich?"

"Doesn't everyone?"

One of Aunt Maggie's magnificently made-up eyebrows arched in silent menace. "A last word of advice—be nice to Etienne. You'll never regret it."

"Hot stuff, huh?"

Maggie Rose laughed helplessly. "What am I gonna do with you, baby?" she asked despairingly.

The third dance had, in fact, been one of the dreaded Strauss medleys and Geni Magari had noted that neither the young Princess nor her handsome partner had really enjoyed it. But the boy had used this pretext to secure a firm commitment on dance number eight.

Magari drifted into the kitchen staging area where canapés were arrayed on trays, made his way to a wall telephone and, once he was alone, dialed a number inside the palace.

"He is called Etienne Rousseau," the agent told his assistant at the other end of the line. "I'll hold the wire open." He waited. This kind of information was held in the Gold Beret central computer, but a terminal with CRT and print readout had been installed in the office Magari used here at the palace. In only a few moments the other agent was back on the line.

"Do you want to make notes?"

"If it's substantive, make a hard copy for me."

"*D'accordo.* Etienne Rousseau, twenty-two, born New York City. U.S. citizen. Two arrests, no convictions. Those were traffic violations, *capo.* Now on the European side—a.k.a. Ettore Russo, Edmond Ross, Ed Russell. Four arrests, no convictions. Those were all in Italy, mostly husbands of amateur tennis ladies who wanted Etienne to stop annoying their wives. No drug busts. Source of income—tennis professional at Cortina D'Ampezzo. That's it."

Magari hung up and stood there, absentmindedly fingering a canapé. When he realized what he was doing, he frowned and popped the tiny bit of food into his mouth. By modern standards, Mr. Rousseau was a solid citizen. The business with the wives was a nothing. The phony name probably went with the romantic intrigue. Okay, call it *gigoloismo,* it still wasn't anything to get excited about.

Not unless the target was *la Principessa Paola.*

The eighth dance was more to both their liking, a set of disco changes, one seamless thud that lasted a quarter of an hour and swept everyone over the age of twenty-five off the floor. Etienne, Polly noted, did all the new moves and most of the older ones. Aside from a glow of health, he didn't get disgustingly sweaty as most boys did. Nor did he try to weave small talk into their dancing.

That was really the nicest thing about him. He approached the dance as a thing unto itself, not an occasion to flirt with the Princess. Dancing was a physical thing, he seemed to be saying, and with the physical, I am thoroughly at home.

So she gave him number nine, too, knowing that the boy whose name was in that box would hate her forever. Gave Etienne Rousseau dance number nine and took him outside into the garden for a walk. This strategy was flawless except that at the moment thick sheets of rain poured down from the thunderous skies. It felt as if they were standing at the base of some immense waterfall. They ran a few yards to the nearest glazed greenhouse and stood inside, staring out through the calsomined windows at the downpour.

"Not such a hot idea," Polly admitted.

"No problem." He turned to her. In the half-light his normally dark face resolved itself into two great eyes and a neat row of small, strong teeth as regular as Polly's, speaking of good genes and expensive dental care. "Tell me something," he said after a long pause. He stopped.

"Tell you what?" Polly had to ask.

"There must be some way a guy..." He stopped again.

There was a peculiar quality to the way he seemed to censor himself and then wait, almost patiently. Polly had too little experience to understand the technique of getting her to worm it out of him. Nor did she understand that in so doing she was implicating herself.

At this stage of the exchange between them there was still nothing terribly serious at stake. But a pattern was being established, a progression of responsibilities.

"A guy does what?" Polly finally asked, submitting to the maneuver.

Etienne had great difficulty following up. In the dark she could see his strong eyebrows knot with anguish. It wasn't as if he would ask for anything more important than a date, was it? God, he was shy with women, she thought.

It even crossed her mind that in a man so handsome and so masculine-looking, such reticence was hard to credit. Twice he framed words that he left unsaid. Then:

"I don't suppose there's a way we could see...?"

Dead stop. Long pause. "See each other again?" Polly finished for him. Instantly the air seemed to clear, as if the storm, with its humidity and tension, had moved off to leave them in peace.

A beatific smile seemed to glow at her in the darkened greenhouse. "Thank God you're a mind reader," he managed to say.

*   *   *

The meteorological record would show that San Sebastian alone took almost four inches of rain that night, amid gusts of up to gale force. Four ships foundered at sea off the Italo-French Riviera but there was no loss of life, according to early reports. Since the rain had dwindled to a drizzle by eleven o'clock, merrymakers leaving the ball—in seventeen years no one had ever had the gall to refer to it as the Tennis Ball—managed to keep dry on their way to bars, clubs, casinos or wherever home was.

In the lobby of his hotel, before going upstairs, Etienne Rousseau had a nightcap with Aunt Maggie, just the two of them in a dim corner of the American bar. Geni Magari watched the tête-à-tête from a distance without the capability of eavesdropping, since he felt sure Maggie Rose knew his face. He dictated a full report and was asleep in bed by 2 A.M.

Polly, for perhaps the first time in her life, especially after so much dancing, found it impossible to sleep. She sat by her window and watched the lightning in the heights above the principality, wondering if she should talk to Mike, but not willing to take the heavy kidding that would go with such a conversation.

She watched the sky lighten slowly in the east and was one of the few in San Sebastian to greet the new day and see that it had dawned clear, well washed and blue. She was tired and hardly knew it. She took a deep breath. Lovely, bright, sunny new day.

· 15 ·

The inquest into Charley Oakhurst's death established only that he was dead. It never quite got around to how.

San Sebastian's police, coast guard and coroner's office at first refused to take jurisdiction. According to witnesses, the regrettable accident had taken place well offshore in international waters. But the fact that the *Finisterre*'s last port of call had been San Sebastian made it impossible to evade forever the responsibility of doing something to "close" the case.

Witnesses were scarce. There was no corpse. People who knew Oakhurst in the principality were not available. Maggie Rose, for example, was in Las Vegas headlining her own show at the time of the inquest. It would have been out of the question, as well as illegal, to subpoena either of Their Serene Highnesses. And no one thought of the elderly fisherman who had foreseen the chaos and death the *Finisterre* would bring.

Even the Faircloths were not available, having been coptered off to Nice and flown directly back to New York, where they were recovering in Doctors Hospital from exposure, hypothermia and depression. The only witness handy to the coroner was the widow, Connie Oakhurst. She was allowed some weeks to compose herself before giving brief testimony that carried weight.

Not even the French captain or crew were on hand for direct testimony. Captain Rattazzi had nearly perished in the storm that claimed Charley Oakhurst. From his hospital bed in Nice, duly sworn to and attested by two *notaires,* came an affidavit, read out at the inquest, that tallied perfectly with the widow's testimony.

The night, black. Cauldrons of water pouring horizontally. Charley on deck one moment, roped to the taffrail. Charley not there the next moment. Under gale gusts the rope had come unknotted.

Everything else was a bit fuzzy, such as who had ordered the *Finisterre* out to sea in such weather, who had plotted her course, who had resisted the thought of turning back or finding shelter down the coast at Monaco or Villefranche.

The widow's evidence came forth with admirable restraint, all tears spent. She seemed to want to do her duty, have Charley declared legally dead and then be allowed to return to New York, where matters of probate and insurance awaited her.

The gossip in San Sebastian was that an estate of many millions had been left to the still youngish, still attractive Connie Oakhurst. There was talk of a double indemnity clause in the life insurance for death by misadventure. Connie's daughter from a previous marriage arrived in San Sebastian with her husband to bring the widow home. They treated her as carefully as a prize package, which she certainly was.

In all this no word came from the palace. Later, to the memorial service in Rye, New York, a small, expensive wreath was sent by

Their Serene Highnesses. But, of course, the palace was busy just now with a project of tremendous value that required everyone's attention.

Yes, the harbor expansion. The rumor was that Prince Michele had headed a committee of local business executives who had gotten a Swiss syndicate of banks to advance two billion Swiss francs at a reasonable rate of interest. When no one denied the rumor it was taken as a framework for further embroidery. The Swiss currency was like gold; it seldom varied as to rate of exchange (half true). The syndicate had been formed among the Swiss banks' younger officers (true), some of whom had been schoolmates of Prince Michele (false). The job would be awarded to Swiss companies (true), as a sop to the banks, but all the workmen would be San Sebastiani (true). Jobs galore.

"And no clause about casino take," Mike explained to his mother. "The Swiss don't gamble." He winked at her.

She had followed his thoughts closely. Now she nodded. "It's a good contract, Mike. Your father's proud of you. I know I am. I've even written to Uncle Billy because I know he was worried."

The two sat on the terrace, table littered with breakfast things, the rest of the family having left. The morning sun no longer carried summer's intense heat. Autumn was almost in the air but no leaf yet fell. Faith had patted her son's hand as it lay on the table. Now she held it, saying nothing but giving it a faint squeeze from time to time as her thoughts strayed.

"Billy was worried?" Mike echoed then. "So am I. We're over this hump of financing the harbor expansion. But something else will come along. I have no idea what, but I know they won't stop trying."

"They."

"The boys, the mob. This place is a thorn in their side. It's not just the money. A businessman can live awhile without extra profit as long as the rest of his empire is doing well. It's a matter of *brutta figura*."

"*Che cosa c'è?*" She smiled apologetically. It was a family joke that Faith's Italian vocabulary and pronunciation were good, but the idioms, the niceties of the subjunctive and other tenses eluded her. So did Italianate concepts like *brutta* and *bella figura*.

Mike executed a very Italian hand-and-shoulders gesture. "Appearance is everything. You show the world a *figura*. You want it to look *bella* because you're judged by your look. But how does it look when the mob owns the entire world of gambling—not a chip is laid, not a dice thrown without their hand in it—except in one particular place? And that place happens to be more glamorous than any other gambling location on earth?"

"It sounds childish."

"San Sebastian is the chink in their armor," Mike went on. "Somewhere a casino owner or small island republic is chafing under Mafia control and looks to San Sebastian and says, 'Hey, the mob doesn't own *them* anymore—why can't we throw off mob rule too?' Maybe they try. Maybe they don't. But it's a risk the mob hates to live with."

"So for reasons of their own security, they want us."

"You got it," Mike agreed.

Her hand tightened on his. "And when he failed to get it for them, Charley Oakhurst had to die."

Her son was silent for a long time. Then: "Charley was basically a cutout, not a banker, a guy who fronted for the boys and formed a layer of shielding for them. They were surely monitoring his performance here. They must have reached the conclusion, once he bombed, that he was too dangerous to live."

"So there's no security either way," Faith burst out. "Fight them or serve them, you still die."

Neither of them spoke for a long while. In the bougainvillea, two small birds, as tiny as sparrows but plumper, chased each other through airy circles, chittering and swooping joyously.

"You said they monitored his performance," the Princess said at last. Her voice sounded heavy.

He shook his head. "I have no information. Neither does Geni Magari. I only have the evidence of my eyes and the thoughts of a very paranoid brain."

She squeezed his hand. "Tell me."

"I prefer not to." He stopped and glanced at her. "The lady's a friend of yours."

Faith nodded slowly, as if she had expected this. "It's not what it seems," she said at last. "There was a period of your life, Mikey, when you were away from here for years on end. The only way I got to see you was during summer vacation. A lot went on here in those days that you'll never know about, nor need to."

"With Maggie?"

"I have my reasons for keeping her close, Mike. And if it turns out she—what's the word?—she *fingered* Charley Oakhurst, I am not about to shed tears.

"Nor I."

"That's not what worries me..." Faith paused.

Already, in just the past few minutes, she had violated all of the best intentions of keeping her children clear of such ugly adult problems. And now she was faced with this report Magari had given her about Polly and the tennis player Rousseau. It was something she had to handle herself.

She gave her son's hand a final squeeze and put it away from her as she got to her feet. She was aware that he was watching her closely without reacting, much as a camera might.

You never knew how you registered with a camera until the film came back from the lab. Probably her own son was finding her older, dottier. She was not aware of what her hand was doing now, coming up under her chin as if to support the flesh there, the telltale flesh.

Mike stood up. "Anything I can do, call on me."

"I know that."

She watched him leave, tall, still not too well coordinated, but clearly the brilliant one of the family. She knew he felt he wasn't given enough responsibility, perhaps because she wanted him insulated from the ugly side of power. But his success with the Swiss had changed all that.

She sank back down in her chair. Sunlight glittered on the silver coffee service. She closed her eyes and thought about Polly: who can I turn to? Not Florian, who had his own daily ration of problems. Not Jill: her judgment was phenomenally faulty when it came to relations with men. Not Billy, she leaned on him too much as it was. The poor man had his own life to lead.

She glanced at her wristwatch. Seven-thirty in the morning. Half-past midnight in Chicago. She picked up the telephone on the side

table, got an outside line and dialed direct to the Brennan enclave
north of town along the edge of Lake Michigan. The phone rang
eight times before anybody picked up.

"Brennan residence."

"Kerrigan? It's Faith. Sorry to bother you at this hour. Who's
home, Gloria? Caroline? Patrick?"

"Dear God, it's the Princess," the butler said, coming down hard
on the word, Prin-*cess*. "Nobody here but me, Miss Faith."

"Do you expect anybody soon?"

"After Labor Day, the lot of them."

"Tell them I called to invite them for a visit as soon as they can
get free."

"Yes, Miss Faith. Which one of them?"

"Any."

As she put down the phone she thought, I have never treasured
advice from any of my brothers or sisters. But there was this Brennan
thing they all inherited from Eamon: a world made up of two kinds
of people, themselves and enemies.

How right the nasty old man had been.

· 16 ·

The tall young man had been pacing along the shingle beach where
the poorer fishermen beached their boats to avoid paying harbor
fees. The heavy wooden double-ended craft, powered by smelly in-
board engines, lay drunkenly on wooden supports under the noon
sun. At dusk their owners would return to begin another night of
trolling for anchovies and sardines in some of the most polluted
waters on earth.

From a distance, unobserved, Mike had watched Geni inspecting each boat, checking its cuddy forecabin, its fuel tank, the space
under its floorboards. Mike found it strange that the colonel who
headed Gold Beret Intelligence would spend time this way. If Geni
were searching for boats that might have been used for smuggling
not fishing, why not send some of his men to do the job?

Mike was moving up silently behind Magari, careful not to make too much noise in the crunching shingle. When he was several yards behind Geni, he called, "Find any H?"

The policeman whirled, his hand reaching for something inside the breast pocket of his jacket. Then he grinned and let his hand fall empty to his side. "Gumshoe, eh?"

"What're you up to, Geni?"

The older man began strolling rather casually in the direction of a small hut nearby where, on weekends, they sold cold drinks. "Sea air. Sun. Solitude," he said. "Much like you."

They spoke a rather formal Italian to each other, although Geni had known Mike since he was a newborn babe. This stilted choice of words was Geni's. He led them behind the shack and, indicating the sand, asked, "Care to sit down?"

The future ruler of this principality, and the man who would protect it from harm, sat with their backs against the hut's wall, legs stretched out on the shingle. Mike eyed the older man, who was definitely not dressed for a casual stroll.

Geni's sallow complexion would have been more attractive with a tan, but when had he time to acquire one? A tan would have toned down the intimidating contrast between his pale skin and his olive-black eyes. Sitting in the warm sun, Magari lowered his lids over those accusing eyes, as if shuttering them.

From time to time he bent sideways, craning his neck around to peep past the corner of the shack at the small fishing boat he had been inspecting when Mike found him. "Something?" Mike asked.

The secret policeman wriggled uncomfortably on the bits of shale and pebble. "I give myself these small assignments. They keep the fishermen in fear and offer an excuse for a stroll."

For some years now Mike had recognized that among the small *consiglio* which ran things in San Sebastian, only Geni Magari was truly intelligent. Mike loved his father, but in Geni he had found something more, a mentor, a source of important knowledge, of insight. If the truth were known, a role model.

"You've got that boat under surveillance," Mike told him.

"If you say so, *Eccellenza*." Geni's voice was mocking, a man not used to being questioned.

"Tell me," Mike continued, "what do you think of this farce they call a coroner's verdict on Charley Oakhurst?"

"One laughs at farces." The older man gently eased himself sideways to peek at the suspect boat again. "Do you find anything funny about the aroma of a Mafia hit, even as artistically executed as this one? Lost at sea. Dear me. Bizarre, I call it."

"The crew had to be in on it," Mike agreed. "Which makes it an awfully elaborate scenario."

A fisherman, carrying an empty wooden box, was plodding along the beach toward them. Geni's hand indicated sudden silence by one of those encoded movements the Italians have made into a language. But the man passed without incident.

"A scenario fit for someone truly important," he said then.

"As the link to the I.U.D.?"

Magari picked up a handful of pebbles. "Or the other way around. He was either the Vatican's cat's-paw or the Mafia's. It's an extremely dangerous occupation. Others have been killed in this field of fire." He let the pebbles trickle through his fingers one by one. "This is an ancient alliance. Neither side can admit its existence. But there has always been someone at the overlap—what do you computer geniuses call it?"

"The interface. Oakhurst was that man?"

"Recently, yes. The man is always a banker. Milan, Rome, New York, his background hardly matters as long as he does his job."

The faint Mediterranean surf washed in and out over the shingle with a whispering sound. "His profit," Mike said then, "must be enormous."

"High risk, high profit."

"Christ, Geni," the younger man burst out, "how can one accept that and still be a good Catholic? To know that the Church at Rome is in league with the most criminal organization in history?"

"Do you ever watch duplicate bridge? Where each foursome gets the same hand to play? Would a bridge grand master think of not accepting such a hand? No, he would pick up the challenge and make the most of it."

"So. You accept the linkup between the Mafia and the Vatican."

"You're being deliberately provoking," Magari said in an easy voice. "That's the American in you, isn't it? Separation of church and state."

He smiled gravely at the younger man. "With us, it's an old story. There is no separation. In Italy, the Christian Democrats represent the Church's interests. But they have something other parliamentary parties don't. When a judge or a bureaucrat, a government minister or senator, a businessman or even a simple parish priest gets out of line, when he grows too threatening to the Church for any of a thousand reasons, he is eliminated.

"The Mafia is thus the cutting edge of the Church. They rarely have to murder the man. Usually they concoct a scandal that blows him out of office. Italian newspapers exist on a daily ration of such tripe."

"But what's in it for the Mafia?" Mike wanted to know. "Why go to such lengths to serve the Church's interest?"

"Because the interests are identical. The Mafia and the Church exist to protect the status quo. They have the most to gain from maintaining it, the most to lose if it's disturbed."

He drew a faint line with his forefinger in the pebbles lying beneath them. "You must stop thinking of the Church as the embodiment of poor ascetics like St. Francis or St. Clair. There is a tremendous amount of money to be administered. Money has a life and demands of its own. They have nothing to do with God or heaven. But, as demands, they *must* be served."

Magari thought for a moment. "The man at the interface, the Oakhurst of the moment, is the instrument of these demands. He cuts corners, fakes papers, transfers funds illegally, suborns politicians. If you or I tried such tricks, we'd end up in big trouble. But when the Oakhurst type does it in the name of the Church, he's protected."

"And then dead."

Geni's face went blank. "High profit, high risk." He edged nearer the corner of the hut and peered at the boat again. This time his slight body stiffened and the hand signal he gave Mike was a clear-cut "Watch it!"

Slowly, both men rose to their feet. Geni edged out into the open, his right hand paused at the V opening of his jacket front. Two men stood at the suspect boat, one in the garb of a fisherman.

They were arguing so fiercely that they failed to hear Geni's stealthy approach. As noiselessly as Mike had sneaked up behind him, he now bore down on the pair of men.

The businessman reached into his own suit jacket pocket. Geni withdrew a small .25 Beretta automatic. Its heavily blued steel glinted very faintly in the hot sun. Mike eyed the businessman, but he had only withdrawn from his breast pocket a long white envelope he now handed to the fisherman.

"That's it!" Geni called. "Up with the hands."

Instinctively, the fisherman's hand went for his knife."

"*Cretino,*" muttered the businessman, his face blanched dead white, "it's Magari. Do what he says."

The knife clattered against some stones as he dropped it. Geni nodded politely, like a teacher approving the good conduct of his students. "Face the boat. Spread the hands. Lean forward. It's just like you see on TV."

"*Colonnello,*" the fisherman groaned, "I am a poor man. The envelope you saw? The envelope is yours, if y—"

"*Stupidoggine,*" the businessman grunted, "now you've angered the man. Didn't I tell you it was Magari?"

Geni winked at Mike. "The incorruptible Magari." He looked around the long beach and waved his arm twice. A gray Renault 5 came bounding along the shingle like a frisking dog. Two Gold Berets got out and saluted, first Prince Michele and then their colonel.

After they had taken away the two men from the boat, Mike stood there, watching Geni slide the Beretta back into its paper-thin holster. "What were they up to?"

Geni produced one of those magnificent up-from-under shrugs, complete with chin jut and a downturn of his mouth at both corners indicating total indifference. "Small stuff. Cocaine, probably, the fishermen smuggle in from Corsica. Who knows?"

"A minute ago you didn't sound quite so casual about crime here in the principality."

"We were talking philosophy, not crime. We were comparing the Vatican with the Mafia. Both these illustrious organizations—"

"Operate on faith," Mike cut in. "Superstitious dread. Both of them."

The truth of this seemed faintly to surprise the older man. He thought for a long moment. "With one you fear death. With the other you fear going to hell." He shrugged again. "But, look, *potere è potere.* Power is power. It demands respect. Not just here in San Sebastian. Everywhere."

He picked up a handful of pebbles and slowly let them drop one by one, his glance on the retreating gray Renault. "Enjoy your stroll?"

"Very much, Geni."

He watched the secret policeman walk off along the beach, stop at another boat and then move on. The pitfalls of power, Mike thought. He was lucky to have Magari, a man still young enough to protect him when he took over from his father.

Comforting thought. Comforting man. Then Mike recalled the look on the businessman's face. He had tried to keep it blank, but the fear showed through. Fear of the man called Geni Magari.

· 17 ·

The sky-blue Jaguar sat up on the hydraulic lift in the palace garage. Geni's father, Enzo Magari, carefully fitted the nozzle of a grease gun to the various tiny cups and points in the Jaguar's undercarriage where the official maintenance manual suggested additional lubrication be applied in the fall after long hot summer use.

Not that the Jag got that much use, Enzo reminded himself. He was not quite as methodical as his son, but garage procedures called for a logbook to be kept on each of the limousines and private cars, even including the shabby, dented, calico-cat VW Beetle Mike preferred to drive when off on his own. And the logbook for this Jag— *l'Altezza's* favorite car, though it was a dozen years old and had the cross-eyed headlights of the "E" series—showed that since the last lube job in May it had been driven barely 800 kilometers, almost entirely by the Princess herself.

Standing under the car looking up at its long bracing struts, cables and steering linkages, Enzo decided he should consult the manual again and see if it was not time to check and recheck all these fittings. The thick loose-leaf folder of printed and Xeroxed sheets was in English, of course. In the old days, when Enzo Magari was a young apprentice mechanic, one needed to speak only Italian, in addition to the local San Sebastian dialect. Since the wedding, English was the language most of the more intelligent palace staff decided to learn.

Enzo had never had the time to do so and usually took the manual home for his son, Geni, to translate. For some months now, however, since July in fact, there had been a lad working for Enzo washing the cars, seeing that they were gassed up and the oil levels maintained, a *figliuolo* of one of Enzo's drinking companions. The boy was Massimo Sgroi and he knew English.

A short, stubby little fellow, Massimo's face knitted into grave lines as he paged through the maintenance manual. *"Ecco,"* he said, pointing to a page. He read silently for a while, then made one of those thin farting noises with his lips by which in this part of the world something of no importance was designated.

"Every four months," he told Enzo, "so don't worry."

"Cretino, every four months means I am now a month overdue."

Massimo seemed uninterested. He paged through the steering-system section of the handbook. "Also every four months. Happy?"

"With you, no."

"And why pick on me? I'm your right hand. Look, I'll help you with the checkup. What could be better?"

"Help from *un asino?"*

Grumbling, Enzo let the boy watch as he carefully checked each joint and fastening, tested the play in each strut and cable. Massimo seemed all eyes.

It occurred to Enzo that Massimo Sgroi was one of those boys whose intelligence lay in mechanical things, not ideas or written thoughts. As long as he stayed in a garage or workshop, Massimo would do well.

"Think you could handle it yourself?" Enzo asked as he washed up.

Massimo was letting down the hydraulic lift. The Jag's tires gently touched the cement floor and in a moment the car floated free of the lift. In two deft moves, one backward and one forward, Massimo swung the car into its normal parking space. He got out and sauntered over to the older man. Enzo found something comic about so small a lad trying out his Gary Cooper walk. Obviously he hadn't heard Enzo's question and the older man wasn't about to repeat it.

But Massimo Sgroi's hearing was quite good. "I could do the brakes *and* the steering with *one* hand tied behind my back *and* a blindfold over my eyes," he bragged.

Enzo's face went dead. Just when you warmed up a bit to this little roach, his mouth betrayed him again. Too bad the father was a drinking pal. Not a real friend of the heart, you understand. Still, it made it harder to get rid of the son.

Enzo frowned. But get rid of him he would.

· 18 ·

The Eamon Brennan Memorial Clinic stood at the western end of the principality, the enclave created by a process of slum clearance. Some dingy three-story Art Nouveau houses from before the turn of the century had been razed. In their place this grand, faintly Grecian edifice in dazzling white marble cladding, with a small captive park, had been erected.

The exterior design was the only part that Eamon himself had taken a hand in before his death, which accounted for the oddly banklike look of the front facade. Neither Gloria nor Caroline had seen any of the inside layout. They'd been on hand for the cornerstone laying two years ago, as had the whole family, including Eamon, two cardinals and a papal nuncio.

Privately, that is to Polly alone, Mike normally referred to the Brennans as the Ecclesiastical Eight Plus One. It was not that any of them were unusually religious people, only that they had the money to subsidize rather more showily churchy works than other Catholic families.

So that now in October, when two of Faith's sisters arrived with their husbands (one a broker, the other a procurement general at the Pentagon), the Princess' first thought was to take Gloria and Caroline to visit the clinic. They were duly impressed by the incredible cleanliness, the CAT scanner and other new electronic toys their father's trust fund was providing for this memorial.

But, to tell the truth, Caroline and Gloria were perhaps most impressed by the small, lovely hospitality pavilion hidden away in the tiny park that lay open only to the clinic and not to the outside world. Here, amid several small fountains decorated by Barbara Hodgkins sculpture, stood a private bar complete with English-speaking barman quivering to provide a professional cocktail hour for the Sisters Brennan.

As Faith, Gloria and Caroline lounged in the shady retreat, letting the murmur of the fountains and the dappled light soothe their souls, Faith discreetly checked up on the other two. They had only just arrived that day. She knew she was overboard on the subject but she had to see if either of them showed fewer signs of age than she did.

Caroline, the oldest of Eamon's daughters, looked quite spruce. She had gained weight through the hips, which a girdle was minimizing, but by the process of turning wobble to stone was betraying its presence too much. Caro's hair, as jet black as Faith's, was short and curly, quite fashionable and probably with just as much suppressed gray.

Glory, the youngest child, barely forty now where Caro was long past fifty, had let her hair go white. In context with her starved figure, she could almost have passed as a glamorous platinum blonde. But too much dieting had given her a haggard look beyond her years.

"Do you always stare at your guests?" she demanded.

"Because if you do," Caro joined the attack, "it's liable to cause an international incident. Put away the microscope, dear. I use the same hair color you do."

Faith laughed softly. They weren't much, either of them, but she could be herself with them as with no one else, not even Florian.

"I've missed you guys."

"The penalty of greatness," Glory responded with some sarcasm.

"Yes," Caro agreed in mock gravity, "it's lonely at the top."

"What do you think of the setup?" Faith continued, indicating the clinic and its grounds.

"George says," Caro quoted her army procurement husband,

"that you have to be netting more a year than the state of Nevada. When he retires can you get him a job sweeping up the spilled chips at the casino?"

Faith paused an instant. "I mean the clinic. Do you think Pop would have approved?"

"It's a lot like him," Glory suggested. "Hard as stone on the outside, but inside pure stainless steel."

All three women chuckled. "This little glade," Caro went on, "would be much to the old boozer's liking. Very refined watering hole, this, and your man knows what an extra-dry mart is all about."

Neither of them spoke for a while, watching the way the sunlight reflected off the fountain pool and the Hodgkins bronzes. "I suppose," the oldest sister began then in a suddenly lowered voice, "what you really want is a reading on that darling Etienne Rousseau."

Faith grinned at her: dear old Caro, straight to the point. "I figured, once I phoned, you'd do some checking on your side of the Atlantic."

"Well, naturally one doesn't want one's favorite niece hobnobbing with just anyone." Caro sipped the last of her martini. As she put it down the barman arrived with another and a saucer of fat salted almonds. The women waited until he had disappeared. Then:

"The Rousseaus are quite well connected," Caro continued. "Etienne's uncle on his father's side is something in the French Embassy. And back home in France, my dear, the Rousseaus are *de trop*. But the boy is half American and it's his mother you worry about."

"Yes?"

"My dear, have you ever sat in the Palm Court at the Plaza and watched some zany little lady in a ball-length chiffon number, with or without hair ribbon, tickle the harp at teatime? *That's* Mrs. Rousseau."

"Oh, good," Glory chimed in cattily. "Faith's showbiz, too, you know."

"Snob," the Princess remarked. Then: "Mom plays the harp? Is that the black mark against him?"

"The parents have been separated for years," Caro added. "The father's too Catholic for a divorce and the mother has been making the most of the separation with a series of part-time stepfathers for Etienne."

Faith sat back and munched an almond. Taken with the spotty record Geni Magari had given her on the boy, prospects looked bad. Unlike ordinary girls, Polly did not have the luxury of enjoying a flirtation or a light affair. Every encounter with a marriageable male had to be assayed as a jeweler checks a diamond.

Faith could feel her heart go out to the poor mother of the boy, if she should ever learn her effect on Etienne's chances. Probably a perfectly decent, talented performer, but in the cruel game of royal matchmaking, a low-ranking card in the deck.

"But then," Glory burst out with that startling knack for mind reading she'd always displayed, "who the hell would you want Polly hitched to? Some kinky old duke?"

"He doesn't have to have a title," Faith explained patiently. "Mike's future wife is a different matter. She has to have rank of *some* kind, even *my* kind."

"Meaning her own money," Glory added.

"Or even her father's money," Caro supplied smoothly.

"You two don't leave a girl much to stand on."

"Come on, Princess," Caro kidded her. "You were always the old man's favorite. I'm surprised he ever let you get married at all."

Faith could feel her cheeks growing warm. Sisterly kidding was one thing. Nasty innuendo was another. "Meaning what?"

"You know what we always figured?" Caro got a grip on her girdle rim and tugged it down an inch. She sipped her new martini and nodded her approval. "You know how in every Irish family there is always one unmarried daughter? I mean aside from the one who becomes a nun." She cackled to herself for a moment. "You know how the whole brood gets married except this one chick because it is her destiny to be the mainstay of her dear old dad's dotage, fetching his slippers and putting a shot of Bushmill's in his tea and taking all his abuse because after all she has no husband or children. We figured Eamon was saving you for that. Otherwise who would nursemaid the old devil when he couldn't keep himself clean?"

"Couldn't keep himself clean?" Faith blurted. "The nasty, evil old lecher!"

"What?" Both sisters asked the same question in unison.

Face scarlet, the Princess sat forward and did a full minute of fussing with the sidecar she'd been drinking. Then, having regained her composure, she went on as if nothing had been said about her father, least of all by her. It was a privilege accorded only to princesses.

"Would you like some olives?" she asked. "Or perhaps we ought to be getting back to our husbands." She glanced at her watch.

Glory looked at Caro. By unspoken accord they agreed to let her get away with it. Watching the agreement being reached, Faith felt that same rush of warmth she always did in the company of her own family. When they wanted to they could hammer you down, but if you asked for mercy, they knew when to hold back.

But that had been such an unlikely outburst. Was she losing her grip on herself? Was age doing that to her self-control? And if her innermost nightmares could surface in this bizarre way in front of two of her most trusted allies, what might her aging brain allow her to do in front of strangers or enemies?

Flash! Just a casual phrase of Caro's. And the whole unclean ugliness sprang up out of her unconscious.

With elaborately casual gestures, Glory examined her own wristwatch. "Right. It's either six-fifteen or it's three-thirty. These damned designer watches."

All three women got to their feet, Caro polishing off her martini as she stood up. "Sorry to leave this woodsy glen," she murmured. "You girls know how much I love nature."

This sent the three of them into giggling of such alarming volume that the barman came running. "That's all right, Arturo," the Princess assured him. Giacobbe smiled, feeling foolish. He had never had the finesse his colleague Geni Magari had with these assignments. On the other hand, he knew he made a good drink.

Still chuckling, the three Brennan sisters took themselves out of the park and into the waiting limousine. A uniformed driver on a motorcycle preceded them through the streets back to the palace.

Not another word passed about Faith's peculiar outburst, nor did any of the sisters discuss the unsuitable pairing of Polly with the admittedly gorgeous but socially awkward Etienne Rousseau.

Only one of the Brennans was a princess, but all of them understood how easy it was to bug a limousine.

· 19 ·

Florian always finished dressing early, despite the fact that on state occasions he was called on to wear one of nearly fifty different military dress uniforms with appropriate decorations and ribbons.

Tonight being an informal family affair—Guldas vs. Brennans, best two falls out of three—he was in a midnight-blue dinner jacket. He dropped by Faith's chambers to watch her prepare for dinner, a spectacle he never found less than engrossing: the tiny eyebrow hairs firmly tweezed, the blending of the foundation base and then its near removal, all the deft expertise that would end, as ever, in a fresh face that looked almost without makeup.

But he found the Princess sitting at her dressing table at least a good forty-five minutes from being finished. Her long neck drooped disconsolately. She eyed herself in the mirror, but only sideways, never head-on. When she saw Florian come up behind her she started guiltily.

"Caught in the act," she muttered.

"Vanity, vanity, all is vanity."

Her mouth flattened in a level line. "Nothing much left to be vain about, my dear," she said in an equally flat voice. "Only the shell is left, behind which God knows what brain damage's hiding."

He chose to take this as a joke. "You always have these fits of despondency when your baby sister's around."

"Glory looks worse than I do. We Brennans don't age well. Look at you," she went on challengingly. "With that thick blond hair, you look younger than Mike. In a few years, when we step out on the balcony, people will say 'There's Florian and his poor old mother.' But that's not the worst part."

She stopped and began applying foundation base with a small, flat foam sponge. "It's the mind, Florian. What kind of foundation base can cover up cracks in the mind?"

"I haven't noticed anything senile about you."

She nodded slowly, as if this only confirmed her view. "We manage two heavy, separate schedules that rarely intersect. That's why you haven't been exposed to the new me."

She gave an exasperated gasp. "What do the others do?" she demanded. "There's that fellow who's married to one of the Dutch princesses. He's constantly in and out of a mental clinic in Basel and a fat lot of good it does him. Depression syndrome, they call it. Of course depression because you have to wash *all* your dirty linen in public. The newspapers never let you alone."

"There are, um, discreet private therapists." Florian's tone suggested that he was not recommending, only noting. "One pays them a large amount, partly for their help but mostly for their silence."

"Blackmail." Faith began dabbing off the base with small, practiced strokes, blending and smoothing it to invisibility.

"Nobody has this kind of trouble without being able to get expert help," Faith went on in a low voice, as if to herself. "The rich can buy it, the poor can get it free. Over there"—her head inclined eastward in the direction of Monaco—"they never had this with their children or their casinos or their..." Her voice died away. She began applying eye shadow and liner. Her face grew more defined.

"We always feel our own problems are unique," Florian said. "When the truth is they're as common as..." He gestured for a word.

"Common as pig tracks, we say down South, honeychile," Faith responded in a suddenly better mood.

With each touch of makeup her face had sprung farther out into life, more real, more beautiful. She brushed the outline of her lips and began filling in. Something like a faint smile curved her mouth. The crisis had passed, Florian noted, because she was still a gorgeous woman whose face needed only a little help. But what would she be like in ten years? Twenty?

As he made his way slowly down a back stairs toward the game room, where the Brennans were waiting for him, Florian's face lit up. He rarely had ideas, especially good ones, but he'd just had one. He was fond of telling himself that in his entire life, now nearing the age of sixty, he had only had one really good idea.

To marry Faith.

One brilliant decision in a lifetime of mediocre coping. But it had lighted up his life and always would.

And now he'd just had a second good idea, not in the same class, but a bona fide gem. He ducked into the library, where he found Jill working on the diary portfolio at her desk. Striding to the telephone, he got an outside line and turned to her.

She rose to her feet. "Shall I leave?"

"No, certainly not." He dialed a Beverly Hills number in the States. "Well," he added lamely, "as a matter of fact, would you?"

The phone had not yet started ringing as she left. Florian hadn't bothered to figure the time lag, but it was about eleven in the morning in California. Nevertheless, when the phone rang no one answered.

It was still a good idea, Florian reassured himself, and it had strong historical precedents. To whom did royalty turn in the old days when hearts had to be unburdened? To their father confessors. And Faith's was not answering his phone.

Just as he was about to hang up on the twentieth ring, a voice said, "Yeh?" Breathless, thin.

"Billy? Florian here."

"*Enschuldig mir, liebe Fürst,*" the gnomelike Viennese director cracked back. "What's cooking?"

"We never see you anymore."

"*Arbeit, alles ist Arbeit.* Excuse me, I was out at the pool and it's my houseboy's day off and I'm dripping wet. All is work, Florian. Not making films but finding the money for them. I don't have the time at my age."

"They tell me there is money in San Sebastian," Florian joked.

"Friends' money I don't solicit. Otherwise I'd have no friends."

There was a pause at Billy Ritz' end of the line. "What's up, Florian? You always were terrible at acting casual."

"*Caro amico,* our girl needs a father figure to talk to." He cleared his throat. "I know you were just here this summer. But..."

A second pause on Billy's part. "I see in the papers that you've got houseguests. When do they leave?"

"Wednesday."

"I'll be at Nice airport just before Wednesday lunch. Can you have a copter meet me?"

When he entered the games room downstairs a few moments later, he found Jill passing around a tray of drinks to two couples who seemed, if Florian was any judge, to be on about their third tray.

Everyone got to their feet. This was strict protocol in San Sebastian and good old-fashioned manners in many another part of the world when one's host entered the room. But Florian knew it did not come naturally to either Brennan sister. Only years of reminders by Faith had finally dinned it into them.

After kissing both his sisters-in-law, Florian gravely shook hands with Bert French, Gloria's broker husband, a short weedy fellow who one would have thought could have afforded a dinner jacket that didn't hang on him like a scarecrow's coat. General George McElhinny, rather svelte in a pale pink tuxedo, gave Florian's hand a tremendous squeeze.

There was a trick to surviving such killer handshakes, a trick every politician knows, a matter of relaxing one's grip in a jellyfish way. Unfortunately, Florian had never had to run for office and was innocent of such guile. He tried not to grimace at the Pentagon man's preemptive strike.

"George, you're looking...sleek."

"If you mean plump," his wife Caro put in, "he'll tell you it's part of his job to take all the wining and dining the industrialists throw at him. I say..."

She paused and took a large swallow of her dry martini while everyone remained silent. It was obvious to Florian that Caro, the oldest, had long ago taken over the role of family monologist.

"What I say," she went on in her own good time, confident of not being interrupted, "is that George may be the only honest procurement general in Washington, D.C., but faced with an *île flottant* dessert, his will power degenerates to minus zero."

"Honest procurement general," George cracked, "is a contradiction in terms. Caro, will you let Florian get a word in edgewise?"

Fortunately for Florian, who had his own opinion of Pentagon honesty, he was spared the need to speak by the entrance of the missing Brennan. His wife looked lovely, as usual, and in age somewhere between thirty and thirty-two.

"We're all on our feet as it is," Glory cracked, "so what's left? Sing a chorus of 'Hail to the Chief'?"

Across the room Jill mouthed a message to Faith, "Sidecar?"

The Princess nodded. During the settling down, the patting of George's new potbelly and the cheek-pecking, Jill produced one of the amber Prohibition cocktails out of brandy, lemon juice and Triple Sec. She made it dry, the way Faith liked it, and handed her a white-wine glass half filled with the drink.

Over the years the sidecar had become Jill's favorite, too, mainly because Faith rarely finished even one drink and there was always another left in the shaker. But sidecars had other, more hidden advantages. Just as gin martinis made Jill quarrelsome and old-fashioneds put her to sleep, sidecars gave her the warm, false illusion that everything was going to be all right.

"And where's my favorite niece?" Caro was asking.

"And where's my brainy nephew?" George demanded.

"And who's looking after your personal portfolio?" Bert wanted to know.

"And how do I get another mart?" Glory pleaded.

Florian sat down in his usual straight-backed chair and tried to cope. He missed Mike's presence. Mike was so much better with these people, for whom he had a rather sneaking affection.

For Florian none of them ever came alive. All four were American stereotypes, more than slightly plastic, with the exception of Caro, who was overpowering in a Maggie Rose way, steamrolling over life. But that was another American stereotype, was it not?

To think that his own Faith had come out of this same bloodline, a kind of genetic sport, a mutant that in no way resembled the rootstock. Some of his most interesting quarrels with Mike were on this general subject of Plastic Americans and wholesome real ones like Faith.

"You have it wrong," Mike would assure him. "I have run into Europeans twice as phony and ten times as insincere. It's that you're not trained to spot the American Real Thing."

In the end it came down to Eamon's seed, filtered vaguely through a mother few of them remembered except hazily. Florian sat back, accepted a whiskey-and-soda from Jill and let the Brennans unfocus before him as he thought about his terribly good idea and the fact that help, in the form of Billy Ritz, was on its way.

Billy would be able to sort out Faith's problems. He had no ax to grind. He loved her. And his judgment about the great world was, for a cynic, impeccable.

When at eight o'clock there was a general milling about as if everyone had suddenly grown hungry, Florian stood up. He caught Jill's eye. Speaking in a very low tone that concealed his words from the Brennan contingent and masked his own sudden fear, Florian muttered, "Where are they, Mike and Polly?"

A sudden bright flash of panic lighted up Jill's eyes. Both children were very punctual, very responsible, especially when it came to family events. They had been looking forward all day to seeing their aunts. Both understood the anguish they could cause by not sticking to a schedule, how quickly fears of kidnapping or some other act of terror would be imagined in the absence of facts.

"Speak," Florian said with such menacing softness that it sounded like a curse.

"P-Polly went out at four. Both should have shown up long ago."

Dreading the encounter, her eyes moved slowly until she was staring into his. "Get Magari on the phone. Something's happened." Florian murmured. "I can feel it in my bones."

Jill nodded and turned toward the telephone. "Not here." Florian's voice was shaking with rage or anguish, it was hard to tell which. "And tell them to remove two place settings at the dinner table, so it looks as if the absences were expected."

Jill's eyes widened. "That's bril—"

"Enough! Leave! Call Magari!"

Biting her lip, Jill dashed out of the room. Faith moved up beside her husband and out of the corner of her mouth asked, "Problem?"

"Not at all, my dear," Florian said, his smile widening far beyond normal. "You remember the children have that youth meeting," he added in a louder voice.

"What y—?" Faith stopped dead, seeing the look in his eyes.

Florian reached past her for Caroline's arm. "Come, my dear, and bring your martini with you."

"Oh, you mean there's food too?" his sister-in-law wisecracked. "Don't worry, Caro," Gloria responded, "drinks come with it."

Over their heads, Florian's glance locked with his wife's. *"Avanti, a tavola,"* he told them. Only Faith heard the slight quaver of fear in his voice. But it was enough to lock its grip, like a hand of ice, around her heart.

· 20 ·

He hadn't planned to miss the dinner. In fact he rather liked Aunt Caro's alcoholic humor and found Uncle Bert so dim-witted about the stock market as to be hilarious in an unintended way. But when at five o'clock Mike had descended to the palace garage to take out his battered VW convertible for a drive, he saw that the white Renault 5 Polly used was not in its stall.

"Massimo," he had called to Enzo Magari's helper. "When did *la Principessa* Paola leave?"

The short young fellow produced a ferocious scowl of thought as he polished the long thigh of the Jaguar XKE's sky-blue fender. "Maybe t'ree-four o'clock," he responded in English.

"When is she due back, soon?"

"They di'n say."

"They?"

"La Principessa and the tennis guy."

As Mike considered this Massimo continued stroking the Jag as if caressing the flank of a lovely woman. Mike gunned the little VW and sent it rattling up the concrete passageway to the side gate of the palace.

Many fender repairs and door dents had produced a variety of colored patches of epoxy filler and rustproofing. The convertible resembled a parti-colored cat of extremely mixed parentage. It moved like one, too, in a series of leapy pounces.

When Mike had returned at seven, with just enough time to dress for dinner, Polly's car was still not to be seen. *"Non è arrivata,"* Massimo said in his normal tone of utter disinterest. He was now washing each tire of the Jaguar with a soapy towel, then hosing it and drying it with a blast of compressed air. Mike had never seen anyone curry a car with such relentless intimacy.

Wheeling the VW around, Mike roared up and out of the palace a second time. It was possible they were at the tennis club. Or a bar somewhere. But what was really *not* possible was that Polly had forgotten dinner with her aunts, who adored her.

After buzzing in and around the principality checking likely places, he double-parked in front of the Gold Beret barracks behind the soccer field.

"Colonnello Magari c'è?"

"Momentino, Altezzo." The sergeant disappeared at high speed, returning at once with Geni Magari. He and Mike went into a small anteroom. Geni closed the door behind them. After only a moment of talk, his face went white.

"Mannaggia, how could this be?

"I don't know," Mike assured him. "I only know we have to find her fast without involving my mother and father."

"I can't keep it from them."

"For an hour or two."

Geni looked miserable. "But no longer. If she is still missing by then, we have to put out an all-points. Your father will have to be informed."

"Geni, no publicity, *per favore.* Let's not escalate this from a kid's prank to a federal case."

"Che cosa, federal case?"

"Let's not blow it up out of proportion."

"La Principessa is young. Her judgment is unformed. But the boy is your age. He knows better."

Mike could hear the jangle of handcuffs in Magari's tone. "No formal charges. No publicity. Let's just get her back to the palace in one piece."

It was always amazing to Mike to see how effortlessly the Gold Berets could cut off San Sebastian from the rest of the planet, and how quickly. Within ninety seconds all roads in and out were blocked, each car to be stopped and discreetly surveyed. The train station on the Ventimiglia-Rome line was frozen, as if in a block of ice. The harbor was shut tight and the principality's three helicopter pads and one STOL landing field were closed to further traffic.

In Magari's office, Mike listened as he polled each border checkpoint, small kiosks most motorists never noticed. The one on the coast road reported seeing a white Renault 5 come through at high speed at approximately four-thirty. The guard could not be sure the girl was *la Principessa*, but a boy was at the wheel and the car's license plate had definitely been that of San Sebastian.

"How many white Renault 5's," Mike asked in desperation, "are registered in the principality? Hundreds?"

Geni Magari was manipulating the keyboard of his computer terminal. "Seven," he responded. "But only one has a beeper."

He picked up the phone and placed a call to Genoa. "Capitano Pulische, *per favore*." He launched into a quick torrent of questions, fired back some radio frequency numbers, then waited. After ten minutes, the Genoa cop came back on the line and spoke for some time. Geni thanked him, hung up and got to his feet.

"*Andiamo.* They're heading down the coast toward Livorno. Probably they'll hole up in Santa Margarita or Rapallo or Portofino." Geni's mouth worked silently for a moment. "Some *fashionable* spot," he added with a surprising note of malice.

"But they're sure to be spotted in a really fashionable place," Mike argued. "And anyway..." He stopped talking. The agent was too anxious to get moving to notice this. He was buckling on his shoulder holster, holding a nasty little .25 caliber Beretta belly gun. As he ran out the door he shouted for a helicopter.

Mike let him go. The rest of the unspoken sentence had been "And anyway, Polly knows her car's beeped. We've both known for years that you can trace our cars anywhere by the mechanism under the floor of the trunk."

None of this had he said because it had struck him suddenly that the car with the beeper was a decoy. Someone, either Polly or the Rousseau kid using her information, was staging a real, true disappearance. They had confederates. That made it either an assignation or...

Or a kidnap.

PART
THREE

· 21 ·

Seated at either end of the long table, Faith and Florian had no way of conferring about the unusual absence from this all-family dinner of both children. This uncertainty lent a note of stiltedness to their conversation but it wouldn't be noticed at a table where Caro Brennan was holding forth, with husband George running her a close second. Florian felt grateful for the diversion.

"...told him they'd been field tested," George was reminiscing about a hundred gross of outmoded Armalite assault rifles left over from Vietnam which he had managed to unload at list price on a Latin American dictatorship.

"I said each and every one of them had been tested in combat," General McElhinny went on, "which was God's honest truth. Tested and found wanting." He broke up laughing. Then, brushing tears from his eyes, he said to Florian,"How's your own shopping list? Need any hardware?"

Florian cleared his throat carefully. "We're a neutral country," he explained, recalling that he had to make this same explanation every time he dined with the Pentagon's demon procurer. "We don't maintain a standing army, simply the Gold Berets. And most of their equipment is Swiss, except sidearms, I should imagine."

The general was shaking his head sadly through all this. "You want state-of-the-art hardware, Florian. The Swiss R and D is strictly Stone Age. We're Space Age and beyond."

"Everything field tested?" Florian asked with a faint smile.

George laughed. "Okay, you got me there. What about surveillance equipment? We've got laser probes that can bug right through a window or one of your thin modern walls. We've got eye-in-the-sky stuff with a resolution of three centimeters at a height of ten miles. We've got—"

"*Do* you mind?" Glory cut in on him. "I spent a week lecturing Bert not to start a sales pitch at dinner for one of his fraudulent offshore funds and you come in here hawking all the obsolete garbage in your inventory. Is this a dinner or a clearance sale?"

"There is a difference," her sister Caro snapped, "between one of Bert's little sermons in greed and a man representing the government of the United States of America."

"Temper, temper," the general said. "We're all jet-lagged out of our skulls. Florian, I apologize. Just got carried away. Forget the whole thing."

"It's forgotten," Florian assured him.

"But where *are* the kids?" Caro demanded to know.

In his extreme youth Mike had been a great reader of almost anything he could find. Beyond the assigned books of his schoolwork, he had managed to sop up everything romantic from *Treasure Island* to *Les Misèrables*. One of his favorites had been an account of Haroun al Raschid, or another apocryphal Arab prince who, dressed in beggar's rags, would roam the streets of Baghdad to find out how things stood with the common people of his realm.

Being more than slightly over what a San Sebastiano would call "tall," Mike knew he hadn't much chance of stalking the streets of the principality unidentified. But as a German backpacker in regulation uniform—short lederhosen, rucksack, open sandals over funny brown socks and wild blond hair—he could trudge some of San Sebastian's back alleys without drawing too much attention.

In this garb Mike covered the smaller *pensioni*, as well as the older apartment houses and the three motels at the northern perimeter of the principality. All that was left would be the deluxe hotels and super-deluxe high-rise apartment houses. But all of them had door-men by now questioned by Magari's men. That left only the harbor.

Here his disguise wouldn't work. He decided to go back to what he had been wearing, chinos, tennis shoes and a T-shirt bearing the slogan "ASK ME ABOUT MY LAYAWAY PLAN." Parking the calico car half a mile from the harbor, he glanced at his watch: nine o'clock. Dinner was half over at home and so was the breathing space he had gotten Geni Magari to agree to. At any moment the Gold Be-rets would have to inform Their Serene Highnesses that Polly had flown the coop. Or had been stolen.

Mike decided to start at the far end where the smaller yachts and day sailers were moored. He had noticed half a dozen house-boats tied up in a row last week and thought what a neat way to live. Such a boat might also make a nice hideaway. Magari's men would not be canvassing boats. They would be monitoring only out-going craft.

As if by accident Faith and Florian met at the small cocktail bar where Jill was preparing nightcaps for their jet-lagged guests. "Any news?" Florian asked the secretary.

She shook her head. "Geni Magari called five minutes ago. He wanted to be sure you knew he was on his way here."

Florian's face darkened. They all knew what it meant when Magari preferred to report something in person rather than over the phone. Florian turned to Faith. "Can you send them up to bed early?"

"They're falling asleep as it is," she whispered, "but if I suggest they go to bed, they'll just hang in. However." She turned and strode back to her two sisters, carrying their drinks. "Okay, kids, time for Scrabble."

Groans. "I insist," Faith continued. "Remember the old days?"

Caro took her drink and got to her feet. "The rest of you can indulge this crazy girl if you like. I, for one, am taking this to bed."

The last of them had gone to their rooms when Magari arrived, red-faced and sweating on this cool October night. "We lost the trail in Portofino," he muttered. "Excuse me. I am not myself. *La Princi-pessa* Paola? It's that damned tennis player. They have eloped."

Faith sat down suddenly on the nearest divan. "He's abducted her," she said.

"With respect, *Altezza*, we believe she is cooperating."

"This has been Maggie's plan all along," Faith's voice had a dark keening note to it. "Implicate her. Blackmail us. Force us to agree to a marr—" She broke down, sobbing. "My fault. Anybody Maggie brought. A poisoned gift. My fault."

Florian sat down next to her and tried to comfort her while, at the same time, pumping Magari for more information. "What do you mean 'lost' them in Portofino?"

"Oh, we'll get them. We have the Italian carabinieri doing a house-to-house right now. We have located her car, so we know it's just a matter of time."

"You have the carab—?" Faith's voice choked off.

Florian shook his head at Magari. "There is to be *no* publicity."

"*Senza dubbio, Altezzo, il Principe Michele mi ha detto.*"

"What did Mike tell you?" Faith demanded.

"No publicity. The carabinieri are sworn to—"

"Fat lot of good that'll do," Jill interrupted. "Any newspaper reporter with a fifty-thousand-lire note can buy the carabinieri."

"My best man is in Portofino," the harassed agent swore. "He will enforce a press blackout."

Florian rose to tower over Magari. "*You* will go there at once. *You* will take charge of the security and *you* will make certain not a word of this gets into the press. Is that clear?"

"Perfectly." Magari snapped a salute and left the room on the double.

"Do you think I was too severe with him?" Florian asked.

"Too kind, if you ask me," Faith commented. "He's somehow bungled this into an international scandal."

"It's only a childish prank," Florian said in a tone that indicated he didn't think too much of the idea.

"Runaway Princess Caught in Love Nest," Faith said, moving her finger through the air as if reading an eight-column headline. Then she glanced at Jill, as if to say "You know how they are," and buried her face in her hands, sobbing.

Florian sat down beside her again, but his mind was elsewhere. He'd dismissed Magari without finding out where Mike was. If this was a crisis in San Sebastian leadership—and it was in a certain way—then he wanted San Sebastian's next ruler free and clear of it. Polly had to be saved. But the continuity of the Gulda line was paramount.

As if she had read his mind, Faith looked up at him. Her mascara had started to run, and as she talked Jill dabbed at her face with a bit of tissue.

"Find Mike," she told her husband. "I want him here with me. Right here," she repeated, patting the divan.

"My thoughts precisely." He made his way to the office Magari kept here in the palace, but without any idea of what the next step might be. The truth was they let other people do too much for them. In the future, Florian promised himself, he would play a more personal role. He had let Faith raise the children by American standards, and see where it had got them.

In the future he would make his will felt in these matters, Florian swore. But right now, at this moment, he had no idea of what his next step should be.

All six of the houseboats, Mike saw, had been made in Kalamazoo, Michigan. They all blazed light except the second from the far end. In his sneakers he stepped silently aboard and peered through a huge Plexiglas picture window into a darkened room.

The people in bed could have been any couple at all. But the black patent-leather pumps with the low cuban heels could only belong to one female in the principality, Little Miss Sexpot.

Mike eased the sliding door open. "You probably forgot to tell him you're not yet eighteen," he announced in a loud, brotherly tone.

"Oh, God," Polly moaned. "Mr. Tact."

Etienne Rousseau came rolling off the bunk, naked as a Greek statue which no succeeding age had bothered to dress with a fig leaf. He tried to tower over Mike but found it impossible. "Wait a second," he said, then, as if voicing an afterthought, "what was that about her age?"

"My boy," Mike said in a ripe W. C. Fields tone, "you are in deep shit."

· 22 ·

Looming above the main channel that leads from the open sea into San Sebastian's protected harbor stands a curious round tower of brick built in the middle of the nineteenth century when the miraculous effects of iron-bound masonry were being exploited.

Something like a traditional lighthouse, the tower's gently curving sides led downward from a seemingly pinpoint apex to an ever-widening base nearly a hundred feet below. While not quite a wonder of the world, the San Sebastian Needle, as it is called, remains a rather impressive engineering feat.

In the apex high over the harbor two men usually sit, each with binoculars. One man is from the Harbormaster's Office, the other from the Gold Berets' Intelligence Section. Between them they control all traffic below.

In Italian *controllare* means to supervise or monitor. That is the harbormaster's job. In its English sense of managing and controlling those who use the harbor, the Gold Beret agent takes full responsibility. Between them they miss almost nothing.

They even picked up the three people walking out of the harbor area from the far end where the houseboats were tied up.

"Two men and a woman," the Gold Beret agent commented.

He scribbled a note in his logbook and, from the fact that only one of the houseboats was dark, deduced that the three might have come from that craft. He lost interest in the three when they reached the edge of the coast road. It was the harbormaster's man who spotted one of the three returning to the houseboat. Since this meant nothing to him, he almost failed to make a note. But he did.

Instead of roaring down into the bowels of the palace garage, Mike stopped the calico car once it had cleared perimeter security. On foot, he ran noiselessly down the ramp to see if Massimo was still making love to the sky-blue Jaguar XKE. Finding the garage empty, he hustled Polly up a set of back stairs to their mother's suite.

They moved in the half-darkness by instinct, having grown up in this congeries of back passages and played a thousand games here of hide-and-seek. Their voices were hushed whispers.

"My problem," Mike was saying, "is that I have to get back to Etienne. I gave him my word he'd be okay, but if they find him before I get back, he's in big trouble."

"How long do you figure my lecture will run?" Polly asked.

"If we stick to our story, maybe you'll get off with a warning. You parked your car and somebody stole it. That somebody drove it into Italy. Then I ran into you two in the harbor area and we came home."

"Long after dinner ended."

"We spent part of the time looking for your car." Mike frowned in the darkness. "Only the truth works," he said then.

"Christ, no."

"I don't mean the whole truth. Love's young dream. A little kissie-face. No copulation, dig?"

"They won't believe me."

"Mom will because she wants to. You're her. At your age she didn't know one end of a boy from the other."

"You have to admit one thing," Polly whispered softly. "I really picked a hunk for the Big Opening."

"A hunk? That's your analysis of him?"

"How'd you like him as a brother-in-law?"

"About as much as root-canal work. When I take over this place from Dad I'm going to get you a brain transplant."

"What's wrong with him, then? He's super in the sack."

"Compared to who?" her brother taunted her. "You've managed to forget that Aunt Maggie was pimping for him. And Aunt Maggie does nothing without an ulterior motive. Look," he sighed heavily, "they must understand that no defloration occurred. He is a nice boy. He loves you but you are intact. *Capisce?*"

"So how did I lose it?"

"Will you knock it off? You haven't lost anything, dodo!"

"Then before I do get married, I'm going to need one of those Sicilian pussy stitchers. Unless I marry Etienne."

"Quiet. I hear Dad's voice inside. And another." They stood in the darkness outside Her Serene Highness' suite. "Geni Magari," Mike said then. "Okay, kid, give it that Academy Award performance. You're going out on that stage a raw ingenue," he added, "but you're coming back...a star. *Avanti!*"

In much less time than he'd counted on, more than half an hour after Polly's tearful reunion with her parents, Mike was able to leave the premises, accompanied by Geni Magari.

"I said nothing inside," the agent began in a grim voice as they started down the front stairs of the palace.

"I didn't want to disturb your parents any more than they already were, but you and I know there is more to this story. The Portofino end of it was meant to mislead us, to give this Rousseau person more time with your sister. No, don't," he added when Mike seemed about to argue this.

"I don't have the time for this, *Altezza.* Either you cooperate with me, as you have not done, and we deal in good faith. Or I go my own way, using my own methods."

And end up in Portofino, Mike added silently, his face bland. He hated holding back information from Geni, but he had promised the handsome tennis player a safe way out of his dilemma. Etienne Rousseau, Mike was beginning to see, was only a pawn. He was being used by people who hadn't explained to him the consequence of failure.

It seemed to be standard operating procedure nowadays that no one was immune, not even Charley Oakhurst, who had surely been far wiser, far more experienced and much higher up than this rank beginner with the terrible backhand.

Mike was sure that someone had painted a quite rosy picture for Etienne. You romance this cute girl. What could be bad? If you get in, it's gravy. You marry a princess and spend her personal budget on your own pleasures. What could be bad? As for the tennis, they give you this sinecure of great prestige, managing one of the world's big tournaments and buddying up with the biggies. What could be bad?

Etienne richly deserved whatever fate was in store for him, the idiot. But Polly liked the guy and in a funny way so did Mike. His backhand was even worse than Etienne's.

So he'd given his word. Foolish, of course.

The obverse side of the coin called power, Mike saw now. When he took over from Dad he had to remember never to give his word that casually again. Ruler or no ruler, Mike put great stock in his word. In the field of finance, people had come to rely on it. It underlay the whole Swiss deal for the harbor development project. He had given it to Etienne Rousseau and now he would have to rescue the poor bastard before the Gold Berets found him.

But he hadn't counted on the two men at the top of the Needle.

By the time Mike got back to the harbor, a crowd of people had gathered around the houseboat, held back by uniformed Harbor Police guards. They let him on board and Mike soon saw why no one else was allowed to see.

No one else could have been permitted to witness the Gold Berets at play. They had wrecked the houseboat, sheer wanton trashing of furniture, glasses, even pictures yanked off the wall and smashed on the floor. Blood had spattered here and there. The brute wreckage of inanimate objects had been accompanied by the murderous demolition of a human being.

A man his own age. His own height. Whom his sister liked more than just a little. God, what was he going to tell Polly?

Some dark hair had been ripped out of Etienne's scalp. It lay with its flesh in a small puddle of congealing blood, as though in addition to a vicious beating there had been a savage scalping too.

And he had given his word.

Mike could picture the truncheons lifting and snapping down. He could almost hear the bone breaking under the flesh. He could visualize the raw screw of wrecked flesh where the handsome face had once been, the broken fingers, the smashed nose, the ruptured organs.

And he had given his word.

The Genoa daily carried the item at the bottom of page three. An unidentified man had been found adrift in a small boat loaded with plastic one-kilo sacks of cocaine worth several billion lire on the street. He was in serious condition, but stabilized.

The *Herald-Tribune* of the next day printed an identification of the man, together with the ponderous guesses of the Genoa police that the young American tennis player Etienne Rousseau had been involved in the international drug trade, specifically among athletes.

In neither story did anything point back to the principality of San Sebastian. Rousseau remained in a prison hospital.

When he realized that only he could explain some of this to Polly, Mike for the first time understood what it would mean to succeed his father as ruler of the principality. As he sat in his study, trying to figure out a way of making the unacceptable acceptable to his sister, Mike realized his parents ruled San Sebastian in a permanent partnership with people like Magari, normal people, not psychopaths, people who went to church and raised families and had a license to kill signed by the state they served.

In the end Mike gathered up all the newspapers that had carried the story and burned them. He could think of no other way to handle this unclean affair of state. If this was power, the power he yearned for, it stank.

· 23 ·

The suite of rooms where Florian slept had been his even as a boy. His father, the oversexed Pippo, had marooned himself on an entire palace floor served by private entrances and exits, the better to thumb through his encyclopedia of vices without his son as a spectator.

Here in Florian's chambers a bedroom thirty feet square was situated, like Faith's, on a corner of the palace to give it two views. The bed, which he had had installed when he became ruler of the principality, gave evidence of a youthful imagination in which one played a continuous game of satyr with as many nymphs as could fit this oversized playpen.

Although there had been exceptions, the young Prince even in those stallion days had limited the bed to one woman at a time, without restricting his guest list in the same way. Everyone had slept here, even Georgiadis' Russian ballerina. But instead of making Florian's Mediterranean subjects pleased with his prowess, it had enraged them.

Tonight, as he lay in bed absolutely unable to sleep, he remembered that in this promiscuous period people angrily accused him of spilling his seed everywhere except where it would produce a son and heir. And now that he had one?

Florian sighed angrily. That his own children should try to make him believe such an obvious story, designed to soothe his suspicions that something carnal had happened. It might have taken in their mother, who was sometimes too innocent for this world, but it didn't fool him for a moment.

That his virgin daughter was virgin no longer, Florian felt fairly sure. It wasn't the defloration, as such. But he had always assumed that it would be he who would choose Paola's ravisher, the way any sensible father did. She had cheated him of his rightful, um, duty.

Secondly, both of them had taken him for a real mug, as his British tutor would have put it. A prime patsy who would believe whatever he was told. That hurt. Deeply.

But of all his many reasons for anger, the strongest was fear. He knew, better than anyone, that what he was seeing were the Gulda genes in action. The first attractive boy who made a pass at Paola got the whole bundle, hymen and all.

The terrifying Gulda sexuality was at the bottom of this. The daughter of the man who had filled this gigantic bed with naked women night after night was stained from birth with the Gulda curse. The fact that Michele wasn't doing the same thing implied to Florian that Brennan blood ran in the boy's veins.

In matters of sex, he told himself, the Brennan posture is self-control. The Gulda posture is down in the muck with the rest of the pigs, swilling away. Dear God, if only the genes had sorted out the other way. San Sebastian could live with a profligate Prince Michele but not a promiscuous Princess Paola.

She wasn't even of age. Was it too late? Could some sort of deep therapy help? Florian's eyes snapped open in the half darkness. He stared at the bedside clock. Nearly 1 A.M.

Someone was turning the handle of his bedroom door. The hairs bristled on the back of his head. Faith stepped silently into the room. "It's me."

"Are you as upset as I am?" She nodded and sat down on the edge of his immense bed, pulling her pale beige robe around her.

"I'm not used to being played for a sucker," Her Serene Highness said in a small, bitter tone. "You might have been taken in by that yarn, Florian, you're a true innocent. But it didn't fool me!"

"Innocent?" He grinned at her. "You flatter me, my dear. I know a cover story when I hear one."

"It's being shut out of it that kills me," she went on in a low, angry mutter. "When a girl loses it, her mother naturally wants to be there to help her through the trauma. Did you see any sign of trauma on that girl's face? Did she look anything but pleased as punch?"

She was silent for a moment. "And I'm not fool enough to blame it all on that tennis player. Or on Maggie, who produced him. I'm perfectly well aware of the kind of signals Polly transmits to young men. I told myself she was unaware of how she came on. But I've been the one who was unaware. That little kid is hugely oversexed. Can you believe it?"

There was a long pause in which Florian's guilt seemed to glow like a neon sign in hot Mercurochrome pinks and blinding blues. It would be only a matter of time before Faith saw the connection.

"Whereas Mikey has been living a monastic existence," Faith went on. "I know he has a girl at Harvard, but should this turn him celibate in San Sebastian?"

"Eileen Maas," Florian said. "Magari keeps me informed. She's a law major from a nice Dutch-Jewish family. What bothers me is that it's a poor Dutch-Jewish family with no social connections."

"You're having our children shadowed like common criminals?" Faith demanded. "Can't they do anything without Geni Magari knowing it? And Polly still gets away with murder?"

"I don't see how Geni can be faulted in this. Michele and Paola misled him at first, but he got the Rousseau boy and he's taught him a lesson he won't forget."

"After the horse is stolen."

There was a pause. "Is that some American idiom?" Florian demanded.

She turned to him with a look of hopeless love. Putting her arms around him, she gave him a long, rocking hug. "It's silly of me, but I never want them to grow up."

He pulled back the covers of the gigantic bed, and still wearing her robe, she snuggled in beside him as he covered them both. They lay for a long time staring at the ceiling high above them. From time to time, perhaps from a car far away on the autostrada to Savona, or it may have been the turn of the Needle's lighthouse, a yellowish beam would flicker across the mosaic of the ceiling, animating the design in a lascivious wriggle of colors.

Florian knew the design by heart, satyrs and nymphs cavorting in a forest glade. What else? he asked himself. This palace and its family were steeped in sex. Once the shock of discovery had worn off, Faith would know where to place the fundamental blame for Polly's looseness.

He found himself wondering if she realized that she had never actually lain in this bed with him before. She sat on the edge, of course. Visited him for a drink in this room, naturally. But always, just before it was too late, Florian would remove them to Faith's suite. If he believed in anything, he believed in the sacredness of married love.

It remained sacred, for him, because he took pains to keep it that way. Since their marriage night there had never been another woman in this bed with him, nor had he ever visited one elsewhere. It would not have been difficult, Florian reminded himself. There would always be women who fancied him. He needn't look any farther than their own Jill Tremont, if he'd wanted that kind of love.

After the apprenticeship he had served in the mysteries of Venus, Florian felt he understood the matter quite well. The former libertine had become the faithful husband, practically a *Commedia dell'Arte* stereotype. But, now that the whole problem had bubbled back up to the surface in the person of his daughter, a load of original guilt had descended on him again after a hiatus of more than twenty years.

"What absolutely kills me," Faith murmured in his ear, "is that these kids seem to think they have a monopoly on sex. We're ancient. We're past it. So, naturally, we don't have the wit to see through their lies."

"Past it?"

As she turned toward him, her robe was pulled partly aside. "That's the real message, husband dear." She edged closer to him.

Florian could feel a faint sense of panic as his body began to respond to her movements. Not in here. Not on this bed. He'd been so strong about this for so many years. Maybe it was silly. A bed is a bed, after all. But he had sworn a great oath to himself on this point.

"We've done nothing but discuss sex, think sex, worry sex," Faith said in a voice so small he had to strain to hear it. "And here we are, losing sleep over sex."

"Let me..." She kissed him. He had wanted to suggest that he escort her back to her bed. Instead he kissed her back.

After all, one didn't have to be strong forever. Some oaths, he supposed, feeling helpless with the realization, are made to be broken.

· 24 ·

Enzo Magari sat in his little office at the back of the palace garage, leafing through new updated maintenance sheets the Mercedes people had sent him for the model 600. Unlike Jaguar updates, these had been translated into four languages, including Italian.

Little Massimo poked his head around the doorway. *"Commendatore,"* he said, using a meaningless honorific as a backhanded mark of respect, "my father wishes to know if you have time for him."

There was rarely an occasion when Enzo was not at home to those he knew, particularly the *Cavaliere,* as Massimo's father was called, yet another honorific of respect. Although they were both called Massimo Sgroi, they did not resemble each other, particularly in size. The father loomed in the doorway, as immense as his son was small, a balloon of a man who seemed always to dance on tiny, pointed feet.

A hairline mustache under a squashed nose of terrifying authority gave him the retro look of a Fascist thug who had escaped from Italy at the end of the war to avoid explaining himself to *partigiani* who were busy rounding up and shooting blackshirt capos like the *Cavaliere*.

"*Dottore* Magari," he enthused, beaming affection as he sidled into the room. His son, Massimo, reduced one would have thought to Minimo by comparison, had totally disappeared from view.

"*Illustre professore*," Enzo responded in a like vein. "What brings you into my dark cave on such a sunny day?"

"It is of Massimo that I would speak," the visitor went on smoothly, offering the ever-present pack of cigarettes, which Enzo politely refused.

The *Cavaliere* lit his cigarette and inhaled ferociously, the hippo nostrils of his deformed nose flaring to such an alarming diameter that they seemed capable of sucking up both Enzo and a few automobiles in the same breath.

"Tell me," Enzo urged.

"A boy with his qualifications," the father continued in an unhurried voice, "who speaks English as well, can surely rise to higher things."

"As time goes by," Enzo agreed cautiously.

The fat man began delving tiny raccoon paws into his pockets, as if seeking his next words there.

"Ah." He withdrew a small envelope "Two front-row tickets to the soccer on Saturday. A friend cannot go. The seats are excellent." He laid them on Enzo's desk. "If you cannot do me the favor of using them, be good enough to pass them along to another honored friend."

"*Grazie mille*." Enzo's voice was always polite. The *Cavaliere* meant well, but surely he must know that through Enzo's son Geni he could get any number of good seats at the stadium.

The fat man's lips pursed. "After the game, old friend, a few of us are having dinner at Mamma Teresa's. She will have calamari and scungilli and I am told she expects a *cernia* from the Ionic Sea of such tender flavor as to melt under your very gaze. We would be honored, my friends and I, to have the pleasure of your company."

Knowing this to be an all-male dinner in the Southern mode,

Enzo found himself wondering how he might explain such an affair to his wife, with whom he invariably ate dinner every evening of his life whether at home, at a friend's or a restaurant.

"But I have embarrassed you," the *Cavaliere* interjected delicately. "You cannot come to the soccer because of a previous engagement. Perhaps another time," he added in a light, unaccented tone. "But please, give the tickets to a deserving friend."

With a sighing grunt, the fat man got to his feet and casually tossed his still-lighted cigarette into a corner of the office. Southern style, Enzo noted; no wonder they have those terrifying forest fires down there every summer. He got up and ground out the smoldering butt with the tip of his shoe.

"Around here...grease...*benzina*...you understand," he said almost apologetically.

The *Cavaliere* nodded ponderously. "A very dangerous place for a fire," he agreed. The two men strolled out of the office, Enzo waiting for an apology about the cigarette butt. It never came.

Instead, as they came to the main part of the garage, Enzo was shocked to see that Massimo had racked the XKE Jaguar up on the hydraulic lift and was running the beam of a trouble light over its undercarriage as he glanced at the manual.

From its height the car's headlamps looked down with cross-eyed displeasure, as if resenting Massimo's intimacies.

Words failed Enzo. The insult was immense. It was not that Massimo was doing something bad. He was probably only familiarizing himself with the different linkages. But the presumption was insulting. Nobody touched these autos without Enzo's specific permission. Nobody, not even *Principe* Michele, was allowed to make free with royal property unless specifically authorized by Enzo and Enzo alone.

His mouth worked for several seconds, framing and rejecting words. Then, coldly: "Lower the car. At once. Replace the manual on the shelf. Immediately."

"Right, boss," Massimo said in English.

All this the boy's father watched with a keen eye while lighting a second cigarette. "He oversteps himself, Don Enzo?" the fat man asked at last.

"Only *la Principessa* drives that car. Massimo can wash it. He is not allowed to service it."

"But how does the lad learn, then?"

Enzo felt the anger rising slowly in his craw. He wanted to shout. He wanted to slap. But something held him back. That something was the extreme, the provocative slowness with which Massimo the Small lowered the hydraulic lift. He kept grinning at Massimo the Large as he did so. The insult was complete.

When finally the car was back in its stall, Massimo the Lesser carelessly tossed the service manual into a waste receptacle, a fifty-five-gallon oil drum in which the sweepings of the garage were neatly kept till the garbage truck came for them.

"Massimo," his father cried with such fake pain that it took Enzo's breath away. *"Che fai, piccolo?"*

As he passed his son on the way to the waste can, the *Cavaliere* cuffed him lovingly on the cheek. Then he dropped his just-lighted cigarette into the can, turned to Enzo and gave him a mock salute. *"Arivederci, amico mio.* Be good to my little Massimo. It's such dangerous work down here."

On tiny pointed feet, the balloon of his body disappeared up the ramp to the outside. Enzo had already snatched a fire extinguisher from the wall. He rushed to the can, removed the Jaguar manual and peered down into the waste rags and grease there. For safety's sake he squirted a thick layer of white foam over the contents of the can.

When he finished he was trembling with rage. He threw the extinguisher at Massimo. "Get it refilled, you little louse," he spat.

"Is that any way to talk?"

"I don't like to be threatened. You can tell your father that." He wanted to add "When I send you home sacked and with no letter of recommendation." But Enzo could not bring himself to take that next step.

Nor the one after, which was to inform Geni of what had happened. To begin with, aside from the affront to his authority and the stupid trick with the cigarette, no specific threat had been uttered. This was ever the Mafia's way with first steps, delicately to see whether or not more force was required.

Very often that was all that was needed, the mere smell of a threat, in an unspoken aura of arrogance and violent solutions.

So it was possible—but not probable—that he was reacting too sensitively to the *Cavaliere's* behavior. After all, what was the man asking but advancement for his son? Surely such a request did not require the deadweight of the Mafia as a convincer.

But Enzo knew he would never bring himself at this stage of the game to bother Geni with it. His son had large problems, affairs of state, not small-time hoodlums seeking preference for their offspring. This Enzo could handle himself.

It would destroy the fabric of the lifelong relationship he had with Geni—or badly wrench it out of kilter—suddenly to run fearfully for protection to the boy who had often run to him in the old days for protection and comforting.

No. Not possible.

· 25 ·

A pall had fallen over the palace, or so it seemed to Florian. He felt isolated from his son, who was his greatest source of useful information. Michele hadn't been out of his room for days. Since Faith's spare time was taken up with her sisters, Florian felt he had somehow become imprisoned in a vacuum.

He decided to take steps. Without warning he flung open the door to Mike's room and squinted into the dismal darkness. "You're driving your mother insane," he barked, a formula that had worked for most of his son's life. "Mikey? Are you there?"

A grunt came from the direction of the bed. Florian strode to the window and flung it open. "This place stinks. Your mother's mad with worry, your aunts are furious. What is this, a sit-in strike?"

Mike revolved slowly in bed and stared at his father. Florian saw that he hadn't shaved. There were smudges under his eyes. "You and your sister are making more fuss over this fortune-hunter tennis bum than World War II. I won't have it."

Mike grunted again and turned away from his father. Florian laid his hand on Mike's shoulder and shook him gently. "Come on, Mikey, be a man, will you?" He turned his son's head toward him again.

The silence seemed to grow in size and thickness like an immense blanket of blotting paper, sucking the life out of both of them. "Mike?" Silence. "Please?" Silence.

Florian's sigh of exasperation escaped like pent-up steam. "I will not have dissension in the family," he said then. "There is still a lot of unspoken tension between your sister and your mother. And with you behaving like a child, it becomes insupportable, Michele. Do you hear me?"

Mike nodded, but said nothing. For a long moment Florian gazed into his eyes, wondering exactly what his son had looked upon to make him this despondent.

"If you ask me," Caro was telling Princess Faith, "and remember, I have three girls of my own, I think you've kept her in Mary Janes too long. It was all right when you and I were girls. Things were different then between the sexes. Nowadays their little hormones start perking at about age thirteen, as near as I can see, and nothing will do but they instantly graduate to womanhood."

Faith's mouth had pressed into a straight line. She knew this produced ugly vertical lines in her upper lip, a disaster in women her age. "What are you suggesting, Caro? Ritual defloration?"

"I'm suggesting she be given a little leeway. She's still swimming in one-piece suits, Faith. Let her have bikinis. Let her have a heel that's more than an inch high."

"And her own pessary and pillbox."

"Pessary! I haven't heard that word in thirty years. You remember Sister Immaculata? She used to hiss it out like it was the name of a snake." She paused. "Are you telling me you haven't had a talk with her about contraception? I mean, you're *not* letting that Polack run her sex life, are you?"

"Don't get started on the Pope, Caro. I'm well aware how advanced you American lay Catholics are about birth control. Behind the Church's back, that is."

"That's the only way the Church will have it," her older sister

assured her. "It exists solely to provide absolution. Forgiveness pays
the bills."

"Very worldly."

"Look, Faith. For a country linked to the Vatican you and Florian
have to provide a lot of lip service on such matters. But not to your
daughter. Give the poor kid a chance."

Faith stood up. They had been having a last cup of coffee on the
terrace. She went to the edge and stared out over the principality.
"This is a very peaceful place, Caro," she said at last. "I have had
people tell me it's one of the few untroubled places left on earth
still with civilized amenities. I suppose that means we're behind
the times."

Neither sister spoke as Caroline joined her at the edge of the
terrace. "Faith," she said then, "this is the little paradise everybody
keeps looking for. George and I haven't found ours. You have, but
nothing remains frozen in place. So you get caught in the middle.
Because..." She stopped, but only for an instant.

"Because," she went on in a stronger voice, "you have no protection. It's just you against the outside world. Let's not kid ourselves about Florian."

"He's more of a buffer than you realize," Faith countered, but
without much force.

"And as for Mike, do I still have a nephew named Mike? I've
seen him precisely once this whole trip."

"It's this harbor development thing with the Swiss," Faith lied.

"I know it's devastated Bert," Caro rolled on. "He hasn't a fi-
nancial idea in his head except what he picks up from people like
Mike who really know what's going on. Don't tell me, you think
Mike's too young too. He must have girls stashed away somewhere.
Does he?"

The Princess gestured meaninglessly. "There's someone at Harvard he corresponds with. Eileen somebody."

"Corresponds?" A whole world of derision lingered in Caro's
tone. "You really are a Sleeping Beauty. And meanwhile a whole
thicket of thorns is growing up around the castle." She sighed with
what sounded like satisfaction. "What you always needed was Pop
on your tail, so to speak. He was your link with the real world."

"My link with filth!" Faith's mouth turned down at the corners and she burst into tears.

"He's back again," Caro said with immense calm, putting her arm around her sister. "The nasty man is back. Something happened. You walked in on him with one of his cunts, as he used to call them when he was really soused?"

"Please." Faith sounded choked.

"That's what every woman in the world was to him, every woman but his own daughters and you above all. He did whatever he wanted with the rest and the things he wanted you simply would not believe a woman would do." She patted Faith's shoulder. "All of us have had our noses rubbed in Eamon Brennan."

Faith twisted sideways and buried her face in her sister's shoulder. Her slim body bucked and shook with sobs against the more matronly figure. "The smell, Caro," she gasped. "The hideous smell in that room. And she was covered with it."

Around them a bright October morning poured pure light down on this blessed place, this oasis of civilized amenities, this fairy-tale principality. Around them a bright new day brought soft, pleasing breezes and small fleecy clouds like sky-born lambs.

And still the harsh, choking sobs racked her body.

· 26 ·

The back corridors of the Gran Palazzo di San Sebastiano were of many ages, some as old as the original castle keep of the thirteenth century. The most ancient passages had been either blocked and filled or widened and brilliantly lighted to keep the newer servants from wandering about lost. But there still remained a few dark, narrow, low-ceilinged corridors hewn out of volcanic rock base that had escaped both the eye of the architect and the attention of the security conscious.

No caretaker knew these silent, spectral passages any longer. They had long since disappeared from any floor plan of the palace. But Polly and Mike knew the secret stairways and corridors intimately. Many a candle or flashlight had been used up in exploring them over the years until their plan was etched into memory.

It was to these lonely, echoing stretches of dusty rock that both came to brood or, as today, comfort each other. The Prince and Princess had chosen a small torture chamber in whose walls great twisted circles of rusting iron had been set, the better to flay a prisoner. As consolation, Polly had thought to bring two chilled cans of beer, which they sipped glumly.

"Hey." Mike seemed to rise for a moment out of his lethargy. "This prince business is a hell of a racket, huh?"

"Yuck."

"Don't give me yuck when it's hooray that I need." He sighed. "Just another of life's ongoing cons, huh, kid? One of Uncle Billy's cynical flicks. Life is no cabaret."

"At least you didn't have your lover beaten half to death by goons." She sipped deeply from her can of beer. "God knows what Etienne will look like...if and when I ever do see him again."

"They tell me he looks okay. To that thrilling Greek God quality has been added the sexy ruggedness of some well-placed lumps."

"Don't," Polly begged. "No more kidding."

"Sorry." He sipped his beer. "But you have about as much chance of seeing Etienne again as I have of seeing Eileen on this side of the Atlantic. For us to meet in privacy I have to don a fake name and slip into Massachusetts. And even then you know the reporters can nose it out."

"Playboy Prince Romances Coed," Polly quoted, doing a terrific imitation of her mother reading a fake headline.

"Privacy is what we lack. Etienne's in a locked ward at the Sanctissima Madre del Saverio hospital near Genoa. What good does that do you?"

"I could dress up as a nun and visit him."

"Lay off the brew, kid."

Polly's eyes shifted around the small cell. "This place is symbolic."

They listened for a long time to the distant sounds of palace life filtering through the rock strata, the croak of heavy furniture being dragged, the homely flush of a toilet. "I suppose," Mike said then, "I could rent a place off-season in San Remo. But you know how long Geni's arm is."

He fell silent and then, as if it had been squeezed from him, he burst out, "Murderous bastard! And how I worshiped that man."

"He's got a small mind, Geni," Polly responded. "His idea of revenge is to turn his cowards loose on an unarmed man."

Mike grunted. "He swore to me his men had exceeded their orders. Of course," he hurried on, "I don't believe him. I don't think I'll ever believe him again."

His sister grinned crookedly at him. Mike wondered where he had seen that odd, leering look before. Grandpa Eamon? And on rare occasions, his own dear mother. "What's that lopsided leer supposed to mean?"

"It's supposed to mean that finally you're wising up."

"Will you listen to what's spouting wisdom!"

"Your problem is you're a romantic," Polly said. "You have faith that everything will work out. So the first time it isn't that way, you cave in. Look at you," she went on quickly, "sulking in bed all week? Is that the act of a realistic, Gulda-type brain?"

"And what were you doing?"

"I?" The leer grew slightly sinister. "I was arranging with one of the palace maids to get fitted with a coil. It cost everything in my piggy bank, but the doctor was so near-sighted he didn't see I was wearing a blond wig and wouldn't know me again in a million years."

Mike's lips parted to say something but, instead, stayed open silently for a long time. Then he laughed softly. "So. You're just like the rest." He stood up. "Let's blow this joint. Gives me the creeps. It's too much like real life, this torture cell."

Polly jumped to her feet. "Take the beer cans."

Her brother nodded. "This prince business," he said then. "Nothing changes. I fart around with bank loans, but that's not what a prince does. A prince imposes order, using his murderous henchmen."

His sister was holding the flashlight so that its upward beam gave them a strange look. "You're such a baby, Mike."

"Knock it off."

"You can't always have everything fall into place," she went on. "You have to expect unplanned screwball twists. And you have to be ready to take advantage of them."

"With a nice new coil?"

"What about a place in San Remo? Could you find one?"

"Knowing Geni, it'd be like transferring the cell from here to there."

They were walking through a turning in the tunnel, where it widened slightly. "You're so goddamned logical!" Polly snapped. "That's always been your trouble. You're Mom's true son, always planning ahead. What I'm talking is grabbing a chance, any chance."

"That's pirates' blood talking."

They found themselves in an open gallery cut in the rock. Mike sniffed the fresh air and beat the dust off his jeans. "Look!"

They watched a tall-masted ketch tacking into the harbor. As it drew abreast of the Needle its indigo sails fell slack and were roller-reefed out of sight. "The black ship," Mike muttered. "Last time out it was Oakhurst's."

People appeared on the foredeck of the *Finisterre*, shielding their eyes against the brilliant sunshine. Even at this distance, Maggie Rose's long legs and great breasts identified her. "The return of the Godmother," Mike announced. "Does she know Uncle Billy's due? They loathe each other."

"There's another chance," Polly said in a quiet, thoughtful voice. "We have to be alert to anything that comes along."

"Chance for what?"

His sister's sea-green eyes stared deeply into his. "The prince business doesn't suit you as it is, right? Then why not take charge of part of it?"

"Rave on."

"Why not begin with Maggie and Billy?"

"How does that help either of us?"

"I'm talking about *doing* something, Mr. Daredevil. I'm talking about shaking things up. About taking a chance. They've had all the good shots. Now it's our turn."

A nervous laugh escaped Mike. He blinked with sudden excitement. "The words don't make any sense, kiddo," he told her, "but I like the tune."

Grinning, he cocked his arm back and sent both empty beer cans glittering into the sun. They tumbled end over end in the air, but made no sound when they landed in shrubbery below. After a long moment in which neither spoke, Polly and Mike ducked out of the sunshine and sped along another corridor into the known part of the castle.

"That head of yours," Mike said with some admiration. "It's pure Gulda."

· 27 ·

The big Vertol chopper settled down tail-first like a dragonfly on the general aviation landing pad at Côte D'Azur Airport west of Nice.

It seemed to waggle slightly, forefeet still in the air, as if not certain it wanted to soil itself by contact with the earth. Then it touched the pad, sending out great rippling clouds of dust. The moment its weight settled, it lost its delicate insectile look and became what it was, heavy machinery.

U.S. Marine guards provided by the American Consulate rushed at the earthbound ship as if mounting an assault, except that they left their sidearms in their holsters. The security precaution was on behalf of Lieutenant General George McElhinny and not, as mean gossips might have it, because two Brennan sisters were aboard.

Formal good-byes had been said at the palace in San Sebastian. The copter had then taken off with the two couples and Geni Magari in a plain blue blazer and trousers. Two golf-cart vehicles streaked the party and its luggage across the tarmac to the VIP waiting salon.

Geni exhaled slowly. The rest of today's transport would be less fraught with problems and of far greater personal interest to him. He got back in the copter and waited for the arrival of the Air France relay flight that brought U.S. passengers from Paris down to the Riviera.

The day was bright. This entire coast had been having a run of brilliantly clear October weather, the kind that makes everyone wish he had scheduled his vacation for this universally magic month. Two of the Vertol's plastic ports swung open to the breeze coming in off the sea.

"One could nap," the pilot suggested in a lazy voice, his eyes heavy-lidded.

Geni nodded. "I'll keep watch."

The pilot's head settled back at an angle against the padded inside wall of the cockpit area, just below the plaque bearing the arms of San Sebastian. Another plaque of slightly larger size was fixed to the outside of the passenger door.

The shield was a sunburst of outward-radiating points like a compass rose. In the top center stood the castle-fortress-palace that had always protected the principality. In the lower half a naked man tied to a tree and pierced by a dozen arrows symbolized the principality's patron saint, the same Sebastian who had deserted his post as a Roman soldier to join the enemy ranks of Christians and, of course, pay the supreme penalty.

Geni watched the pilot's young face smooth out in sleep, all worries gone, no cares, no problems. He was probably only a few years younger than Magari himself, but the difference in the two made an unhappy impression on the police colonel, who, still in his thirties, was racked with problems and cares far beyond his desire for such punishment.

He had completed the unhappy job of disciplining the four Berets who had almost terminated the young tennis bum. This would not win back the rapport he'd lost with the man who would one day be his superior, young *Principe* Michele.

The boy's half-baked liberal mind, confused with all sorts of American fantasies about justice that no American cop believed, had now assigned Magari and the Berets to a niche somewhere between Attila the Hun and the Gestapo.

Well, rapport wasn't everything. Let the young Prince learn respect and, yes, fear. It would steady him miraculously to feel how much power Geni could wield if he chose. It was not a large problem since it could be solved by the application of just a little pain.

But the other problem was not easy since it concerned Geni's father. As he sat beside the snoozing pilot, he watched a stretched DC-9 come in over the landing runway nearest the sea. It taxied slowly to the terminal building. Geni glanced at his watch. Too early for the Paris connecting flight. He snapped on the cockpit radio and tuned in the tower talk of the traffic controllers but kept the sound low. The pilot shifted in his seat and remained asleep. Wonderful to have so few troubles.

The problem with his father was not something Geni himself had noticed. It had been his mother who called his attention to it. He tried to eat at least one meal a day with his parents but usually ended up simply having a snack at the kitchen table while his mother filled him in on family affairs.

"Secretive" was the word she had used for Enzo Magari's new behavior. "You know your father," she expanded. "He is an open book for all to read, especially for you and for me. Every evening at dinner, he always gives me a full account, whether I want it or not." She had smiled slightly. Between mother and son there was a nerve-ending telegraph system that required very few words to convey whole worlds of meaning.

"And recently, no such report?" Geni asked.

"Awkward silences. If I did not know him so well, I would suspect him of having an affair with another woman." Both mother and son chuckled at the idea.

"All this is new to me," the son said. "How is his health?"

"How is one to know?" his mother countered. "Normally I am treated to a full physical report the moment something comes up like a strained back or a head cold. Now...silence."

Geni nodded slowly as he chewed over the idea. Sitting in the Vertol now, he continued to think about it in the light of a few discreet inquiries he had made since his talk with his mother. He didn't dare come barging in with an up-close investigation. His father would be livid. At arm's length, things looked about as they always had. A new boy, one Massimo Sgroi, had been added for clean-up jobs, but that had been six months before, so it could have little to do with the change his mother had noted.

A man loathes the idea that his father is cheating on his mother, but this was the only explanation left open. Geni could not possibly assign a man to shadow his father, nor did he have the time to tail his own parent around town. It would simply have to wait, this problem, until that mythical day when he had some spare time to devote to it.

An A-300 Airbus lumbered in on the same runway now. Geni turned up the tower-talk radio slightly and verified that it was the flight he expected.

"*Allora*," he said, nudging the pilot awake, "my bird has arrived.

Wake up." He slipped out of the copter and made his way on foot to the terminal building, where he had a word with the customs people and the baggage master.

When the little Viennese director stepped off the plane, blinking in the brilliant October sunlight, a pretty flight attendant ushered him via a circuitous route that united him with Geni and his bags long before the rest of the passengers had cleared customs.

This was a special privilege few new arrivals were accorded, either by the French on their own or as a favor to San Sebastian. Geni almost never requested it, but he had this time.

"Mr. Ritz, sir."

"Ah, it's..." His gnome-like face puckered for a moment in recall. "It's Eugenio," he said with a grin. "Do I have you to thank for the free ride through customs? I've only smuggled in a few extra cigars."

"This way, sir."

One of the same golf-cart-like vehicles that had ferried the Brennan contingent now took the two men to the helicopter. If the occupants of the VIP lounge had been watching, they might have found the arrangements interesting. But Caro and Glory were both asleep, George was on the phone to Washington and Bert was nervously scanning the London *Financial Times*.

The visit to Princess Faith had not been an unqualified success, both sisters had agreed in careful undertones. Faith and Florian had not been "their old selves" obviously because of something having to do with the children. As a result, Caro told Glory, it had been entirely "too one-sided a visit. We've given her the pleasure of our company and advice and hard-earned experience and she's given us neurotic fits and poses."

"And did we meet anyone new?" the younger Brennan sister asked rhetorically. "I'm having to defend myself from idiot Bert, who absolutely depends on meeting worthwhile new people."

"Tell him it's a write-off in the interests of family unity," Caro wisecracked. "That's what I told George. Someday we will need Faith and she'll come through because she owes us."

"God, how cold-blooded."

"It's the way you and I were brought up, dear. Every relationship is a calculated one. A daughter of Eamon Brennan should never forget that. Oh, yes," she went on in her seamless conversational style, about to introduce to Glory the subject of their father's depraved sexual excesses, then decided Faith had given away too much with that lurid report. It had to be hoarded.

"Oh, yes, what?"

"Let's get some shut-eye. You know I can't sleep on planes."

Which was why they hadn't seen Billy Ritz—who certainly ranked as somebody worthwhile—board the Vertol back to San Sebastian. Missing the Brennans was precisely what Billy had in mind when he booked his visit. Over the years, starting with Eamon, he had had enough Brennans to last for several lives.

He found them a bossy, immoral gang in the tradition of many a family unit that came out of oppression. A loner himself, who could hardly remember the parents and the brother who ended up in the Treblinka death camp, Billy had an outsider's view of big-family life.

Perhaps if he'd been allowed by Hitler to grow up in his own family, his view of it would have been less jaundiced. But to Billy, families like the Brennans—Irish families, Italian ones, Jewish, in fact families from any part of the world where society could be hostile if not downright murderous—such families were organized like gangs.

There was an essentially illegal or, to be kind, extralegal lawlessness about them. They were laws unto themselves and to hell with the rest of society. It was a recipe for survival if you lived in fear of Cromwell's Protestant zealots, or the Czar's pogroms, or the varied oppressors of Italy, or the Nazi sadists: the family above all.

He himself had seen it applied in such unlikely places as Hollywood studios, where every kind of lie was justified as necessary to the success of the product, where every immorality was covered up by slathers of mealymouthed patriotism and religiosity because each studio was organized as a family, sometimes a real one in which every executive was a blood relation, more often a replica in which all were accomplices. Thank God that era was over.

He stared out the helicopter window, his chin propped on one hand, as some of the most expensive real estate on earth unrolled before him.

He found himself spotting the homes of those he knew personally, the actress in Vence, the producer-director in Cap Ferrat, a former wife in Grasse, the screenwriter in Eze. Yachts flashed by in swarms, like beetles. Velvety lawns watered by automatic sprinklers passed in review, along with houses in every style, a kind of architectural encyclopedia of the sort found in Beverly Hills, where Norman towers in conical slate roofs stood beside bunkerlike, modern brushed-concrete boxes, half-timbered Tudor manors and Rococo extravaganzas.

Perhaps here the extralegal family was extinct, he thought. But he had been in other, Third World places, where famine and disease and massacre were daily facts of life. The Brennans and the Guldas had grown careless with their family power. But in two-thirds of the planet, the gang-family was still the only survival technique.

Ahead loomed the terraces and turreted outline of the Gulda palace, almost precisely as depicted on the crest of San Sebastian. Billy turned to Geni Magari as the agent pointed out the palace to him.

In these situations Geni rarely spoke unless spoken to. Now he eyed the director almost greedily. He happened to have seen every film Billy Ritz had ever made, not just the ones with Faith Brennan. The best of them, if you had asked Geni, were the early "B" movies he had cranked out for Sol Pantages just after the war, cheap, somber crime movies that now had an international reputation as *films noir*.

In revivals they had been the teenage Geni Magari's most formative life experience. Sitting in the single theater San Sebastian had in those days, he had watched the crime unfold and, after many setbacks, had seen the detective create a cynical semblance of justice.

He had never spoken to Billy Ritz of this influence, but in a world where the secret police are perhaps even more cynical than those who make movies about them, Geni Magari did have one hero. And he was sharing the helicopter with him.

Aware that he was staring too long at the little Viennese, Geni shifted his glance to the small landing pad they were using for this flight, the one that occupied what had in the fourteenth century been the castle's courtyard. It reminded him abruptly of a scene in one of those *films noir* in which a hijacked autogiro landed in a prison yard to help the gang's leader escape.

"It's the same scene," Geni blurted out.

Billy turned toward him to see him staring down as the copter pad below seemed to rise to meet them. "And that's where Frank Kane would be standing," he went on unable to stop, "there by the archway. And the guard with the machine gun was over there, by the old well."

He glanced up, saw Billy's eye on him and blushed deeply. The Viennese nodded. *"The Big Crush-Out*, Paramount, 1946." His funny gnome's face crinkled with a lopsided grin. *"Ma che memoria!"*

"My memory," Geni was horrified to hear himself confess, "covers precisely fifty-six of your features." It was like a nightmare. He couldn't seem to do anything but blurt.

The Vertol had settled on the ground in a whirlwind of dust.

"I have made only fifty-six features," Billy said gravely. "Good God, don't tell me. I have just met my number one fan."

"You must excuse me, sir."

"You've made my day," Billy said. "Let's you and me have a drink one of these evenings and wander down memory lane."

"A great honor, but—"

"It's a deal. Tomorrow night at six. I'll be at La Muta," he added, naming a working-class bar in the center of town.

Before Geni could disgrace himself any further, servants began to unload Billy's bags. Across the courtyard Princess Faith was running to him, arms outstretched.

· 28 ·

The small gray Renault 5-TS rounded the corner of the Eamon Brennan Memorial Clinic and paused in front of the half dozen parking spaces marked PARCHEGGIO UFFICIALE.

Geni Magari had a certain right to park here, even though it was reserved for hospital staff, but to do so would be to reveal his official identity. He had few illusions about remaining anonymous in and around the palace and other seats of government, but he did cherish the hope that this visit could be kept "unofficial." So he slowly turned the car into a side street, found a metered space, dutifully put his 1,000-lire coin in the slot and walked with a certain gravity toward the small private park inside the compound. His guess was correct. Arturo was busy polishing glasses in the bar there.

"*Mannaggia*, Geni," the other agent apologized. "I have neglected this place all week. It's a shambles."

Geni nodded, still with the solemness of a fellow Gold Beret but a bit self-mocking now as a friend of Arturo's since high school. "It's an even better place to talk than inside that den of quacks," he murmured softly, picking up another towel and helping with the polishing.

"The *Finisterre* is back," he said after a while.

"*Porca miseria*," Giacobbe muttered. "That's nerve, isn't it?"

"Perfectly in order," Geni responded. "Same crew, even the same captain. Not well enough to attend the inquest in summer. Perfectly fit now to crew that accursed boat." He polished another glass until it shone. "And the passengers. Maggie Rose, *ricordi?*"

"Now that's *real* nerve. Can we reopen the inquest, do you think?"

"Forget the inquest. The interesting thing is that she was not invited by Her Serene Highness. There is a certain coolness since the affair of the tennis player. We have to mount another all-night radio watch. Tonight."

"But this Maggie Rose is no Oakhurst. She's an entertainer."

"Her affiliations are similar. I haven't yet identified the remainder of her party. Until then we have to monitor the *Finisterre* closely. Can you begin at sundown?"

"Do I have a choice?"

"None."

Both men produced similar looks and gestures, a kind of orchestrated Italianate duet of shoulder and chin movements which, if set to words, would run along the lines of "What a job this is for two grown men, eh?"

Geni Magari held a narrow, elongated champagne glass to the light, huffed a layer of mist on it and briskly polished away a fingerprint. "All is tranquil in the clinic?" he asked, more to make conversation than out of curiosity.

The other agent paused. "The gambling again, more or less."

Geni made a face. Gambling was part of human nature, especially when people congregated in one place, as the staff of the clinic did, or perhaps the employees of a large office anywhere else in the world, he reminded himself.

"More or less," he repeated back to Giacobbe. "Obviously it's more, not less, or a crafty *ebreo* like you wouldn't mention it."

He couldn't be sure, but he thought Arturo's face grew minutely darker. It wasn't that he didn't want to be known as a Jew. After all, Giacobbe is Giacobbe, the son of Jacob. It was, Geni knew, that the Gold Berets had about as many Jews among their number as they did Abyssinians.

"This *ebreo* smells something," Arturo said at last. *"Who* gambles? All right for the cleaning staff. All right for orderlies and drivers. I am even willing to agree that sisters of mercy can place a bet if they so desire."

"But?"

"But doctors?" Giacobbe asked in a faintly scandalized voice.

Geni nodded solemnly. How Jewish, he thought, to believe that a doctor, or any other professional, should be above the petty temptations that afflict common folk. He put his arm around his agent's shoulders and gave him a fatherly squeeze. "Turo, what is so sacred about a doctor?"

"The young ones, fresh out of medical school? And since we are a teaching hospital, we also have interns. Geni," he said, "where do they get the money to gamble?"

"They have salaries."

"Minuscule."

"Allowances from parents, if they're still students."

"Picayune."

"The older doctors are allowed small private practices."

"If they're older, they have families," Arturo argued relentlessly. "If they have families, they have no loose change for football pools. No, if the man who sweeps the halls wants to pauperize himself, it isn't a matter of life and death. But when a doctor is worried about paying his bookie, that's an entirely different matter."

"Arturo, in a principality whose chief source of income is gambling there are no laws being broken here, unless the bookie welshes on a bet."

The agent led the way out of the bar and locked the door behind them. They stood in the sunshine, admiring the Barbara Hodgkins sculptures in the fountain. The sharply slanting rays of afternoon sunlight ricocheted off the rippling surface of the pond, making the statues come alive in their varying hues of bronze, pale copper, faint green, narrow drips of green-black patina, each angle and point dazzling in sun.

The two men sat down for a moment of peace. It was typical of them both that although they felt that they had won this respite by hard, driving, secret work, neither could enjoy the quiet for more than a few minutes. It would be a contest to see who jumped up first.

Geni got reluctantly to his feet. "A pleasant pause." He glanced sideways at Giacobbe. "All right, how can they afford to gamble?"

"It's the drugs, Geni."

"Drugs?" The word hissed oddly through the sylvan peace of the small park. "They pay off gambling debts with drugs? Taken from the dispensary?"

Giacobbe nodded. "Only the desperate ones."

"Only the desperate ones," Geni echoed in a melancholy tone. "The bookie's name?" He held out his hand, palm up, as if waiting to be handed a coin.

"He's the fat man down in the harbor area called Massimo Sgroi," Arturo said then. "They call him *Il Cavaliere*."

Geni sat back down on the bench and looked at his open palm. "Does he have a son of the same name?"

"I believe so."

"The boy works in the palace garage, washing cars?"

Knowing that this was Geni's father's domain, Giacobbe hesitated to reply. "As you say," he responded lamely.

"*Dio mio*," Geni murmured, still staring at the palm of his hand as if, instead of a coin, his fellow agent had presented him with a live scorpion.

Minutes passed. Finally Arturo Giacobbe stirred. He put his hand on Magari's shoulder. "Geni, are you all right?"

There was an even longer pause. "No," Geni said then.

PART
FOUR

PART
FOUR

· 29 ·

One must try to understand one's own motives, Billy Ritz lectured himself. Otherwise nothing in life makes sense.

He was sitting in an uncomfortable upholstered armchair drawn up to the southwest windows of Princess Faith's dressing room. She sat across from him in a similarly bad chair, the sun pouring down on them a golden inundation of happiness and health... everything, Billy thought, but what this poor girl is telling me.

One must know why one tortures oneself, he kept thinking. Why on this brilliant day late in what's left of my life, I sacrifice God's glorious sun for the interior darkness of this poor girl who is no longer a girl.

In the fan magazines and gossip columns of a bygone age the close relationship between Billy and the woman he had made a star had been presented with terrifying ignorance and lack of original-ity by writers and editors who fed on such leavings of the film in-dustry. Svengali and Trilby. Master and novice. The usual crapola, Billy recalled.

In journals of the film intelligentsia—if he could manage that word without throwing up—the relationship was reversed, as if for shock effect. It was Faith Brennan who had rescued Billy Ritz from the obscurity of "B" crime films, according to these magnificent asses.

No one had the wit or the nerve to speak the truth of it: he had been in love with her from that fateful night in Chicago in 1943.

He had never had sexual relations with her, which only sharpened the poignancy of the thing until it pierced his heart like a permanent surgical drain, leaching away any love he had for other women and sending him through five extremely expensive divorces that had left him scrambling for money for each new movie he wanted to make.

We both know it, Billy thought as he stared at that beloved face, now drawn with remorse. She won't let herself think about it and I can't stop.

With the passage of years—decades—it had become grotesque. The fires were supposed to die down. I've become a vaudeville joke with my unrequited passion, Billy thought. And she's finally allowed life to jell her. She's become the one thing she never was, the Ice Queen.

"...little things at first, unimportant things," she was saying. She had said it all before, through an entire afternoon. Billy Ritz wondered how many official appointments had been stricken off her book to make time for this soul-baring.

"...then it was vital things I couldn't remember. Names of people. Common ordinary English verbs. The key action word, the verb. Absolute blank."

"I know," he said, lifting to his lips what must have been his four hundredth cup of tea that day and putting it back down untasted.

"But it's more sinister than that," she said.

He knew what was coming because she had told him this several times now, an actress rehearsing for her director until she was able to give her lines their maximum effect. She would now repeat the business of how one unwanted memory grew sharper and crowded out the parts of her mind on which she relied for daily speech.

"Is that possible?" Faith asked him yet again. "You must know about such things, Billy."

"Because I'm so old?" he parried. "An expert on aging?"

He eyed his tea and wondered, since it was after five o'clock, if he might have a triple scotch on very few rocks. But, if he could get away, he was meeting the secret policeman at a bar in town. Best not to arrive skunked out of his skull with palace booze. Besides, he couldn't handle it the way he used to.

That was part of aging he could tell her about. How even the sweet nepenthe, the blessed oblivion, was no longer available to smooth the sharp and dangerous corners of life, nor enliven the drab, dull stretches.

But why depress her still further? He gazed into those pure green eyes and remembered her at seventeen on the stage of the Goodman, permanently altering the beat of his heart.

"...ugly, ugly scenes of the past. Like figures in a horror flick," she was telling him. "You know, those cutaway shots you flash to for shock effect?"

He nodded. "Very effective."

"They block off my mind, Billy. There are scenes I have done my level best to forget. And you know I have a strong mind. Had," she corrected herself. "I was always able to control my thoughts. And now they control me, nasty, vile, sordid scenes of..."

Silence. She had come to this brink twice now. Each time Billy had hesitated to shove her over the edge. But it was five o'clock and he was tired. The outpour of her problems had eroded him. Now was the time to get her to go the extra inch and be done with it.

"You're going to *have* to tell me," he spoke up suddenly. She blinked as if he had shouted. "If not me, some expensive shrink. What scenes come back to you? What can be that vile?"

She sat numbly for a moment, turning her head on her long, swan's neck to stare blindly out at the afternoon sunlight. "I couldn't even tell Caro. I could only hint at it and, since she seemed to know what I was talking about, it never really got said."

"What about Jill?"

The princess shook her head. "She wouldn't be able to help. I don't think anyone can but you."

"Not if I can't guess what you're talking about." The little Viennese waved his hand in a negligent gesture. "As for the rest, all your memory problems, it's only a matter of aging, Faith. In 1943, when I first fell in love with you, you were not yet a woman. I have seen you mature into one. There's a two-edged word. You're still maturing, only now we call it aging. Faith, you're over fifty. You don't look it so you're one of the lucky ones, as far as appearances are concerned. Don't bitch and moan when you suffer interior changes. They're the price you pay for still looking good on the outside."

She reached across to pat his hand, a gesture he particularly hated. "Flattery gets you everywhere," she said smiling. "But what good is it, Billy, if underneath the looks I'm senile?"

"A crock," he announced with an exaggerated Austrian roll to the *r*. "You sustain your star part in this production with all the aplomb of the true professional. You run this two-bit Graustark. Without you, Florian would be a busted truss." He took a breath and then launched into the shock part of the tactic.

"What scenes obsess you?" he demanded. "Scenes with your late lamented father?"

Her face went white. She pulled back in her chair. "Billy," she whispered "you know how close we two were. My only parent."

"Speak up."

"Domineering. And as he aged, filthy."

Billy Ritz moistened his lips. "Eamon Brennan was always filthy," he said at last. He took a slow, careful breath. "Outside the bosom of his family his reputation stank."

"As a businessman?"

"As a dirty old man."

Neither of them spoke for a moment. Then the Viennese cleared his throat somewhat nervously. "You know, Hollywood has a lot to answer for. Some of the producers and directors developed tastes for the kind of tricks you could buy only in a very raunchy Bessarabian brothel. But in Hollywood, lovely young girls wanted so much to be in the movies that they would perform for free what a hardened old whore would think twice about and them demand a double salary. That power deforms a man for any normal human relationship with women *or* men. To wield so much power that you could get people volunteering to turn themselves into sexual sewers... Although he came to it from banking, Eamon Brennan turned loose in Hollywood was like a pig in shit."

"In shit!" Her voice was a shriek. Her eyes stared wildly at the director. *"In shit!"* she howled. "He had covered her with it and was forcing her to *eat* it!"

"Oh, God, what did you walk in on?"

"She was *devouring* it. She was *gobbling* it. And he was crowing as he straddled her, crowing like the cock of a dunghill, the two of them smeared like—"

He could hear the click in her throat that cut off her words. They say glaring into each other's eyes, two golems out of a Frankenstein epic, Billy thought, each electrified by Lionel Atwill with twenty thousand volts of ersatz vitality.

One must, he told himself, put names to things. It is the function of the human animal on this planet. The list of women's names he didn't want to hear was long. He especially hoped it hadn't been Jill because in the scheme of holding Faith together during this part of her life, Jill was a crucial binding agent.

Then it came into his mind with such certainty that he had the illusion the name had been spoken. "Maggie Rose."

Faith nodded. Her underlip was caught between her teeth. Billy Ritz could see a thin line of blood rill up. He jumped to his feet and gently slapped her face. "Stop that! Look what you've done to your mouth!"

He shoved her head around so that she could look into her dressing-table mirror. She could see the line of red slowly crawling down from the corner of her mouth but she did nothing about it. He reached for a tissue and patted it off, then stared at the crimson stain on the tissue. Some obscure thought told him: don't let a maid find it in the wastebasket. He stuffed it in the pocket of his jacket.

He held her head against his small, trim body. The tiny potbelly he'd developed in his later years served as a pillow. He stroked her hair slowly. He'd gotten it out of her. Now she had to be returned to normality. "You see, it isn't so bad," he heard himself telling her. "You've said it and the skies haven't opened up and nobody's zapped you with a thunderbolt."

He could hear her whimpering but he couldn't see her face, except in the mirror. She had pressed herself so tightly against him that she was bending that lovely nose sideways. "It's an aberration, a very old one. Even the Greeks had a word for it. Puppy dogs do it. And, if you believe Freud, Eamon Brennan would have been precisely the man to enjoy such a gourmet treat. Freud equates shit with money. What the hell, we all do."

"Stop," he heard her beg.

"Okay. No more Viennese shoptalk."

She moved away from him and automatically glanced at herself in the mirror. The line of blood had reformed. She patted it off with another tissue and seemed struck by the same caution as Billy had. She handed him the tissue and he filed it in his pocket.

"Thanks, Billy." She examined her lower lip in the mirror, frowning and making noises of disgust. Vanity takes over, Billy thought. Now she delved into a dresser drawer and brought forth a small styptic pencil which she touched to the bite she had given herself. She winced. "Yipe!"

"But why did you keep Maggie Rose close to you all these years?" he asked her then. "Revenge?"

"Retribution."

"You picked the wrong villain, my dear. She was as much a victim as any other performer who—"

"I know." She turned from the mirror. Her face had been almost gray. Now there was a faint color in her cheeks again. "But, Billy, I couldn't admit to myself who the real villain was. I...I fantasized that she'd...I don't know, *trapped* him into such a scene."

"You know better now." The Viennese glanced sharply at her. "Don't you?"

She nodded. "Caro warned me about that. Isn't it pretty clear now that on this one thing I could never think straight?" She paused and seemed to listen to her own words again. "And from that one refusal...came all the rest. In a lifetime of being strong, there was this one weak link. And it was breaking me up."

He sat back down in the armchair. His whole body seemed to be crying for a drink. "You're missing part of it," he told her then. "This, whatever you call it, this mental confusion of yours. It's gotten bad only very recently. Am I right?"

She sat perfectly still, staring at him. He knew her well enough to know that, once again, she was repeating their words to herself, going over them in that logical, careful way of hers. "Yes, since he died. Only since then."

"Because retribution is something you can have only with a living person," the director remarked. "It won't work on a dead man."

"Yes. He escaped me."

"And if he were still alive, what do you think you could have done to him? People like Eamon Brennan," he went on in a heavier voice, "never pay the bill. When the waiter arrives, they have already left the table."

Her eyes were dry, bright with knowledge. "He *was* evil," she said, "but so is Maggie. She's played me false in so many devious, underhanded ways."

"Forgive me, my dear. That's just business. The business of the people who control her recording contracts. Who finance her films. She calls them her family. What they really are is her masters. She's traded Eamon Brennan for the Mafia."

"And I should let her go? Just like that?"

"Yes."

She smiled grimly. "You really don't understand the Irish," she said then. "You really can't feel what it's like to have hated the wrong person all these years, to have been cheated of revenge, the frustration of miscalculating and the agony of knowing that he was my own, true, dear, loving *father*." She spat out the last word with such force that it shocked both of them.

"There's more to this tale, Billy," she warned him.

"Not today there isn't."

"There's a whole story you haven't heard yet about Polly."

The director grimaced. "Some scandal?"

"You might say that." She stared intently at him. "It's not as important now as it seemed at the time. But it illustrates something about bloodlines."

"I don't follow," Billy said. "And that's just the way I want it."

"You and I," she went on as if he hadn't spoken, "grew up thinking the Gulda family was a hothouse of sex fiends, perverts and libertines. Am I right?"

"But you can hardly call Florian a—"

"I know. I know. But he blames himself for something that happened to Polly. He blames his genes." She suddenly started to laugh. The noise sounded so ugly to the little Viennese as it rose in volume like someone choking.

"Billy, he blamed *his* genes!" She was helpless with laughter now, shaking with it.

"Faith. Take it easy."

"Don't you see? What's a Gulda gene compared to the inheritance I have from my dear father?"

"Give it a rest, Faith. I can't take any more."

"Right. Right. Right." She nodded three times, as if winding up a charm.

Then she turned back to the mirror and reexamined her lip again. She seemed lost in this closed-off reflection. Typical performer, Billy Ritz thought. Unload on the nearest friend and it's back to the looking glass for the only real relationship of their life.

"Let's break," he said. "We've had enough for now." He stood up.

"Yes," she said from a great distance. "Mark it and strike it and save the lights," she quoted from studio jargon. "Tomorrow's a big day. A weekend conference of fellow nobility." She giggled, as if in perfect humor. "Us, Monaco, Luxembourg, Liechtenstein, the Bishop of Urgel, who runs Andorra. It's a—what did you call it?—a summit conference of Graustarks."

"What happened to San Marino?"

"They're Communist. Turned us down politely."

The little Viennese began laughing. He knew it wasn't all that funny. But he'd managed to get out of her one of the horrors making her miserable. In a life of recent failures, he'd at least been able to accomplish this one thing. He stood up.

"*Permesso?*" he asked.

"You need permission to leave the royal presence?" she asked. "Remember, dinner's at eight sharp. And..." Her mind wandered, just as her glance did, back to the mirror. She examined her lip. She had stanched the blood, but wasn't the lip the tiniest bit puffy now? Perhaps ice? She rang for her maid. Billy passed the girl as he left the room.

He could hear Faith ordering a bowl of ice as he sped along the corridor and down the stairs to his own suite. Too much of his life was spent with performers, he told himself.

· 30 ·

In the guest suite assigned to Billy Ritz, with its large drawing room, dressing room and bed chamber, leaded-glass windows looked out over one of the castle's many courtyards. Each bowed window contained an upholstered seat from which to contemplate the pleasant view.

At this point, however, all Billy required was the rather small but adequate bar in the drawing room, where he quickly popped two ice cubes into a glass and poured whisky over them. As he stood there, trying to shed the tension of the day, he rattled the ice cubes to cool the scotch and wondered what the other priests did after hearing a particularly lurid confession.

"Uncle Billy?"

He flinched, turned and faced the window. There sat his lanky god-nephew, Mike, looking, in that hallowed phrase, like an unmade bed.

"I'm warning you," the small Viennese began, "I've had enough *tsouris* from your family today. What's up?"

Mike got slowly to his feet and approached him, hand extended. They shook formally but for quite a while, the prince towering over Billy and slumping as much as he could to minimize the contrast.

"What's *tsouris*?" Mike asked.

"Trouble. Aggravation. And you got a face full of it."

The younger man's hands went up in front of him, not protectively, but as a form of disclaimer. "Let's do this tomorrow then," he said. "Sorry I barged in."

"I got five minutes. Can your tale be told that quickly?"

"Quicker."

"Sit, then. Drink?"

"A beer." Mike swung open the small refrigerator door and extracted a can. He popped the top and took a long pull before sitting down. "It's Aunt Maggie," he said then.

"Please. When referring to that one, omit the honorific. What's the problem with Maggie?" The director sat down beside Mike on the window seat. The evening sky behind them had already turned from pink to mauve. Billy found it soothing to hear Mike's low-pitched, almost hesitant voice after Faith's strong, keening tone.

"She's back is the problem. Uninvited."

"Mmm."

"Just mmm?" Mike asked. "That last little effort of hers nearly got a guy murdered by our private Gestapo."

"Mikey," the Viennese begged, "I've been away. In *Variety* not a lot of San Sebastian news gets printed."

"She introduced some Mafia shill to Polly. Geni's goons nearly beat him to death. Now she's back and I know Mom, she won't be able to say no to an old friend."

"You sure know Mom," Billy agreed. He found himself wondering whether, in her new mood, cleansed of all hatred for Maggie, Faith would have her defenestrated or merely staked out on an anthill.

"Why not leave Maggie Rose to the Gold Berets?" he asked then.

"We've left too much to them," the young Prince said in a low voice. "Anything we don't want to touch we hand over to Geni Magari. He's got the finesse of a gorilla."

"I thought you liked Geni."

"I idolized him."

"And now he's Heinrich Himmler?"

"Huh?"

"Runs a Gestapo?"

"Now?" Mike shrugged and threw both hands out sideways, sloshing beer foam on the padded window seat. "Now he turns out to be part of the problem, not part of the solution."

"So what do you want?" Billy persisted. "A world in which all secret police are Parsifal and all pop singers with big tits have the souls of angels?"

"I don't want Aunt Maggie back here stirring up shit."

Billy fell silent, realizing that, between them, he and Mike could set something ugly in motion. "You want her to get the bum's rush," he said then. "It's a job for the Gold Berets."

"The hell with that."

"You can't have it both ways," the director warned him. "Either you have a secret police or you handle all this stuff yourself, you and your parents. Which would you rather have?"

The younger man stared at him for a long moment. "I guess I'd rather be a checkout clerk in a Safeway supermarket in Dayton, Ohio."

Both of them laughed, but in different keys, Billy noted. He got to his feet and drained the last of his whisky. "Five minutes are up," he announced.

"So you're not going to help me?" Mike inquired.

"Help you do what?" Billy walked to a mirror and inspected his face. One of the very few advantages of baldness was that one's hair seldom got disarranged. He felt a hundred years old. "Tell me what you want."

"I want that woman..." Long pause. "Neutralized."

"Is that anything like liquidated?" the Viennese asked with a slight edge to his voice. "Or that new South American trick, disappeared?"

"I want her out of our hair."

Billy went to his bathroom, dampened a washcloth and carefully rubbed his face with it. He now felt ninety-nine years old. "See what I can do," he said then.

La Muta had always been a small friendly bar near the harbor where divers and dockyard workers congregated to nurse cheap shots of grappa and munch boiled trotters in vinaigrette sauce.

But Billy saw, as he entered the place, that times had changed. La Muta had been discovered by the rat pack of trendy young people who came to San Sebastian for gambling or sports. Some of the girls had style but the boys universally reminded him of typecast Mafia hit men, not the old-fashioned pug-ugly types, but the new, slim menaces. Perhaps they got their money by dealing drugs. Perhaps they worked as checkout clerks in Italian Safeways. Perhaps he didn't give a damn about any of them except that they had usurped what had once been a pleasant, quiet place for a drink.

As he listened to some wordless jukebox cackle he saw that in addition to the loud music the proprietor had put in a microwave oven and a line of factory-made warm-up foods for the new, younger clientele. He had also tarted up the decor with fake gas lamps of the 1880s.

The sign that had once hung outside now served as a wall decoration, a woman with no head, bloodlessly decapitated. Billy yawned and reached into his pocket to throw away Faith's two bloodied tissues. The headless woman was a play on *la Muta*, the Mute Woman. But in diver's slang the wet suit they wore to keep warm was also called a muta. Sipping a really small ounce of whisky, Billy found himself dozing off in the corner booth.

When he awoke the scene had changed. Under the sign sat a grossly fat man with the ruined face of a gladiator and a squashed nose whose nostrils flared like the muzzles of a double-barreled shotgun. Sleepily, eyes half closed, Billy watched various people come and go. Money changed hands. Billy noted the delicate raccoon paws of the fat man, tiny Japanese-painting fingers that deftly twitched money out of sight so that one could have sworn it hadn't passed hands at all.

The little Viennese made a face. Too Fellini. Nobody could be this grotesque, miniature feet in pointed shoes, miniature hands on a bloated ruin of a body. He dozed again.

By the time Geni Magari arrived the great director was fast asleep, two bloodied tissues on the table before him.

Respectfully quiet, Geni ordered a grappa and debated with himself whether or not to let Billy Ritz sleep. He watched people arrive under the sign of the Mute Woman, as if for an appointment. But nobody sat there. Geni reached for the tissues, sniffed them. Perfume.

Geni recognized the scent, just as he recognized that someone had been sitting under the sign. He was an expert in such blank spaces. Often they were the only clues he had unless he invented new ones. In a little while his men would be staging something of an invention in the harbor, a bit of fake excitement Geni needed to have happen. He was an expert in such matters too.

With great care, he reached across and took Billy Ritz's arm in a gentle grip. He repeated the pressure, waiting for the elderly eyes to open, those eyes that had watched thousands, perhaps millions, of staged scenes. Another illusionist, Geni thought. Like me.

· 31 ·

Carrying her great leather portfolio under her arm, Jill Tremont entered the palace library, made sure it was untenanted and sat down at her desk. She opened the immense folder and began sorting small envelopes and sheets of notepaper into several piles. Because in half an hour dinner would be served and because they had an illustrious and beloved guest, Mr. Ritz, Jill was dressed up.

She sat back in the chair and removed her half-moon reading glasses. The small smoked mirror on the wall beyond the desk showed her that her sleeveless mauve dress was perhaps too summery. But she could always wear a dark purple shawl across her shoulders. Her hair...

Tomorrow Jill would be in full fig. She had taken over from Florian's old majordomo, his uncle il Conte di Maremonte, the job if not the title of Protocol Chief. The Count, like his brother, Pippo, had been carried away by spinal spirochetes. He had led a hardworking life and, by God, at the age of ninety-one, it had killed him.

A crooked grin quirked up one corner of Jill's soft mouth. Then she glanced down at the agenda for tomorrow's events and the smile died. Hell's own amount of work, a gaggle of guests, each with his or her protocol. The Grand Duke of Luxembourg was never a problem, nor were the Prince of Liechtenstein, Prince Ranier or Princess Grace of Monaco, the latter being an old friend of Faith's and of Billy's too. No, it was always the Bishop of Urgel who created protocol problems.

Andorra being jointly administered by the President of France and the Bishop, there existed a vast imbalance of influence, all in favor of the big European nation and very little on the side of a tin-pot priest from a dinky Spanish town. But the dinkier the man, the greater his demands.

She grimaced, making careful notes beside the names of each guest, assessing rooms and serving maids. This adventure in microdiplomacy would require the full palace staff and eighteen in hired help. But for the dinner and ball tomorrow night, not counting kitchen staff, a dozen musicians were to be hired, an equal number of waiters and two dozen security men from the Gold Berets, doubling as wine waiters, bartenders, busboys, footmen and the like.

All this added expense was on behalf of a fond fancy of Florian's. Jill smiled softly, not at all the crooked grin that Count Maremonte's life and death had produced. Fond, foolish Florian. As unlike his father and the Count as anyone could be and still lay claim to Gulda blood.

Living under the same roof with him all these years, Jill realized, had very much contributed to her peace of mind. The world saw only Faith, its eyes riveted by her blaze of star power. But Jill felt Florian's gentle influence in so many ways, Old-World, oddly innocent, gravely calm, a pocket of the nineteenth century that had somehow survived in the blare of the twentieth like a winter garden with one all-but-forgotten palm tree.

Jill went to the broad expanse of curtained windows that fronted on the harbor. The October dusk was the color of her dress, mauve, but only for a moment. Then it deepened to violet, then purple, then indigo as she watched. In the distance the sweeping double beam of the Needle made its circuit, blinding her for an instant. On the dock below, two men paced along a walkway made of great blocks of granite. She instantly recognized Billy Ritz. The other she couldn't identify at this distance or in this light.

Behind her the telephone rang.

"Baby, it's me," Maggie Rose announced in a hearty, nasal tone. "S'prise!"

"This is Jill, Maggie. Nobody told us you were expected."

Jill had never needed lessons in cooling down her voice. It now fell several degrees below anything Faith normally used to express disinterest.

"Not tonight. We're at dinner and then it's beddy-bye. Big day tomorrow."

Silence at Maggie's end. Then, casually: "Oh, yeah, the minisummit. Rayn-yay and Grace told me they'd be here."

The grim look on Jill's face colored her next words. "So nice for you, dear. Have to hang up. Bye."

"Hold it!" Maggie Rose snapped. "Not so fucking fast. Let me talk to Florian."

"He's dressing for dinner, I'm sure."

"Either tell him I'm on the line or I'll hang up and dial his number. Makes no difference to me," the singer added brusquely.

Jill understood she'd been outflanked. "Hold on, then." She dashed along the corridor and up the next flight of stairs, arriving at the door of Florian's suite breathless, heart thudding. She knocked.

"*Avanti.*"

"Hello," Jilly called as she entered, in case he was not properly dressed.

"I'm in here," he said from his dressing room. She found him in his shirt sleeves and stockinged feet reading the pink *Financial Times* of London. "What's cooking?" he asked in one of his doomed attempts at American slang.

Still out of breath, she gazed down at his blond hair and felt her fingers itch to touch it, rumple it. "I'm sorry to bother you. It's the Rose woman, on Faith's line. Insists on speaking to you."

"The rose woman?" Florian's stare was blank. "The lady who sells flowers t—?"

"Maggie Rose."

He jumped to his feet. "Here in San Sebastian?"

"And sniffing around for a palace invitation. She knows about tomorrow's do. Claims a couple called Rayn-yay and Grace told her."

They eyed each other a moment and then both grinned like co-conspirators. "In that case," the prince said, "she being so well known in such high places..." He lifted the phone and punched the lighted button. "Goombar," he began. *"Come stai?"*

He listened, nodding, then glanced at his watch. "No, too late. We eat at any moment, I'm afraid. What?" He listened again. "No, tomorrow is all diplomatic comings and goings." He let her talk some more. "I don't th—" He listened. "Maggie, if it were up to me—" More silence. "Yes, but she may have other plans." Now he was silent for a long time. Jill could see by his face that he had relented. Was that the word? Or was it weakened?

"But only half an hour. *Ciao, bella.*"

He hung up the phone and sank back into his dressing chair as if he had been shoved. "God, that woman is a Sherman tank."

"She's coming here after dinner," Jill surmised.

"I had no choice." He avoided her glance, his stockinged feet feeling for the shiny black dancing slippers he would be wearing to dinner, not for the formality but for the comfort. "Anyway, Faith will be pleased to see her."

"As welcome as bubonic plague."

Florian's eyes widened. "I had no idea they..."

"Since the business with the tennis player."

"Ah. Maggie was very remiss, introducing that poor young man. I don't blame Faith for being cross with her."

"Cross." She said it not as a question but as an echo. "How did you feel about Maggie after that episode?"

"Rather cross," he admitted. "But you know me and women. I seem to have inherited the Gulda inability to say no to them."

Again they eyed each other curiously and again they both broke into conspiratorial smiles, as if Florian had been telling her something in code—which he had—and she had deciphered it accurately. "So then what do we do about this evening, after dinner?" he asked, giving her a mock stricken look.

She watched his toes feeling about for the slippers. Slowly she got on her knees in front of him and lifted each slipper in turn, its patent leather gleaming, for him to put on. Her heart resumed its wild beating.

"Thank you, my dear," he murmured. "You have a much more gentle touch than Alberto. It's too bad, isn't it, that I can't have a female valet."

This time, with their plotter's glances crossed, they both broke into laughter, hers quite breathless with joy.

· 32 ·

"On the contrary," Billy Ritz was telling the secret policeman, "what I always look for in a movie is a situation that can't remain at equilibrium. Something that *must* change."

They were watching the last light of day fade out of the western horizon. To their right the urban mass of San Sebastian was coming quickly to life in a series of white flares, neon smears and dancing points of red and yellow. To their left the slight Mediterranean surf, hardly more than a gentle upsurge and retreat, washed the great granite blocks of the jetty. They had stopped among the more romantic of the yachts moored in the principality this evening, the big, tall-masted sailing ships.

"Life is never supposed to come to rest," the director went on. "So in my movies, I tried to find charged examples of that restlessness. In your line of work, each new day must bring some major change too."

In the growing darkness Magari offered a cigarette, was refused, lit his own. By the flicker of his lighter, cupped inside his hands, he eyed the elderly Viennese more closely, as if this were suddenly an interrogation. "That's true enough," he said then, "because when things don't change, we're in trouble."

A slow smile came and went across the director's lips. "And sometimes you sort of, kind of, nudge it along till it does change."

The policeman held the flame a moment longer, checking Ritz' eyes for any hint of sarcasm, but there didn't seem to be any. Geni couldn't pretend it didn't matter if this little man liked him or not. He wanted Billy's approval. It would also be very pleasant to have him as a friend. And, possibly, another ear at court, one close to *la Principessa*.

"What a sinister craft," Ritz said then, speaking not of police work but glancing beyond to the black-hulled ketch nearby. "It's always a mistake to paint a ship a dark color."

"The *Finisterre*, out of Nice," Geni said without looking around at it.

Billy Ritz was silent for a long moment. Geni didn't like such silences. During interrogation one evaluated someone even when they remained silent, as some did despite one's best efforts to crack them. Geni judged that this pint-sized Viennese might be too self-possessed to crack easily.

"Involved in a recent inquest," the director responded at last. "I do read the papers."

"An inquest," Geni said then, "is one way we try to create a motionless state of equilibrium. You wouldn't get a very good movie out of an inquest verdict, would you?"

"What brings the *Finisterre* back here so soon?" Billy wanted to know.

"Hard to tell. Perhaps her passenger, Maggie Rose." Billy made a face. "Not a favorite of yours?" Geni persisted.

"She's nobody's sweetheart now," the director responded.

In the pause that followed Geni could almost read the older man's mind: here's this San Sebastiano who wasted his teens on Hollywood flicks; would he remember a golden oldie quoted out of context?

There were those who said Magari had no heart whatsoever, a machine, a humanoid robot. But they were wrong, Geni told himself, trying to fight back the urge that now swamped him like tall surf. He sighed once, faintly:

"Painted lips," he quoted. "Painted eyes."

Billy Ritz doubled over with glee. "Yours was a totally squandered youth, young man." His face grew serious. "She's never been my sweetheart."

"Do I gather she's *non grata* at the palazzo?"

"She is, in your glorious language, a *fastidio*, a nuisance, an eyesore, a blight, an unwanted object."

"Thank you."

"For what?"

"For...let us say, for another situation which cannot remain at equilibrium but must change."

The small man eyed Geni for a moment. He started to say something then stopped, then began again. "You deliberately brought me here," he said at last.

Geni glanced behind him in time to see a small gray Renault 5-TS bumping slowly over the rocky roadway toward them. It seemed heavily laden. When it drew abreast, four beefy Gold Berets in civilian clothing jumped out, leaving the car motor running. Ignoring Geni Magari as if he didn't exist, they thumped across the wooden gangplank of the *Finisterre* and pounded along its decks.

Billy Ritz and the secret policeman could hear shouts, curses, doors slamming, a shrill yelp of pain. Then a man seemed to erupt from the hatchway, as if shot from a gun, take one giant bound and jump over the side of the ship.

The splash sent ripples out to the jetty, where they broke at the feet of the two onlookers. A moment later the four secret police were on deck shouting a babble of Italian curse words. In the distance

Billy Ritz could see the man's head, sleek as a water rat, as he swam away, trying not to splash.

One of the Berets noticed the head at the same time, drew his .9 Browning automatic and leveled it in two hands, aiming. He glanced at Geni, who shook his head so briefly that Billy Ritz almost missed the gesture. Two Berets ran off the jetty to intercept the swimmer at another place. The remaining two paced the dock, trying not to lose sight of him. Their handguns were now prudently out of sight.

"Who the hell was that?" the director demanded.

"Captain Rattazzi of the *Finisterre*."

"But what has he done?"

The secret policeman's shrug was massive. "Nothing, to my knowledge. But to *his* knowledge something that requires he run from us."

The swimmer was hauled roughly out of the water, coughing and spluttering. A few kicks. Some fists to the gut. He collapsed in a puddle and was hauled by the neck of his sweater, like a sack of meal, along rough stones to another waiting gray Renault 5.

"Exit the captain," the director said. "Have we got equilibrium?"

"We have about as much equilibrium," Geni Magari remarked in a muffled tone, "as he has civil rights."

Billy Ritz glanced at his watch. *"Lieber Gott,* dinner in ten minutes. Can you get me to the palace by then?"

Geni ushered him into the Renault, whose motor was still running. They rattled over the cobbled streets of the old town at a moderate speed.

"Why did you want me to witness that arrest?"

"I?" The policeman looked surprised. "You and I were taking a stroll before dinner and talking of cultural matters, were we not? But I had to supervise the arrest. As you saw, they might have shot the man if I hadn't been there. If it offended you..." Apologies were not Geni's line.

"Let's say it reminded me," the little director corrected him. "It was scenes like that, even before the *Anschluss*, in my native city of Vienna, that sent me away from Austria permanently."

They had drawn up in front of a private side entrance to the palace. Geni had the sudden urge to detain this man whose opinion of him meant something.

"I assure you," he heard himself saying then, "my men are not Gestapo killers."

"Neither were those people in Vienna who liked to beat up Jews," Billy Ritz explained in a pleasant voice, as if remembering something quite neutral. "They were simply good Austrian citizens. You haven't forgotten, have you, that Hitler was Austrian?"

"Yes, sometimes I do," Magari admitted. "But why were they taking the law in their hands, these good citizens?"

Billy got out of the Renault 5. He stood before the palace door. "They called it 'doing their duty.' Like your men were doing."

For a moment, neither of them spoke. Geni felt at a sudden loss for words. The little man hadn't left him much ground for excuse. When you let amateurs watch the police at work they always misunderstood.

To cover his embarrassment, he glanced at his watch. Arturo Giacobbe would have begun monitoring the *Finisterre* radio traffic by now. The excitement of the captain's arrest would surely give people on board ample cause to send radio messages.

"It's precisely eight," Geni said. "Sorry to have delayed you."

"Not at all. It was quite educational."

"Just as long as it doesn't show up someday in one of your films," Geni said good-naturedly. "Would it?"

"You remember what Frank Kane told the warden in *The Big Crush-Out?*" Billy Ritz responded. "That last scene before they close in on him?"

A broad grin split Geni's face. He tucked his chin into his chest, Cagney style, and growled, "Like hell, Warden. Like hell."

The two men shook hands and went their separate ways.

· 33 ·

Both of Florian's children had graced the table with their presence, a rare enough event. Jill and Billy had been chirpy and amusing. For a welcome change, his own dear Faith had been herself, laughing at Billy's reminiscences, smiling across the table at Florian and their children. It had been quite a treat.

Faith brought the occasion to a close by catching Jill's eye. "We have to get down to the vault. I'm not sure any of that stuff has been cleaned lately."

Jill glanced at her watch. "The guard with the combination has gone home by now."

The Princess shook her head. "Tomorrow's too late. I have to wear the tiara first thing in the morning. For the dinner it's the full socko production, Gulda emerald and all."

Florian frowned nervously. "You can't mean to take it out of the palace?"

"Our security is tight."

Across Mike's forehead ran a copy of Florian's frown. "Then wear the fake. Nobody'll know."

"They'll all know," Faith assured them. "Any royal worth his title has an instinct for paste versus the real thing. We're as sensitive as a bunch of jewel thieves."

In the ensuing laughter, Jill, Polly and her mother all got to their feet. "Cigars, gentlemen?" Faith suggested as they left the dining room.

Florian looked from his son to Billy Ritz. "What do you say? The whole works? A bit of port?"

"A few dirty jokes," Mike added.

"And a wonderful case of dyspepsia," the director concluded. "No, Florian, many thanks. I do about one cigar a day now. Penalties of old age." He glanced after the departing women. "As a matter of fact, I was hoping to get a glimpse of the loot up close, if that isn't too much to ask."

"I'll take you," Mike volunteered.

The way down through the palace to its vault was a high-security elevator shaft that dropped a hundred feet through the rock of the foundation. The women already had the elevator car in use. But Mike led the way down a spiral staircase that quickly gave his elderly guest a case of vertigo. Five minutes of downward circling and Billy was ready for mercy. But they had reached the vault level.

"Shh," Mike said. "Listen."

In the silence the little Viennese at first heard nothing. Then, far away, a faint, pleasing sound of water. "The sea in the harbor?" he asked.

"Yes. We're below it by now. In fact there's a system for flooding the vault with seawater if someone breaks in."

He led them around a turn in the tiled corridor and they stood before a double door of tempered Herculite glass. Beyond it, in the bluish glare of fluorescent lights, Faith and Jill compared notes on the lock combination while Polly, who needed no reading glasses, twisted dials.

"Cold down here," Billy said.

Jill rubbed her bare arms and shoulders. "We were having trouble with the other combination, the one the guard takes home with him every night."

One wall of the vault was a Diebold door with time-lock capability. From the library, in another part of the palace, this lock could be activated for the night, but hadn't yet been. Polly now swung the handle and pulled the thick vanadium steel door open.

The three women stepped inside a room with two walls of rock and one of stainless steel boxes. Polly pulled over a high stool and draped a piece of thick black velours on it. Jill inserted keys into two boxes, unlocked and withdrew them. The ceremony had a kind of ritual quality to it. Each act had a place in the sequence.

Finally, Faith stepped forward and pulled the two boxes out of the wall. She opened one and removed a blue velours bag with a drawstring closure. From the other she took out a large blue leather box almost the size of the steel container itself. Standing on tiptoe for a better view, the Viennese watched in silence.

Faith withdrew a diamond tiara from the bag. From the large leather box she took the heavy, almost brutal solid-gold breastplate with its great Gulda emerald. She laid both pieces on the black velours that covered the stool. The overhead fluorescent illumination sent chill sparks through the diamonds but its bluish color only seemed to heighten the mysterious jungle gleam of the emerald.

"Lovely," Billy Ritz breathed.

"And now," Faith said in a mood still gay from dinner, "for my next trick...hey, presto!" She lifted an inner lid in the leather box and produced a second Gulda emerald, gold setting and all.

The tiara was definitely upstaged. The two massive, barbarically beautiful breastplates gleamed with sullen splendor, twin pairs of hawk wings joined at their centers by identical emeralds.

"Can you tell one from the other?" Billy asked.

"Can you?"

The little man advanced to the velours-covered stool and stared down at the real and the copy. "This one seems, um, newer."

"Just more recently cleaned." Faith's glance went to Jill. "You see what I meant about checking these tonight? Can we get the jeweler in here and finished by eight A.M.?"

"He'll have to."

"Mom," Mike's voice boomed too loudly in the small vault. "Wear the copy. Please?"

Faith was about to demur, but seemed to pause. She eyed her son for a long moment. "I'll wear the real one for them at the private cocktail party before dinner. Then I'll switch to the copy for the rest of the night. How's that?"

"*Meglio di niente,*" Mike admitted. "But who has to transport the real one back to the vault?"

"You."

He gave her a hopeless look. "Always one jump ahead of me, huh?"

"That'll be the day," his mother said. "Look, we can simplify this still further, Mikey. The copy doesn't need cleaning. I'll take it upstairs with me now and put it in my bedroom wall safe. Tomorrow, after cocktails, I'll make the switch in my room and you get the real one back down here. Okay?"

He was about to say something when all of them heard the elevator door close. An instant later they could hear it rising in its shaft.

"What the hell?" Mike asked.

In silence the five of them waited, listening. The elevator car reached the top of the shaft and its doors opened. They could hear footsteps, then the sound of the doors closing and the car descending. A moment later the doors shot open at the vault level and Florian stood aside to usher Maggie Rose into their presence.

"What the hell!" Mike repeated in anger.

Maggie's great eyes, in their exquisite nests of makeup, switched from side to side, scrutinizing faces, jewelry, doors, before they came to rest at last on Faith's stony face.

"Surprise!" Florian said.

"Oh, dear God, I forgot to tell you," Jill began compulsively, "but she called just before di—"

"And I invited her for after dinner," Florian finished.

"Look, I can see I'm intruding," Maggie Rose added in a tone devoid of apology.

"Not at all," Faith said with mechanical warmth. "Good to see you. In fact..." She stopped and her lips twisted slightly. "In fact, your timing is perfect, Maggie. But then it always was."

In the same keyed-up but patently fake tone, she showed the newcomer the pieces of jewelry and then managed to bundle her off with the men. The four of them stuffed the small elevator to capacity. As it sighed upward in its shaft a dead silence fell over the three women. Jill eyed Her Serene Highness and decided that silence was her best course of action.

"Some nerve," Polly said then.

"Your father is much too generous for his own good," Faith remarked. But both her daughter and her secretary could catch the held-in note of menace in her voice. It was obvious to them that Her Highness was anything but serene. They quickly locked the vault, working in silence, before bringing down the elevator. As she got into the car the Princess carefully adjusted the massive fake across the upper curves of her breasts.

"I'm sorry," Jill said.

"For what?" Polly asked.

"Shut up, both of you."

In silence they rode upward. "Set the time lock for seven-thirty," Faith snapped as she left them and strode toward her suite. "Get that jeweler on the phone. Have him here when the vault opens."

"It's after ten now," Jill murmured, as if it were her fault.

"Wake him up."

The door to her suite slammed shut.

"Shees!" Polly breathed. "What brought that on? Maggie?"

"She had no business down below."

"Neither did Uncle Billy," the girl pointed out. "But at least she didn't arrive with some new heartbreaker who's supposed to make me cream my jeans."

Jill smiled slightly at Polly's language, which was used only in the absence of her parents. "Do you still think about Etienne?" she asked.

"Do I." But the girl's face failed to show longing, or even chagrin. "Anyway, who asked her to start beating the bushes on my behalf? I can find my own studs."

"That, young lady," Jill said in a prim voice that camouflaged the need to giggle, "we all know. It's what has us worried most."

"That they go gaga when they sniff my spoor?"

This time the deadpan English facade dissolved in laughter. "Polly, honestly, you are a riot!"

The Princess Paola stared challengingly at her and then, unable to keep a straight face, broke up into maniacal giggles.

The door to the Princess' suite swung open again and Faith strode down the hall. "Polly, *bedtime*. Jill, *on the phone*." She stalked off in the direction of the games room, where Florian had taken the others.

They hovered around the bar, making up their minds about having drinks. Faith stood in the doorway and took a long, steadying breath. She had put the Gulda emerald copy in her wall safe. Now it seemed almost as if she missed its reassuring weight on her breast. She held a hand against her where the barbaric ornament had been, as if defending it...and herself.

Keep your friends close, she told herself. Keep your enemies closer.

"What a surprise!" she said, then in a voice that was suddenly warm, "What brings you to this part of the world, Maggie?"

All of them turned around with a faintly guilty air, Florian looking perhaps more culpable than the rest. When they saw her bright, friendly smile, they relaxed, all but the little Viennese director. He moved out of range, taking a seat as if before a stage on which the curtain had just risen.

Maggie Rose came forward, a small sable wrap around her shoulders. She kissed Faith on both cheeks. "You're looking swell, Dolly," she quoted. "Sorry I gave such short notice, but this is a blitz visit. I'm with a boating party and our next stop's Rome. I think you know Bert Kleidermann, the arranger? And Harry Armitage, my manager."

"You should have brought them along tonight," Faith suggested sweetly, making the outrage sound almost acceptable.

The silence that followed the suggestion seemed to grow, fungus-like, till it threatened to fill the room. Mike cleared his throat. "Drinks?" No one responded. "There's a chilled bottle of champagne."

"Fine," his father agreed.

"And a sidecar for me." Faith sat down in her usual chair by the windows.

Prince Florian took a seat across a small backgammon table from his wife. "You see," he began, then: "Maggie called earlier and, since she's only here such a short—"

"Billy," Faith cut in, "champagne for you?"

The director seemed to consider this for a while. Faith could tell he was not enjoying the tension. "Champagne can't hurt that Viennese ulcer of yours."

"Sounds great."

Again silence fell over them. Mike made tinkling noises. Faith wondered if he'd serve the guests first, or her. She got her answer a moment later when he brought her a tray on which stood a lone white-wine glass containing the amber-colored cocktail she'd ordered. She watched him pour champagne for the rest and decided her only son, heir to the principality, had a very good idea of which side his bread was buttered on.

"Harry Armitage," she said then. "Isn't he new for you?"

Maggie nodded, holding her glass of champagne. "Well," Florian said, lifting his, "here's to auld lang—"

"Here's to us," Faith cut in abruptly. "And confusion to the enemy." She gave it the full Irish brogue Eamon Brennan had always used with this, his favorite toast. "Confyushyun t'th'inimy, sez oi," he would intone.

Faith sat absolutely still, not sipping her drink while the rest did. She would never master her love-hatred of her father if she kept quoting him, aping him. Even his whore could tell her that. Even this—what was the word? Billy had said the Greeks had a word for it and Faith had looked it up in several dictionaries until she'd found it.

Even this coprophagous whore could tell her that she was still in bondage to a dead father. It had to stop. Perhaps, Faith thought, having her here tonight wasn't the disaster it seemed at first. Perhaps she could exorcise the two of them.

When she sipped the sidecar she felt suddenly soothed, at ease, in command again. She musn't be too hard on Florian. He had no idea the kind of woman this was. Men didn't. Men never saw beyond the boobs.

"Please," she told Maggie, "sit down. Relax. This isn't a state visit. Just old friends."

Mike watched her over the rim of his champagne glass. "I think I ought to check Jill on the time lock," he said then. "Night all."

"Good idea." Faith watched him put away his drink and leave the room. If only Florian had business elsewhere, she and Billy could settle Maggie Rose once and for all.

"Well," her husband said, glancing at his watch. "It's a big day tomorrow. You two won't keep her up too late will you?" he asked, getting to his feet. He drained the last of his champagne, leaned over Faith to kiss her cheek and bid them all good night.

Telepathy, Faith thought. Everything's working tonight. She glanced at Billy Ritz. He stirred in his chair. "You want me out of here too?" he demanded. "You're very good with the nonverbal projection, always were."

"You stay. I want to explain something to Maggie and it needs a witness."

· 34 ·

The games room, designed for easy entertaining in an informal atmosphere, had taken on the atmospheric pressure of a submarine, moreover one stalled thirty fathoms deep under enemy depth-bomb barrage.

Nobody here but us players, Faith told herself. She glanced covertly at Maggie. The poor whore hadn't a clue as to what was going to happen. As for Billy...

The chair he had chosen seemed strangely out of the central arena and Faith recognized his attempt to distance himself from what he knew would follow. Typical director. She stared at him for a moment longer, then:

"Lights?"

He blinked. "Faith."

"Lights," she said. "Camera. Action."

"Wait a second," the little man cautioned her. "I thought we agreed to go easy."

"Me? I'm always easy."

"What're you two hatching?" the singer asked them. She had settled into a comfortable armchair, crossed her long legs and was dangling one strap sandal by her toes, swinging it back and forth.

"All day," Faith said then, "I've been trying to call back the past. Trying to remember details. For instance," she told Billy, "that scene I spoke of. That goes back quite a way. I've been trying to remember and it's amazing how much my memory's improved."

"Brava," the director breathed. "But there's such a thing as recalling too much. Drop it, Faith."

"You remember," she went on, swinging toward Maggie Rose. "Fifteen or twenty years ago was a historic moment in your career. How could any of us forget?"

The fantastically made-up eyes narrowed. "It was a shitty time for me. I'd lost my recording contract. I wasn't into the rock style yet and my records were selling like matzos to Arabs."

"Stole the picture," Billy Ritz recalled. "Nice comeback. Warmed the cockles of everybody's heart on the Coast. Did you ever wonder what cockles were?" he asked, trying to derail the conversation.

"Small cocks," Maggie spat out. "You people can make jokes, but that was Pitsville for me. Without that part in the movie my name would have gone right out of the language."

"It took a lot of guts for Phil to give you the role," Faith said then. "I mean, *now* we know you're a terrific actress. But who knew it then? He took a big chance signing you."

The jockey-sized director nodded slowly. "He wasn't in such hot shape either, Phil. He lacked a third of his financing."

"I didn't know that," Faith chimed in. "Did I know that? It's coming back, faintly. So Phil was going to have to drop his option on the property? It was an act of tremendous courage to sign an untried actress at that point."

"It was sensational smarts," Maggie spoke up. "That flick made Phil a multimillionaire."

"The last-minute backer, the guy who came in with the missing part of the budget, he grossed big," Billy Ritz explained. He shaped something round before him with his hands. "Phil had about a third of the pie missing. The backer paid the third but took half the gross."

"I'm surprised he didn't take more," the Princess mused.

"You don't know who I'm talking about?" Billy asked.

"The backer?" Faith blinked. "Who?"

"Fella name of Eamon Brennan."

"Really?"

"That's right," Maggie said, her voice sounding defensive for the first time. "I thought you knew."

"Did I?" Faith asked in that same vague, Billie Burke style she had adopted for tonight's memoirs. "It has to be more than coincidence that my father completed the financing and you got the part. That was the summer I was pregnant with Polly. Right? Eamon was here on a visit in June or July and so were you."

"Faith," Billy warned her. "Cool it."

Another oppressive silence fell over the room. Faith found herself hoping no one would interrupt them now, no unwanted entrances from bit players like Jill or Mike. Because this was it.

"So here's how it was," she said then. "The picture was financed and you got the part that saved your career and all you had to do was eat his shit."

She took a long, steadying breath. "All you had to do was lie down on the floor of your room, across the hall from his room. Let him mount you and the rest was fun and games. No wonder you didn't eat much at dinner."

She whirled toward Billy. "Coprophagy!" she shrieked.

Maggie Rose was on her feet. "You spied on us, huh? And all these years—"

"And all those tons of shit—"

"You didn't have the common decency t—"

"Offer you a Kleenex and a puke bucket." Faith was standing up now. "You're a disgrace, Maggie Rose. You're a disgrace to show business. My God, you're a disgrace to the human race. I'm

ashamed to be the same species as you. You can leave now," she
added mildly.

The singer took a step toward her and seemed to stumble. She
recovered, face suddenly white, but whether with fear or rage Faith
couldn't tell.

The director's glance swiveled back and forth between them and
for a moment Faith felt a great anger against Billy Ritz. The ultimate bystander. She felt a sudden sympathy for this miserable
woman in front of her. Performers lay it on the line, she thought.
Directors sit off to the side and make notes.

Maggie seemed to have difficulty breathing. The breath was surg-
ing in and out of her, making her immense breasts rise and fall like
great ocean billows. "Sneaky bastard," she gasped. "Waited all this
time."

"Suffering with the memory of it."

"*You* suffered?" Maggie shot back, gulping for air. "I had to win
it from him the hard way. Have you ever had it any way but easy?"
the singer asked. Her voice seemed to break in mid-word. Then her
body was racked by a spasm of coughing. She tried to master it.
"Didn't he hand it all to you on a plate?" she demanded at last.
"How much of his shit did *you* eat?"

Faith gave Billy Ritz a stricken, searching look. The Viennese
nodded in an almost grandfatherly way. "It's different when you
don't know what you're eating. When you can pretend it's just...."
He made a Tinkerbell gesture with both hands. "Show biz?"

"He never let me pretend that," Maggie Rose said in a deep,
nasal tone like the forlorn toll of a faraway bell. "Christ," she begged
Faith, "did you have to do this in front of him?" the singer asked,
tilting her head toward Billy. She seemed off-base with shock,
wounded by a heavy-caliber bullet but not actually dying. "Where's
my wrap?"

"Around your neck."

The magnificent eyes swung this way and that. Her cheeks
looked white as suet. "Christ, can somebody point me out of here?"

Faith took her arm and led her from the room. They stumbled
down the stairs, along a corridor and down another flight. At the
front entrance, under the porte cochere, a chauffeured Bentley
waited.

"I'm sorry about this," Maggie said in a confused voice. Faith opened the door of the Bentley for her and helped her totter across the cobblestones to the car.

"What're you and the Kraut gonna do with this story?" Maggie asked in a low croak.

"Nothing."

"Don't shit me." Her voice went up several notches. "Maggie defends herself and Maggie has friends who help her." She was keening now in that high muezzin voice. "Don't fuck with Maggie or you'll end up..." She stopped herself and lurched into the Bentley.

The two women watched each other for a long moment. Then Maggie Rose's glance shifted to the back of her driver's head. "I must be insane yacking like this out here...Driver? Let's go."

He failed to respond and both women realized that, behind the plate-glass divider, he was insulated from their voices. Faith kept the car door open.

"The truth, Maggie. Isn't that what you want? My funeral?"

The singer stared at her almost drunkenly, without focus. "Oh no," she said in a suddenly faint voice. "You'll be at mine. I can see you now, by the graveside, in something simple and black to match your hair. Looking like a million bucks because money is no object." A breath shuddered in and out. "You've always had it handed to you, right? Looks, clout. And poor old Maggie will be lying there under six feet of dirt, God's reward for working my ass off every second of my life. Thank you, God."

"Maggie."

She stared up at Faith with a bewildered look. "You never were my friend after all?" she asked then.

"Were you mine?"

Maggie's glance wavered. "Before you walked in on the two of us, were you my friend? Were you?"

The Princess nodded. "Oh, yes. And after that I was in torment."

"You should have kicked me out. Then I'd know where I stood with you. I thought I was your friend. People...." The singer stopped. "Certain people thought I was your friend. Jesus, Faith, Jesus!" Maggie Rose looked wildly around her as if for help. "Don't you...?" She stopped and tried to get control of herself. "You must understand the bind this puts me in."

"If you were a friend," Faith said, "you wouldn't be in any bind."

"I don't have your protection," Maggie told her in a small, tight voice. "Miss Born Lucky. What do you know about the binds people get in, normal people, born ugly and poor."

"I'm sorry. That's no excuse, Maggie."

Those great, mascaraed eyes focused deep into Faith's face. "Did you hear what I told you before? Do you ever listen to anybody? You're in the same bind I am, Miss Born Lucky. You cannot play games with these people, not forever. Those famous high standards of yours? There comes a time when you either lower them or they get chopped. You don't call me a friend anymore, but only a true friend would give you that warning."

The singer rapped on the limousine window. "Home, James."

Her Serene Highness moved up the palace steps. She paused at the top and turned, but the big car was gone. As she walked inside the sound of her heels grew fainter on the marble floor. From behind an entrance pillar, Geni Magari stepped forward in the soft October darkness.

He felt sick at heart. *La Principessa* might think such a warning an empty threat. Colonnello Magari did not.

· 35 ·

Arturo Giacobbe, sleepless and needing a shave, arrived at the Eamon Brennan Memorial Clinic about seven in the morning, having spent a totally fruitless night monitoring the *Finisterre's* radio.

It had not once sparked into life, not even after the provocative raid and the arrest of the captain.

He stared at himself in the mirror of the tiny washroom that adjoined the garden snack bar, lathered his face and shaved. This would not be the first time one of Geni's supercautious ideas hadn't paid off. In the Intelligence Section of the Berets they were used to going without sleep because Geni wanted to be absolutely sure of something.

Arturo switched on the electric espresso machine and made a full demitasse of the sharp, acrid black death that snaps the eyeballs wide and sends waves of caffeine-induced vigor through the heart muscles. Adding a lot of sugar, he swallowed his breakfast in two gulps.

Eamon Brennan Memorial Clinic had been laid out to serve two purposes. Small, airy wards holding no more than eight beds were reserved for the free treatment of San Sebastiani with serious ailments. Large, airy rooms were reserved for rich visitors whose fees, plus a Brennan trust fund, kept the clinic solvent. Arturo Giacobbe always checked the wards first, since any assault victims would likely be found there. That was why he didn't get around to Room 9 until almost eight in the morning.

Rattazzi, Jean-Paul, was the way the patient's chart was headed. Arturo recognized this as the name of *Finisterre's* captain. Otherwise he would have been unrecognizable.

It couldn't have been the roughing up he got on arrest, Giacobbe decided as he read the chart: multiple contusions, lacerations and abrasions; fracture of the left tibia and femur; double concussion. On the way from the harbor the wrecking crew had gotten in a few extra licks.

The agent sat down by the bedside and reached for Rattazzi's pulse. It felt strong to him. Under the bandages that masked his face, who knew how many stitches had been taken? The presence of the captain in this, the principality's best hospital, signified to Giacobbe that Geni had not meant the man to be eliminated. Yes, snatched to stimulate fear on board the *Finisterre*. But had Geni bargained for a stretcher case?

The caffeine in Arturo's veins had long run its course. He got wearily to his feet and went to the small cubbyhole in the cellar where a direct line led to Gold Beret headquarters a mile away.

"...seems stabilized," he concluded to Geni after making his report.

"Your opinion or the doctor's?" his boss demanded.

"Both. He's having no trouble breathing through the bandages. These sailors are a hard bunch."

The line was silent for a long time. "Geni, are you there? Do you have any instructions?"

"I gave those four goons explicit instructions to rough him up and release him after a few hours. This is how they carry out my orders. This is the second time a wrecking crew has gone too far in the last few weeks."

"So you'll have to crack down on them, eh?"

"How else can I exert control, Turo? This isn't some South American dictatorship where the cops are all killers." His sigh carried along the wires. "And today of all days, with loose dukes and princes wandering among the peasants."

A look of malicious glee crossed Giacobbe's face, but he said nothing. It was not that he wished his old friend ill. It was simply that within the Berets a few crypto-Fascist sadists had found a home and it now looked as if they might be evicted.

"*Bene,* Geni. I'll nurse this one along."

"I want him out of there as soon as he can walk. And his goddamned black boat with him. No," he added abruptly, "you don't have to tell me about last night's monitoring. I know you came up blank. The object of our attention wasn't even on board. She was at the palace. Now she's on the Blue Train to Rome."

"You expelled her?"

"Are you crazy? She's expelling herself." The line went dead.

· 36 ·

As far as the world was concerned, the weekend conference of small European nations was a major publicity triumph. The presence of both Princess Faith and Princess Grace tripled the television coverage such a dull event might normally command.

As far as Prince Florian was concerned, his lovely wife had never seemed more radiant. Always a gracious hostess, she seemed to rise to the occasion with a warmth and pleasure their guests were quick to feel as genuine.

As far as Billy Ritz was concerned, the dyspepsia he'd forecast the night before was in such full blast that he spent the entire historic day in bed sipping Maalox and chewing soda crackers.

As far as Jill was concerned, she was on her fourth aspirin. Get-

ting pageantry right, she realized, wasn't easy. Old Count Maremonte had had an instinct for flash and color. Any member of the
consiglio would have gotten that kind of baroque display in his mother's milk. But Jill, who came of stiff-upper-lip county people in
Cheshire, had been trained to avoid peacockery.

Her instinct, for example, was not to spend the money on the
flag twirlers imported from Siena. Was it worth it, this warmed-
over event from the Sienese *palio* that everyone had seen on Euro-
vision? But it was positively heart-stopping to watch the great flags
swirl high into the sky over the grand piazza of San Sebastian, take
flight like gaudy eagles and plummet safely into the hands of the
actor-acrobats who controlled them.

Her rudimentary sense of pageantry was stirred even more, she
found, by the close-order drill of the Gold Beret marching team. A
hundred of them wheeled and stepped through intricate patterns,
to the thundering rataplan of a drum corps. Silver cornets split the
air with their high sweet notes. Bass drummers flipped their sticks
in the air and caught them as deftly as the Sienese flag handlers.
Jill's heart pounded with pride. So did her head.

Nor had it been a mistake to schedule a preview of the auto race
San Sebastian would have in the spring. Sleek, space age cars
vroomed and roared through the narrow streets of the old town.
Someone had brought a jet-engined vehicle that with a great flash
of orange and a belch of smoke took off along the autostrada entrance like a homing bullet.

Bands played in every odd corner of the principality. Flowers
showered down from cathedral windows. Three hundred varicolored
helium balloons floated free after Prince Florian's welcoming speech.
The elephants from the Zoological Garden did a stately parade of
their own, balloons hanging from their harness. Two of Europe's
top-ranking tennis players gave an exhibition in the square.

And everywhere the various visiting dukes and princes walked
among commoners with only a barely visible cordon of plainclothes
Berets guarding them. Geni Magari and his men swarmed around
each royal appearance, whether a walk through a new shopping
mall, the formal opening of a microcomputer plant or impromptu
appearances on balconies to receive the cheers of a happy crowd
and make sure the CBS crews had all the footage they needed.

Prince Michele had brought a small agenda of his own to the formal meetings and was making progress toward a kind of mini-common market in which the tiny states would accept a mutually fixed exchange rate. Since Liechtenstein's currency was Swiss francs, this paper maneuver was intended by Mike to keep all the other currencies pegged to the Swiss. If it worked, he had plans for a kind of customs union that would extend Swiss banking secrecy to San Sebastian and start attracting hot money in great quantities.

The formal visit to the Eamon Brennan Memorial Clinic was supervised by an Arturo Giacobbe struggling to remain awake. He was now operating on an "upper" one of the nuns had slipped him from the dispensary. Somehow he got through the visit without letting anyone see the *Finisterre* captain in his room. He even managed to serve drinks to the two princesses from Hollywood, who posed against the lovely garden fountains with their bronze statuary.

In faraway places like London and New York, film researchers racked through files for footage of any film in which the two had appeared together. There'd been none, but a lucky girl at NBC located newsreel footage of a Hollywood premiere at which both had been photographed among maddened fans. The clip, so old it was in black and white, showed both actresses looking like teenagers. This footage was neatly matched with live coverage being taped via satellite for the evening news. By the time it was midnight in San Sebastian, New York was ready to roll with heavy dinnertime coverage.

If the effect on the outside world was of a conference of former film actresses, the effect inside San Sebastian was far more profound. At the dinner, with its many courses, its changes of wines, its obligatory citrus sorbet halfway along, its endlessly beguiling desserts and lavish carved-ice statues, its extravagant floral displays and accompanying music blending finally into the dancing party of the evening, it seemed to most San Sebastiani that their little principality with its up-down-up history had truly come of age.

There are national characteristics of long standing. The French, for example, automatically assume that if something is French, it must be good. Americans share that delusion. But Italians suffer the reverse. To an Italian only foreign things are worthwhile. If something is Italian, it must be second-rate, déclassé, faintly awkward or countrified.

Watching the televised festivities from his bed of pain, Billy picked up a growing feeling from the local crowds that in this one enclave of the ethnic Italian massif, something first-rate had finally been achieved. It cost. But coming of age was worth any amount of expense.

He had tried to gird his loins for the dinner, but couldn't make it. However, with the aid of Lomotil, he did pull himself together enough to don white tie and make an appearance at dessert. "No, nothing to drink," he told Jill, who fussed till she had him seated at the dais table precisely between the two princesses.

"And no TV," Billy called after her.

It was too late. The little gnome's head shone like a light bulb as crews zeroed in on yet another show-biz personality. He could feel the top of his naked skull heating up as disturbingly as his innards. Of course it didn't hurt his money-raising stature to be seen in such company, he consoled himself, pushing down spasms of nausea with yearnings of greed.

Each time he refused food or drink one of his two Hollywood chums would lean toward him with concern. "Are you all right, Billy?"

"You look positively green, Billy."

"The hangover of all time, Billy."

"Try some of this, Billy."

At the back of the ballroom, where the orchestra was starting its first Mantovani-style medley, Jill ran into Geni Magari, staring gloomily out at the largely young crowd of dancers. "Cheer up."

He glanced in her direction, ready to snap off her head, then saw who it was. "Good evening," he said. One had to be careful with this woman who stood so close to l'Altezza. "Are you enjoying yourself?"

"About as much as you are."

They eyed each other for a long moment. Jill broke the silence at last. "What do you take for your headache? If it's stronger than aspirin, let me have some."

Geni managed a smile, although he felt his face cracking in places. The orchestra was into a Latin medley now. *"Permesso?"* he asked, taking her hand in his.

Which was how she managed the next day to retrieve from the court photographer's files a shot of the two of them, looking very stylish, in the midst of what looked like either a rhumba or a meringue, the secret policeman and the not-at-all-unattractive Miss Tremont.

Magari had turned out to be rather light on his feet but given to traveling about the floor with some rapidity. Jill understood that he was keeping the dancers under surveillance, but it had to be more than that. After all, hadn't he kissed her hand as they left the floor?

At the same moment, she saw, the young man who had been dancing with Polly also kissed her hand as he started to leave her.

The look on Polly's face was clear enough, even a dozen paces away across a crowded floor. While she chattered on about men sniffing her spoor, she knew precisely what she was doing to them. The look on her face—with that same uncanny nonverbal skill as her mother—said as plainly as words "If you weren't in such a rush to leave, you'd be in for a very pleasant surprise."

Whatever the content of the message, it stopped the young man in his tracks, as if she had actually made some sort of improper proposition, which Jill would have sworn she hadn't. Polly didn't need words. The young man remained rooted to the spot, rosy-cheeked with embarrassment, as if some jokester pal had nailed his shoes to the dance floor.

Jill could see Polly's next partner moving toward her. The makings of something awkward seemed at hand. Jill moved in Polly's direction, not quite sure what one did to prevent two young studs in heat from rattling antlers against each other.

But then the blushing first partner suddenly removed himself and the second partner took Polly in his arms. The crisis was over. For now. Jill looked about her for her own next partner, who was supposed to be Mike.

At affairs like this one, dressed in her finest dinner gown, her hair newly done, her makeup personally applied by *la Principessa* herself, Jill hated to be a wallflower. She could count on Mike for some kid-brotherly help.

But she hadn't really seen Mike for some time. He'd been at the cocktail party for the honored guests, as expected. Had she seen him thereafter?

With an unlikely blare of trumpets, the band struck up a waltz medley and Florian and Faith took to the floor. Jill watched the tall, slim Prince pivot his partner in tightly controlled swerves, the very pillar of perfection, calm center of the swirling, flashing dance. As she orbited with him, Faith glittered like some extraordinary comet, tiara glinting and the deep green glow of the Gulda emerald like a forest fire across her breast. Twin spotlights had been trained on the couple, perhaps at the request of TV crews, and the emerald smoldered with chilly fire, winking as she twirled.

Marvelous what they did with paste these days, Jill found herself thinking. Then she remembered why Mike hadn't been around. He'd had the job of transporting the real emerald back to the vault. But hadn't that been some time ago, after the cocktails? Jill was checking her watch when an American with a pitted face asked her to dance.

She knew him vaguely as one of the military attachés at the U.S. Embassy, which made him either CIA or Army Intelligence. In either event she wouldn't make the same mistake with him as she had once before. Amazing how they never stopped trying. She must be well down in their books as an easy mark. But he did dance rather well. Not too many Americans knew how to waltz.

On the dais, Billy Ritz watched the throng. There was the feeling at first of being out of it. His upset insides were giving him an advance taste of what it would be like for him in a few years when he was too old to think about dancing even in a wheelchair. But the waltzes spoke to him as they always did.

"Wien, Wien, nur du allein," he sang under his breath.

Have myself in tears at any moment, he thought. Ersatz schmaltz. Vienna, city of my youth. But to whom in this crowd does this music speak as it speaks to me?

What am I doing here, he wondered, far from my craft? I'm not a dais performer. I'm behind the camera. Here in the lights it's for mountebanks. You put on a fake mustache and pretend to have a sabre fight. Cut. Print.

"*Wien, Wien, nur du allein,*" he sang. "*Soll stets die Stadt meine Traume sein.*" God, it was catching in his throat.

He turned to the pretty girl across the table from him. "*Enschuldig mir, Fraulein,*" he began, getting to his feet. He led her to the dance floor as the orchestra segued into one of the waltzes from *Die Fledermaus*. Billy Ritz twirled his partner so that her skirt billowed and flared like one of those Sienese flags turning end over end through the sky.

He hoped the music would never end.

· 37 ·

After the ball is over, most places go to sleep. In this respect San Sebastian was no different. The starry array of visiting royalty had been bedded down in the palace by not later than three in the morning, with the exception of the Bishop of Urgel and his monsignor, who had been asleep since midnight.

The younger guests at the dinner and dance, nearly all from foreign embassies, had gone on to other pleasures of a night to be followed by a Sunday. Elders of ambassadorial rank were safely in bed. Gold Berets assigned to guard all these royal, noble, pious, or at any rate diplomatic, bodies were also asleep.

Geni Magari surveyed the empty, clean-swept ballroom and glanced at his watch: 5:40 A.M. Many things remained on his mind, but at the moment he was reckoning how long he had been without sleep. He made it to be forty hours.

He was operating only on nerves, but he no longer felt that things might come apart at the seams. The main events of the conference were over. Tomorrow—today—being Sunday, the honored guests would make appearances at San Sebastian's cathedral, where the Bishop of Urgel would celebrate Mass. There would be one last garden lunch and everyone would wend his way homeward.

Between now and then there would be an hour or two for Geni to catch a nap. But he had a most important detail to attend to before he could sleep. He entered the spiral staircase to the vault and carefully circled his way down, not quite sure what he would find.

He had assigned two of his best men to this job, men of the caliber of Giacobbe, who could think on their feet. Still, one never knew. They might prove as imbecile as the goons who had fixed the French captain's hash. As he reached the vault level, with its tiled corridor, he turned the corner and faced the big Herculite doors. Beyond them the vault lay in darkness.

He checked his wristwatch again. Hours seemed to have elapsed since last he'd read the time, yet his watch showed only five minutes to have passed. Magari was familiar with this phenomenon. Extreme fatigue made time crawl, made minutes feel like hours. Time was extremely important because a series of deadlines came due almost on top of each other.

To begin with, a 5-cc injection of Tuinal given to a normally healthy adult produces approximately six to eight hours of rather heavy sleep, whether the adult wants to sleep or not. That gave Geni no more time on the first deadline. On the second he had some leeway; the Blue Train, which was due to arrive in Rome about now, would most assuredly be at least one hour *in ritardo*. It always was. Even in Mussolini's time the amazing talent of the Italians to run trains consistently slower than the schedule was already the marvel of the century.

The Beret normally assigned as vault guard here would not come on duty for several hours. Geni knew the combinations by heart. He opened the tempered glass doors and switched on the lights. He reached for the dials on the Diebold door. He froze.

Mannaggia, the time lock!

If he opened the doors with the time lock not set to release, he would trigger the fail-safe system that flooded this vault with seawater. He'd almost committed the ultimate mistake. Beads of sweat formed on his brow. His heart thudded. To think how close he'd come to touching the dials, turning them! *Dio mio*, how close!

As he felt his way back through darkened corridors and crept up carpeted stairs, he marveled at this brush with utter disaster. How stupid a man got when he lacked sleep. How easy it was to undo the entire principality by one careless act.

Moving through the library now, he found the time-lock panel behind Jill's desk and studied it by the muted glow of a penlight. He glanced at his watch. Almost 6 A.M. He reset the time lock for six and raced back the way he'd come, moving recklessly down the spiral stairs, wishing he could use the elevator but afraid of the noise it made.

He reached the vault just in time to hear the time lock release itself. Now he attacked the dials, flipping them left and right. God, how close he'd come to catastrophe!

He turned the Diebold handle and the great door silently swung open. They had been extremely careful, the two Berets he'd assigned to this. They had been masked, of course, when they had waylaid the victim. He slept on the floor, hands tied with clothesline cord to one of the safe box handles.

Il Principe Michele Gulda, heir apparent to the throne of San Sebastian, lay at Geni Magari's feet. A few minutes before, helpless inside the vault, he could have drowned. Would have. The vault would have been his tomb.

Geni could feel the sweat running down the inside of his armpits as he squatted beside the man who would one day rule the principality. Geni untied his hands and lowered his long arms to his sides. The Tuinal would wear off any time now.

Geni picked up the open blue leather box which normally contained the Gulda emerald and its copy. The copy was undoubtedly upstairs in *la Principessa's* wall safe. But the real one was not here.

The big central terminal in Rome is not that city's only train station. But everything comes to it, locals and big international Tee-trains all the way from Madrid or Vienna. Even the airport busses arrive and depart from the terminal. It is a city in itself. In addition to the usual banks and eating places, it has a fully equipped subterranean *diurno,* a kind of hotel and bath where weary travelers can strip, shower, change clothes and be on their way.

Confusion was the general note of Maggie Rose's arrival here. Someone had tipped off the press that she was overnighting on the Blue Train from San Sebastian. So to the normal everyday confusion that Italians choreograph in such public places was added swarms of sleepy paparazzi photographers, a camera crew from RAI television and several wire service people routed out of bed at this early hour.

Well, after all, Maggie thought as chaos erupted around her, it's a homecoming, isn't it? Why shouldn't she get a fancy welcome in the capital city of her ancestors?

It was only after half an hour of orchestrated confusion that Maggie began to understand she was being detained. Very pleasantly, with many a gallant jest, but detained. Since everyone insisted on speaking Italian to her—and Maggie's command of the language was pretty much limited to ordering in restaurants—she was not getting any clue as to why she was being detained, except that everyone seemed to be waiting for something.

This turned out to be her luggage. All eight cases of it arrived on a long trolley pushed by two unshaven attendants. Was anything missing? She didn't think so. Now the captain of the Guardia di Finanza stopped smiling.

"May I have the keys?" he asked, switching to perfect English.

"To my luggage? Why?"

"To avoid breaking the locks."

His face had gone from deadpan to grim. Maggie handed over the keys and watched the captain and three of his men go through every article of clothing, makeup and jewelry. Fortunately, she never carried a stash of anything, knowing that border guards were paranoid about drugs. But since when was Rome a border? Hadn't she been inside Italy this whole trip from the moment she left the San Sebastian frontier?

In her small overnight case, the one with the medicines, cosmetics and good jewelry, they found it, wrapped in a Hermès scarf.

"*Ecco,*" said the frozen-faced captain.

He held it up to her in all its massive glory, the two solid gold hawk's wings flanking the immense emerald. She gasped.

"*Ecco, signorina—lo smeraldo Gulda, no?*"

In a lifetime lived rather fully, Maggie Rose had never fainted. She thought of the confrontation with Faith. She thought of the press waiting outside this grim room, not content with what they already had but craving something more, something juicier, something with blood on it.

She fainted.

PART
FIVE

· 38 ·

It is most unusual along the lazy, fun-loving Riviera, where people go for relaxation, when Sunday is not a day of rest.

In the memory of those involved with the full span of events, there had never been such a Sunday. It was their fervent hope that there would never again be another one. Even to those who did not share the broad overview, it was a very unrestful day.

The nuns at the Eamon Brennan Memorial Clinic, for example, at eight in the morning came to the realization that Captain Jean-Paul Rattazzi, French national, skipper of the oceangoing ketch *Finisterre,* had died.

A quick examination hinted at cerebral embolism, perhaps a bloodclot associated with the concussions, which blocked one of the cranial capillaries while he slept, cut off the brain's supply of blood-carried oxygen and silently turned him first into a vegetable and, minutes later, into a corpse.

Che peccato. Such a strong-seeming man, so virile. Why, only yesterday, after they had finished stitching his face, he had come out of the anesthetic and winked at Sister Concetta.

So upset were the nurses that they failed to notify Arturo Giacobbe of the death of the man for whose convalescence he had been so concerned.

So, in Room 9 of the clinic, and particularly for Captain Rattazzi,

Sunday was rotten. Later it would also prove so for Arturo, when Geni Magari got the news. It is always left to the living to suffer more.

All night on the vault floor had left Mike with a foul taste in his mouth, a wry-neck spasm in his right shoulder and a hatred of Geni Magari that no longer smoldered. It flamed.

"You call yourself a security man?" he taunted Geni. They stood in the small serving kitchen that adjoined the games room, Geni trying to make coffee without waking anybody at this early hour.

"You're a worm," Mike continued. "You have the instincts of a worm and the mentality of a snake. You have never been straight with me in my entire life. You don't *relate* to me. You *handle* me. And your ability to turn nothing into a raging federal case is beyond belief. Moreover, you don't even lie convincingly."

"I swear to God, *Altezza*, I have no idea who those two men were. As for what they want with the Gulda emerald, they can't sell it. Perhaps it's a kidnap scheme. Perhaps we'll get a ransom note."

"Perhaps your two agents will bring it back after you've stopped playing worm's games," Mike said in a bitter undertone. The kettle came to a boil. "Let me assure you, the morning I sit on the throne of this place, you're out of a job."

Magari spooned instant coffee into two cups and filled them with hot water. He stirred both but took only one for himself, not wanting to presume to hand the other to this angry young man for fear of a louder outburst.

As for threats of being fired, he knew all too well Prince Michele's mind, especially after the affair of the tennis player. What he had done to the young Prince last night was only more of the same, *if* he admitted to it. His only chance was to deny, deny, deny, until the news came in from Rome, which it soon would. Then he could blame, blame, blame.

For, to Geni, it didn't matter if Maggie Rose would get the full blast of adverse publicity or buy silence. The important thing was to spoil her so that she was no longer of value to the men who used her here in San Sebastian as they had used Charley Oakhurst. Damage her value to them and they could be relied on to finish the job.

Regina Coeli prison is a big, squat, raw-looking pile in which both the innocent and the guilty languish sometimes for years. Here in Rome the innocent wait to be charged and tried and the guilty wait for their lawyers to bribe a judge. Like most places designed to curb crime, it is overcrowded inside and out. Relatives and associates of prisoners loiter in the streets for a chance view of their loved ones inside and a hasty shouted greeting or coded message.

Technically, Sala Dodici is not a cell. It is carried on the books as an interrogation room but, in fact, Sala Dodici is meant for those not yet charged but already judged affluent enough to be interesting. It was here that the illustrious *cantatrice*, born Magdalene Ruzza in faraway New Jersey, was brought by a special Guardia di Finanza flying squad that managed to hide her identity from scores of waiting paparazzi.

Spiriting away illustrious prisoners under the very lenses of the waiting press is a specialty of Italian law enforcement. Mafiosi temporarily detained until sprung pay generously to elude the cameras. Thus, by sheer on-the-job training, Italian police are adept in the art.

Maggie Rose glanced around Sala Dodici and tried to estimate her chances of ever leaving it for the outside world again. The institutional smell of this place—half carbolic, half urine—was already giving her a headache. If to it had been added the stench of roach killer, it would have been a match for the elementary school she had attended near Hackensack.

She found it impossible to think that Faith was behind this frame-up. Despite her veneer of cold common sense, Faith was a sentimental slob. Although finding Maggie with the old bastard might have unhinged her mind. Still....

Somebody back in San Sebastian was playing hardball with her life, she reflected. Somebody had set her up for this with all the finesse of a protected criminal.

Maggie knew firsthand about protected criminality. It came in two forms: people like her family and friends, who bought protection from crooked cops and politicos, and the cops themselves, who shielded each other's crimes. The overlap was also familiar to her, in which weak-minded psychopaths like Oswald and Sirhan, one on the payroll of the New Orleans family, the other in hock to the L.A. boys, played starring roles in scenarios concocted by people on both sides of the great divide between the law and crime.

She smiled. What divide?

She had already spoken to her recording company's American attorney in Rome, sleepy and out of sorts at being awakened so early on a Sunday, but anxious to serve. "I have to tread lightly," he'd explained to her. "It's some kind of mine field, Miss Rose. But as soon as I find a familiar palm, the grease will fly. You'll be out of there by dinnertime."

Well, it was now somewhere between breakfast and lunch, Maggie told herself, and my stomach thinks my throat's cut and I haven't heard a burp out of Mr. Legal Eagle.

Her manager, Harry Armitage, who had come down on the Blue Train with her, was also among the missing, "pulling strings" he promised. Maggie suspected he'd taken the first plane out of Rome before they decided to arrest him too.

No one had come near her except a youngish matron who begged her to stay away from the windows of Sala Dodici. "The street is right outside, *carissima donna,* and the paparazzi are poised with their telefoto cameras."

"Thanks for the tip, cousin."

By noon the results of the autopsy were complete. The French captain had indeed, the pathologist averred, died of an embolism, although none had been found. This was not uncommon in the kind of cursory medical examination most hospitals make before a next of kin can be located to authorize something more deep-delving. Since all the other signs were consistent with the embolism hypothesis, Rattazzi's death certificate would bear that as cause of death.

By noon, too, Geni Magari was at the hospital, giving his old school chum Giacobbe a violent dressing down. Having successfully transferred his own humiliation at Mike's hands onto Arturo, he paused for breath.

"I have no excuse, Geni," Giacobbe said contritely.

"How could they have slipped past you, Turo?"

"They? They?"

Geni frowned. "Those who murdered him."

Giacobbe's eyes expanded. "What are you talking about, Geni? It was an embolism."

Magari stared at him for a long moment. "Turo," he said, "sit down here." He patted the unmade bed recently filled by the corpse. "You know what an embolism is?" he began hopefully.

"Something that blocks a blood vessel. A blood clot."

"*Complimenti.* But have you forgotten the Palermo Air Bubble?"

"Here? In this clinic?"

"Twenty cc's of air syringed into a man's artery by hypodermic needle. Within a few minutes it's reached the brain and done its work. Half an hour more and the air has filtered out through the tissues of the capillary. There *is* no embolism."

"*Gesù Cristo!*"

"Listen to the *ebreo* curse." Geni eyed him for a long time, as if trying to make up his mind about something. "You didn't inspect the cadaver for puncture marks?"

"Who knew this was necessary?" Arturo defended himself. "Besides, they'd already given Rattazzi sedatives that way. At least twice. And anesthetics too."

"A hospital is the best killing ground. People come and go. Injections are given. It's all very...natural."

"So now you can reopen the inquest, eh?"

"On what evidence?"

"The murder of Rattazzi," Arturo said.

"Who can prove murder?" Geni gave him a pained smile. "No, Turo, the inquest stays closed. What bothers me is more important."

"Who did the job?"

Geni nodded somberly. "We already know how they got him to do it. Look for a doctor who gambles and we'll find the man with the hypodermic."

*   *   *

"But then where were you?" Faith asked her son. She had returned from Mass to change into the more colorful apparel she would be wearing at lunch, an outdoor affair the press attaché called a "photo opportunity."

"I told you, right here."

"I can accept that you didn't feel well enough for the dinner and ball," Faith said, sitting down on her son's bed. He lay stretched across it, a damp cloth on his forehead. "Even though Uncle Billy was sick as a dog he managed to make it for the Strauss waltzes. But no Mass this morning? And now you want to be let out of lunch?"

"I feel as if a ten-ton safe fell on my head," he lied.

The Tuinal had left him with no such symptoms. It was the missing Gulda emerald—the one he knew to be the real one—that was giving him this sick chill in the pit of his stomach. And it was Geni Magari's obvious involvement in this episode—which he kept denying—that nauseated him even more.

"I'm disappointed in you," the Princess was saying. "What about your currency agreement? After lunch none of the other financial people will be here anymore."

Mike groaned, sat up and tossed the damp rag at his bedside table. She had to be told about the emerald, but not now, not till this whole minisummit crowd left and San Sebastian had some peace and quiet. Then! Then Eugenio Magari would get his! You heard of high-ranking military and police flipping out. It wasn't that rare. They'd have Geni's ass on the carpet the moment everybody cleared out. But until then...

He swung his long legs off the bed. "Okay," he said. "What'm I supposed to wear? Business suit?"

"That dark blue one with the wide pinstripe," she said. "It's got a very reassuring financial look to it."

"White shirt?"

"Of course. And that nice wine-colored tie with the club stripes."

"Black socks?"

"Natu—" She gave him a pained look. "Very funny." She got up from the bed and stood beside him, glancing at both of them in his mirror. "You *will* shave?"

"Yes, Mother."

"If I didn't know better, I'd say you'd been up all night."

*   *   *

Florian's valet had just finished knotting his tie and sliding it firmly into place. It was wine-colored with diagonal club stripes. He stepped back and surveyed his master, flicked an imaginary bit of dirt from the sleeve of the Prince's dark blue pin-striped jacket. He nodded firmly. *"Bellissimo."*

Florian dismissed him just as his switchboard-line telephone rang. "Your Highness," Geni Magari said, "I'm sorry to bother you. Is it possible for you—" He paused. "Do you know the comb—" He stopped again. "Her wall safe, Highness, can you be sure if the paste copy of the Gulda emerald is still there?"

"I can ask her. But why?"

"A very disturbing report has just reached me, *Altezza*."

"Geni!" Since he had come to the throne of San Sebastian, Florian had feared this moment. The Gulda emerald was more than an extremely costly bauble to him, as to all Guldas before him. It was the clan talisman. The luck of San Sebastian rode with it. It was also the nestegg which gave him the nerve to persevere in the early days when bandits like Georgiadis were sucking San Sebastian's blood. Then it was the treasure of last resort. Now it had even greater power as a kind of amulet or charm. And now, Geni...

"It's gone?" Florian demanded.

"Not at all, Highness. But something very strange has happened."

"The emerald is safe?"

"Absolutely, sir. It's on its way back from Rome at this very moment."

"Rome!"

"Two of my best men are bringing it back in a Guardia di Finanza aircraft. It's due here in an hour."

"How in God's name did it get to Rome?"

"Ah," Geni said. "Now that...that's quite a story and it's another reason I'd like *la Principessa* kept out of it for now. You see, her friend..." Geni paused and gave a small, delicate cough. "The singer. You know the one?"

*   *   *

In midafternoon, having been locked in Sala Dodici since early morning, Maggie Rose began to wonder if she would ever see the light of day again. She drew a rickety chair over to the window and, mindful of the matron's warning, slowly exposed one eye over the edge of the window frame to survey the street outside.

She was at ground level. Although two photographers lurked down the street by the entrance, the crowds of paparazzi had probably gotten bored and gone home. Where were her fans? If Armitage, her manager, was out there somewhere, why wasn't he organizing a demonstration?

Across the street lay a kind of piazza where people stood about in twos and threes eyeing the windows of Regina Coeli prison. They ignored the windows of Sala Dodici, Maggie noticed, but seemed to be looking at those far overhead, sometimes waving or blowing a kiss.

Beyond the piazza stood several nondescript old houses that might have fallen down long ago if they hadn't had each other for mutual support. On the fourth-floor roofs of this row of buildings more people stood and watched the prison, some with binoculars, one with a bright red flag she shook from time to time.

They seemed to Maggie to have been there all week, perhaps all month, waiting for a glimpse of someone inside or for their release. The sight of them, free but fettered to this place, squeezed Maggie's heart like a great leaden weight. She got down off the chair and went to the door of Sala Dodici.

Maybe if she pounded and let out a few streams of invective, someone would at least bring her a cup of coffee and a sandwich. Not that danger made her hungry. It made her sick. But the sight of all those people had now finally sunk in. This was a place of permanent waiting.

She sat down on a long bench, folded her sable wrap as a pillow and lay back. She hadn't slept well on the train. They'd refused to give her back her makeup case, saying it was "crucial evidence" because the damned jewel had been stashed in it. So by now she must look a fright.

But where was the lawyer with the bribe? Whoever had framed her for this couldn't seriously support a charge against her. Christ, she had enough money to buy the damned emerald, bird and all. Well, almost.

A squad of police clumped by outside on the street. Maggie closed her eyes and tried to sleep. Sirens ee-awed. Beyond her window a woman's thin voice kept repeating *"Dove sei, Rinaldo? Dove sei?"*

Right, she told herself. How the other half lives.

· 39 ·

His Serene Highness Prince Michele, holding a half-filled champagne glass, moved without apparent haste from one attaché to the next. The afternoon sun beamed down through a sparse layer of small clouds and threw brief moving shadows over the close-cropped lawn.

A striped tent of colossal proportions had been erected, a round, peaked, tasseled tent from some fantasy carousel. Inside, guests moved from the long table where the buffet was laid to an opposite table where bartenders poured drinks.

Any who cared to be waited on could install themselves rather democratically on a first-come-first-served basis at lawn tables outside, their oak surfaces partially covered by octagonal cloths bearing the green seal of San Sebastian. To one side of the lawn an accordionist and two other musicians produced soothing, familiar sounds, soft but firm enough to make confidential talk possible. At the moment they were playing an old Cole Porter song called "Friendship."

It was more or less the text of what Mike had been murmuring under the music to various financial aides of the other small countries. He could see his sister, Polly, dancing with one of them now, a prime young fathead who did something very highly placed in the Liechtenstein treasury.

Until now Mike hadn't thought of enlisting his sister in anything as serious as one of his own business schemes. Now, as he watched the way her arm circled the young financier's neck, her glance like a hatpin through the thorax of a gassed butterfly, Mike saw that he had been neglecting a valuable ally. He supposed he could thank Etienne for turning Polly into a rather calculating female. Fully equipped with her IUD, she would be formidable, if still underage.

The prospect of having to live with a suddenly nubile and sexually ravenous sister filled Mike with dismay. He had to be insane, thinking he could harness all that rawly awakened lust on behalf of a currency union. As he watched her get the Liechtensteiner steamed up to total blubbering incoherence, Mike started to grin. Who would've thought it of Poor Poll? And without even one overt physical grope.

He glanced down at his champagne but still refrained from sipping it. Clear head, he told himself. Big day. Big results, if he didn't let all the background noise confuse him. The Case of the Kidnapped Emerald, or Assault in the Vault. God, what childish stuff lurked in Geni's head.

By now Mike had spoken to representatives of each minipower. The consensus was promising. It needed only his father and the Prince of Liechtenstein to nail it down firmly. Mike started to put down his flat champagne.

Instantly, Geni Magari arrived with a fresh glass. "I can't tell you how sick I am," Mike murmured, "of having you pop up everywhere I look."

"With good news. The emerald is back in San Sebastian. The Italians found it in the luggage of Maggie Rose."

Mike stood in shocked silence a moment, trying to digest this news. Across the lawn an American Embassy spy with a pitted face was monopolizing Jill Tremont's attention. The musicians were playing "Love Me Tonight."

Her Serene Highness Princess Faith had limited the CBS team to only one crew and no interviewing. This overworked trio of camera operators and sound men was darting from one group to the next, taking full advantage of the brilliant sunshine.

Last night at the gala hundreds of guests were happy to pose, posture, gesture and mouth endlessly for television. Today, with barely fifty people on hand, all of them high-ranking, everyone showed great reluctance to having themselves immortalized on videotape. Normal protocol would have kept the crew out, but this chance to elevate San Sebastian's prestige was too good to let pass.

"What'll the Italians do to Maggie?" Mike asked in an undertone.

"I don't know. Your father wants her punished."

"And my mother?"

"She hasn't been told yet. Not even that the real emerald has been missing since last evening."

Mike got a sullen, mulish look on his face. "No mystery there. She'll side with my father. They'll throw Maggie to the wolves."

"If she's guilty, what more can she expect?"

"Can the crap," Mike snapped. "I'm going to tell *la Principessa* about this. It's stupid to keep her in the dark."

"Can you wait until our guests leave?" Geni requested.

"Why? Their stomachs are easily as strong as ours. Don't think they each don't have their own personal Geni Magari to touch the untouchable."

"Why?" Geni echoed. He drew up his compact body. He was still a head shorter than Mike, but so was everyone else in San Sebastian. "Because when you are the ruler—*and* you have fired me as you promised—you will find out that power depends on interchange of favors. For finding the emerald, I now owe the Italians a favor. For giving you the time a month ago to get your sister out of that houseboat, *you* owe *me* a favor." His voice had dropped terribly low, but it came forth with great intensity. "Please tell your mother later."

"I don't believe what I'm hearing," Mike responded in an equally low tone. "You have a man nearly murdered, a man to whom I gave my word he'd be safe, and you claim I owe you for it?"

The two princesses who had been Hollywood stars were posing for photographers now in a beautiful corner of the lawn where banks of autumn flowers trembled with color. The accordionist went softly into a song called "There's No Business Like Show Business." Flashbulbs flared, filling in the sun's strong shadows. The hand-held lights of the TV camera crew were blinding.

"That was a gross overreaction by my people. They have been disciplined. And you might as well know it, some of my men also beat up the captain of the *Finisterre* the other night. This morning he died in the hospital, of other causes."

Mike gave him a startled look. "Jesus, Geni, your people are savages."

"Worse. Some are killers. You can be sure they will be weeded out," the agent promised. "I demand precise obedience. But when you have sadists on the payroll, you get atrocities."

"I do love that cool, managerial tone," Mike said with mock admiration. "We might be discussing the cucumber crop."

The princes married to the film stars now joined them in still more informal tableaux. The musicians moved smoothly into "That's Entertainment."

"We can surely discuss this in some better place. All I ask," Geni went on, "is an hour's delay. Then tell your mother the whole story or any part of it you choose. I'll stand mute."

Mike looked down at his champagne, then suddenly lifted it to his lips and took the whole drink in four quick swallows. "I'm not all that eager to watch her sell Maggie out," the hereditary heir said then. "I've seen too much of this power business from too close up. You tell her."

"No, you," Geni insisted, "because you were part of it. They attacked you. You were the one who spent the night in the vault. It's your story, even to the happy ending."

"You call it happy? Do you have any idea what will happen to Maggie?"

"*State calmi,*" Billy Ritz said in a conspiratorial tone. He had come up behind the two men and how swung them around toward him by pulling on their elbows. "This is an upbeat scene, you two," he chided. "Stop hissing at each other."

"*Mi scusi, Commendatore,*" Geni apologized.

"How much did you overhear?" Mike asked cautiously.

"Enough to know it'd make a lousy movie," the little Viennese retorted. "I want you two smiling. I want you gay, in the old-time sense of the word. Okay?"

He touched each of their mouths in turn and both reacted by flinching. Then they produced fake grins. "Plastic enough for you, Uncle Billy?"

"I love it. Cut and print."

The accordionist was playing an old song called "Hooray for Hollywood."

· 40 ·

Gold Beret headquarters occupied an old building behind the soccer stadium. Space was crowded and Geni Magari kept his section trimmed down. His parents' apartment, where he lived, was only a five-minute walk from headquarters. On a slow day he could even take lunch at home. The last slow day had been the summer two years before.

This hectic Sunday he had summoned Arturo Giacobbe and another of his Berets, Paolo Croce, for a conference as soon as the last visiting royalty had left the principality.

"I have given my word," he began, "in the highest quarters"— his glance flicked sideways in the direction of the palace—"to clean up this department and try to put an intelligent face on the Intelligence Section. *D'accordo?*"

"*Si, capo,*" Croce responded. "But how?"

Geni sat back in his chair, producing a long, complaining creak. "Turo will be transferred from the clinic assignment to head a Special Investigations squad. You will be his deputy, Paolo. You two will take depositions, bring charges and call departmental hearings. No man will be dismissed or disciplined without a full hearing. But make no mistake about it"—he leaned forward to a second creak from his chair—"one way or another I want the dozen or so killers removed. Out. No longer on the payroll. *Capite?*"

"*Si, capo.*"

"In some cases you'll find a man is demented. He likes causing pain, spilling blood. But in other cases you'll learn that he has political motives for death-squad activities. He serves on two payrolls, ours and another's. His secret employers will exert great effort to keep him where he is."

Giacobbe looked worriedly at Croce. Then, to Geni: "You think we have a lot of politicals."

"A handful."

"But, *capo,*" Giacobbe went on then, not using Geni's nickname in front of another Beret, "to get rid of these politicals we must go up against their employers. We know who the major secret employer is in San Sebastian, as everywhere else in Italy."

"In intelligence work," Magari told him, "one follows the trail till it reaches a stopping place."

"All well and good," Croce burst in, "but how long will we stay alive stalking some big-shot maf—"His voice dropped to a murmur and his glance shot around the room. "some *pezzo novanta* mafioso," he nearly whispered.

"This is the universal problem," his boss agreed. "When you uncover such a connection, come to me. Then we decide on the next step. Fair enough?"

Both agents nodded rather dismally. Geni Magari let a moment elapse before addressing himself to Giacobbe. "Turo," he said at last, "at La Muta, Massimo Sgroi hangs out under the sign of the headless woman taking bets and dealing drugs. Start squeezing the fat man about his clinic connections. Our men didn't kill the Frenchman, they only set him up for someone in the clinic. Work backward from Sgroi, through the corrupt clinic people to our own bad guys. It may prove a shortcut to weeding out the politicals."

"Or a shortcut," Giacobbe said, "to Paolo and me being found at the bottom of the harbor wearing cement shoes."

· 41 ·

It was a council of war, Billy Ritz thought, surely the first in which an outsider like himself was on hand.

After a weekend of great stress, none of them needed this kind of wind-up. But Mike had called for it. In so many ways, Billy saw, the boy seemed to echo his grandfather Eamon's insensitivity to the feelings of others. Or rather, since Mike seemed to be suffering more than the rest, his ability to put his own angst well ahead of anyone else's. What a ruler he'd make!

He had chosen the outdoor terrace where the family normally had breakfast. The sun still illuminated the western sky and the air was still warm enough, but the beginnings of an October chill hung in the air. Jill shivered and went to get herself and Faith wool shoulder scarves.

By the time she returned, Mike had finished the incredible story of being waylaid and locked in the vault and the subsequent arrest of Maggie Rose. Moving behind the Princess, Jill draped a scarf over her and then covered her own shoulders. Prince Florian watched grimly, saying nothing, his handsome face etched against the darkening background by the last rays of the sun.

"Now," Mike concluded, "some sort of statement has to be forthcoming from the palace. It doesn't have to come directly from one of you. But it has to comment on this obvious frame-up."

"Why obvious?" his father demanded. "Why frame-up?"

"Because we all know Maggie was set up for this."

"By whom?" Florian persisted. "For what?"

Mike gestured wildly. "Who knows? But it sticks out a mile."

Faith glanced at Billy. "It does, doesn't it?"

The director seemed to shrug down in his chair, as if trying to make himself even smaller. "I'm only an elderly practitioner of fiction. About real life you need an expert like your man Magari."

"Not Magari," Mike burst out. "He's in this up to his eyeballs."

"Make sense, will you?" Florian said in a hurt tone. "What good does it do to blacken Geni's name? You have no proof."

Again Mike made a churning gesture, as if trying to fight off a swarm of insects. "Stick to the basic issue. The crown jewel of San Sebastian was stolen. A comment must be forthcoming. Some sort of apology is due Maggie Rose."

"Why?" his father snapped. "She was in league with that Oakhurst fellow. She introduced Polly to that wretched tennis tramp. You remember the story of the Trojan horse? That's been her role in San Sebastian. We owe her nothing."

He glanced at his wife, who sat in silence. Billy watched Jill, whose eyes never left Florian. The little Viennese automatically noted and filed away this fact.

A long silence settled over the group.

"Well?" Mike said then. "Does anybody see it my way?"

"Sort of," his mother confessed. "I know what you're getting at, Mikey. But nobody forced Maggie to be our guest. If she got into trouble as a result, it's her affair, not ours."

"I knew it!" Mike exploded. "When the chips were down, I knew you'd throw her to the wolves."

"Utter nonsense." Florian's face had darkened with a royal kind of anger. Billy noted that Jill seemed thrilled. "Apologize to your mother for that remark," the Prince demanded.

Mike wheeled on the Princess. "Is that what you want?"

"Calm down, Mikey. You're getting too upset."

"Look," his father cut in. "If you won't listen to sense, let's take it at your level. You've just put together a very advantageous financial arrangement. This weekend conference has redounded to our advantage in many other ways. And what do you think will happen to all this goodwill, to your currency agreement, if we have to stand up and be counted in the Maggie Rose affair? It reduces us to the level of a tin-pot comic-opera Disneyland. Stolen jewels. A fleeing soprano. My God, it's a plot out of Offenbach."

Mike stood across the glass-topped table from his father, two tall, blond men almost silhouetted against the oncoming night by the horizontal light sweeping in from the west. The young Prince ran fingers through his mop of hair. "Okay," he said then. "You have a point. But there's a more important point, Father, and somebody has to make it."

"What could be more important than the honor of this nation?"

"That's *it!*" Mike pounced. "You are making my point for me. If this family governs this land honorably...if we Guldas stand for enlightened leadership...if San Sebastian is really not a half-assed Disneyland...then we *must* take a position. You call it the Maggie Rose affair? It's the Gulda affair, featuring the Gulda emerald. We're not living in the reign of Great-Grandpa Umberto. We're in the electronic age, Father. Everyone knows Maggie's being held on a possible felony. Everyone looks to us to clear up the confusion. It's the duty of enlightened leadership."

"Rot."

"Or else," Mike went on in an overbearing tone of menace, "we're just a nasty little dictatorship camouflaged by a lot of rose-garden publicity, fronted by a movie star and backed up by paid assassins."

"*Mein Gott,*" Billy Ritz intoned.

"Michele!" Florian thundered.

"Easy," Faith said in a quiet, penetrating tone. "This terrace is hard to wiretap or eavesdrop. But if you start shouting, the whole world will know. Mikey," she went on with impressive calm, "how long has all this been festering inside you?"

He glared down at her. Then he seemed to get control of himself. Billy watched the dangerous bulge at his jawline soften slightly. "Oh, what's the use," he inquired plaintively.

"I'm willing to listen," his mother continued. "I'm willing to hear your side of it."

"And *then* sign Maggie's death warrant."

"How did you get to be her champion?"

"That's not it, Mother. I don't like her at all. But I really hate the idea that we're a pack of arrogant, heartless reactionary bastards, cloaked in a lot of fancy-dress sleight-of-hand. I mean, we're not even elected. Back home in the States, when the public finds out a guy's a phony they can replace him at the next election. But here..."

"Back *home?*" Prince Florian asked in a quiet voice. "Did you hear that, my dear? Your son's *home* is not here?"

"That was a dumb thing to say, Mikey," Faith chided him. "What's got you so upset? In a principality a prince doesn't have to answer to anybody if he doesn't want to. If he were a bad man, that would be bad. But he's the best ruler San Sebastian ever had and well you know it."

Mike's lanky body seemed to collapse. He half fell into a chair, leaving his father the only one standing. "You people get me too upset to make sense," he muttered. "I didn't mean to bad-name my own father. It's just..." He stopped and shook his head.

"This prince business—" he began again. "It's not what it seems to be. It runs smoothly because people do our dirty work for us. When some of the dirty work starts to stick out so the whole world sees it, we have a duty to take the responsibility on ourselves. That's what I meant by honor, Father."

Billy decided it was the moment for Florian to rise to a new height of statesmanship and produce some healing concept, a directive, a way out.

But it was the Princess who spoke. "What do you want of us, Mikey? Do you want your father to call a press conference and tell the world our own security people might have been mixed up in this? Be sensible."

"Be sensible," the young Prince repeated. "That was Maggie's line, wasn't it, about signing up with Charley Oakhurst?"

Faith blinked. "Yes," she admitted. "And I was the one taking a high-minded attitude, as you are now. But that was a matter of dollars and cents and Mafia control of our casinos again. This, as your father says, is only a plot out of Offenbach."

"It's a lot more serious for Maggie Rose."

The Princess' glance went to Billy Ritz, then to Florian, then to her watch. "In any event, Mike, I don't see the need for haste. Let's sleep on this." She stood up.

"Predictable," her son groaned.

"What?"

"That you'd delay this. Till it was too late."

Without responding, Faith left the terrace. Jill stared adoringly at Florian. Billy Ritz found himself wondering why. He watched her trail behind the Prince as both of them left the terrace.

The meek, he thought, shall inherit the Prince. Yet another problem for Faith. He glanced at Mike. "You happy now?"

"Huh?"

"You," the Viennese said more sharply, "the one who wanted Maggie Rose out of the way. Or don't you remember that conversation?"

A peculiarly young look came over Mike's tired face, half pout, half grim willfulness. "So what?"

"Terrific," Billy responded. "You have that arrogant look that goes so well with being a heartless reactionary bastard."

Although the last of the sun had left the sky, the elderly director could see Mike flush. For a long time only the sound of his breathing could be heard, uneven and heavy. Then he seemed to calm down.

"I never dreamed you'd get such quick results," Mike said, then in a lower, more chastened voice, "I was just playing power games. I was just stirring up the animals. I never dr—"

"Never dreamed," Billy cut in bitterly. "There are no games, Mike. There is only real life and real death. It may look like a game to the winner. But to the loser it's plain ordinary death."

"You don't think Maggie's life is...?"

"I have no idea," he interrupted again. "I've stopped carrying your messages, Mike. People like Maggie turn them into poisoned darts."

"But surely you knew I didn't mean..." The younger man stopped himself. "Surely you..." He paused again and his glance sought Billy's. "I guess I'm the one who switched Magari on. Is that what you're saying? I'm the one who...who triggered it off?"

"Not too sure about that one," the Viennese admitted after a moment. "Let's put it this way—he had already marked Maggie for punishment. All he needed was something in the way of an official nod."

"And that's what I blundered into?"

"Was it a blunder?" Billy snapped back.

Mike sat in silence for some time. "You don't understand what it's like being me," he burst out then. "Being on permanent public display like a fucking canary in a cage? No privacy, no power, no hope of your own life? You get the urge to smash things, shake them up."

Billy Ritz nodded. "When you succeed to the throne," he said then, "remind me to keep well out of your way."

"That's not nice."

"I'm too old to be nice."

"But if I can get my parents to take Maggie off the hook?"

"Then I'll know," the director told him, "that at least you can feel guilt. Like the rest of us."

"Your hands aren't totally clean."

"That's what makes me so sharp with you, Mike. I'm part of the plot to sink Maggie Rose." The darkness had come up around them quickly. They could barely see each other now. "But I don't want to be part of the plot to sink Geni Magari. Do I make myself clear?"

"You'd protect him?"

"Magari's a good man, underneath."

"Christ! I'm surrounded by *good* men."

"You'd prefer villains."

"It'd help," Mike confessed.

"When you sit on the throne here," the Viennese told him, "you'll be inundated with good men. Nobody wearing a black Stetson is going to get off the Albuquerque stagecoach and kick the first dog he meets. Life is not like that."

"Now you tell me."

Enzo Magari had been in a state of anxiety since the day Massimo Sgroi had threatened him. The last week, with the tremendous load of work it put on the palace fleet of cars, had also taken a toll. But Enzo was wise enough to know that the real source of his uneasiness was himself.

He stared out the open door of his office at the little animal, Massimo Sgroi the Lesser, lazily hosing down dusty limousines that had earlier been ferrying royalty back and forth. He was concentrating now, like a lover with his girl, on the light blue Jaguar XKE on which he lavished so much attention. Even the way he handled the hose and rags left a bad taste in Enzo Magari's mouth. The truth was, he now loathed the very sight of the boy, not just because he was impossible vermin but also because he was a symbol of Enzo's shame.

A man of standing in the community, a man of responsibility, letting himself be pushed around by scum. Moreover, a man whose son could give him every assistance.

Enzo pulled over his ledger books to begin making entries in them. So many liters of benzine, of oil. So many replacement tires. Dates. Prices.

"Scusi, Dottore," an oily voice said.

Enzo looked up. A raw thrill of fear shot through him. The hippopotamus-man in the doorway of his office, known as *il Cavaliere*, held his hat in tiny paws and flared his nostrils as if sniffing dinner. *"Professore, come stai?"*

Enzo's fear seemed to settle in his diaphragm, just under his lungs, giving him a sick, breathless feeling. "Sgroi," he said, naming the fear, "I'm busy."

"We're all busy," the fat man said, dancing in on tiptoe. He shoved ledgers and logbooks off the desk and planted his immense behind on a corner next to the telephone. "We must talk, *Illustre*."

Enzo glanced down at the ledgers scattered on the floor. What he wanted to say was "Not while my books lie in the dirt and grease. Pick them up, pig." What he said was:

"About what?"

"About your attitude, *maestro*."

Behind him his son stepped into the office and slammed the door shut. Enzo wanted to shout "Get out of here, you carrion!" He said:

"What is the meaning of this?" Very stiffly, because he had to keep his voice from trembling.

Massimo the Greater removed a penknife from his pocket and began cleaning his nails. He let the little black bits fall on Enzo's desk. "I came here in good faith, *Egregio Signore*," he said then. "I came as a dutiful father to ask that you look with interest on the work of my son."

Massimo the Lesser came up behind his father and managed to step on an open ledger book, leaving a greasy print. "He hardly speaks to me," the boy complained. "How am I to advance in my profession?"

"What is more," his father rolled on, carefully cleaning the blade of his knife before using it delicately to pick at his teeth, "it has come to my attention that far from helping *my* son, you have decided to complain to *your* son."

"What is that to you, fat scum?" Enzo wanted to ask. "W-What are you talking about?" was what he asked.

"Yes, my humble accomplishments are coming under the scrutiny of the Gold Berets," Massimo Sgroi said. "*Onorevole*, is that the act of a friend?"

"I have never mentioned any of this to my son. Never," Enzo repeated, listening to the unsteady, blubbering note in his voice.

Geni would be ashamed of him, behaving in such a craven manner. He was ashamed of himself. What was so invincible about this fat blob of pus?

"Let me tell you what must now be done, *Commendatore*," the fat man told him. "You must call off your son."

He got up from the desk and, seeing two ledgers still on it, swept them to the floor. Enzo watched the books—carrying years of entries needed in the accounting of the garage's expenses—being stepped on now by the slimy son and the man called *il Cavaliere*.

"I have no authority over him." Enzo was shocked to hear how hard it was for him to voice even such a cowardly thought.

"But you do," the fat man advised him. "He has only one father. Only one mother. Something could easily happen to one of
his parents. Either one," he added carelessly.

Enzo was on his feet. He could feel his whole body trembling.
Screams, howls of rage, imprecations seemed to froth at his lips without being uttered. But what came out was:

"I see."

As if Geni could ever be blackmailed by this tub of guts. As if
he, Enzo Magari, would let his brave, honest, brilliant son be hob-
bled by this man's threats.

"*Senatore*, you'll tell your son to drop this foolish new idea of
his, won't you?"

The silence grew. At last the fat man smiled broadly. "Good,"
he said.

Then he turned and headed for the door, almost tripping over
the ledgers. He reached down for one and, with his penknife, cut
a dozen pages from it. These he stuffed in his pocket as his son
opened the door for him. They left the office and the garage.

Trembling, Enzo Magari sat down at his desk. He had been a
cowardly fool to keep this matter from Geni all these weeks. But
now he would be brave. He would redeem himself in his own eyes.
He would refuse to breathe a word of it to his son.

Only in that way could he ever live with his shame.

· 43 ·

Florian had gone to sleep. So had Jill. Polly had been asleep for some
time. Faith sat in her dressing room and stared at herself in the mirror. Probably Mike and Billy are asleep, too, she told herself. Only
people with unresolved problems can't sleep.

She gave herself one of the Eamon Brennan sneers. Poor Mike
had been so upset. She hadn't seen him that way since he was a
small boy. Of the two, she expected rebellion from Polly, never
Mike. Polly was more like she was, able to stand off an army if need
be. Mike was always too logical not to see both sides of everything.

It was killing him now. He'd begun to see the two sides of

what he called the prince business. The new insight dismayed him. Obviously he wasn't ready yet for power, the way Florian thought he was.

Maybe she could get him interested in another college degree. Was there a Ph.D. in economics or political science or something?

That had been a terrible blunder, referring to the United States as "home." It had really shaken poor Florian. But Faith knew the feeling. The States would always be home to her, even if she never set foot in them again.

Florian would never understand this duality in her nature. It was as if she were cheating with another man. He took the position that San Sebastian was him. A very dear, old-fashioned man, totally out of his depth in the waters Maggie Rose had dragged them to.

Someone knocked on the door. "Princess," Billy Ritz said. "Want to watch the late-late show?"

She let him in. "Don't tell me one of ours is on the tube."

"I meant the news," the little director explained, snapping on the set hidden in a kind of commode-style piece of furniture. He fiddled with the remote-control box and managed to bring in the RAI second channel news sign-off in Italian.

At this time of night the male news readers had all gone home. One of the fluffy blond women whose job it normally was to tell viewers what was scheduled for all channels of RAI now stared at the camera through a panel on which her words were invisibly projected.

"*Buona sera*," she began with a smile better suited to launching a toothpaste commercial. "It has now been eighteen hours since the international singing favorite Maggie Rose was placed under guard in Regina Coeli prison."

She managed to pronounce it Maggie Ruz but it hardly mattered since on the screen the image changed to a glamorous shot of the celebrated personality, looking lush with success.

"Police have given no explanation," the blond woman read on, "but informed sources suggest the possibility of activities related to an unidentified missing jewel."

The video changed to the scene favored by news programs the world over when they have no real footage. The screen showed a nighttime view of the piazza in front of the Regina Coeli prison.

The camera zoomed in for a view of a window, then panned about the grim facade of the building and the even grimmer hangers-on in the piazza.

When the image returned to that of the blond woman, she produced a second dazzling smile. "Miz Ruz had come to Rome from San Sebastian. Her longtime friendship with Princess Faith of that principality is well known. The San Sebastiani have been playing host this past weekend to sovereigns and rulers of a number of other small European nations outside the EEC framework. Meanwhile, in Milano a chemical factory near Malpensa Airport went up in flames late this afternoon after an explosion that—"

Faith switched off the television set. "Mike's right."

"Is he?"

"We have to issue a statement."

"Saying what?"

"We can't just sit here in silence. We're already being linked to the thing."

She picked up her telephone and dialed an internal number. "Mike, did I wake y—?" She listened. "No, I can't sleep either. Come over, will you?" She hung up.

"And what'll his father say about this?"

"Let's take this one problem at a time," the Princess cautioned him. "First the statement. Then I'll get Florian to okay it." She glanced at her watch. "Midnight. Can you believe this dragging on? The worst Sunday I can ever remember."

"Tell me before Mike gets here," the director urged her, "If you had your druthers, what would you tell the press?"

"I'd druther say nothing." She watched him closely for a moment. "I'm not carrying a grudge against her anymore, if that's what you mean. Once I told you, once I told her, I've been free of it. I don't really mean free," she corrected herself. "Maybe I mean reconciled to the fact that I can never make him pay for it. Maybe unloading on Maggie was therapeutic."

Mike appeared without knocking. He seemed a bit miffed at not finding his mother alone. "I thought we could have a heart-to-heart," he complained. "This old coot is everywhere. He's like Geni Magari. Along comes the electrician or the window cleaner and it's

Geni Magari in disguise. Who's Uncle Billy supposed to be, the garbage collector?"

"Something like that," the little man agreed mildly.

"If you had to issue a statement about Maggie," the Princess began then, "what would you say?"

Mike sat down on the chaise longue next to the Viennese. "What would *you* say?"

Faith strode to the windows overlooking the harbor. Outside the palace the city was sinking slowly into slumber. In bunches, lights were going out. The twin beacons of the Needle swept across her field of vision. She frowned and swung the window open a little wider. "Music."

They joined her at the window. "Accordion," Mike said.

"Far away. Is it the fellow we had in the garden?"

"Could be. What's he playing?"

"My song," Billy Ritz told them. "A Viennese waltz."

Faith hummed along for a moment. Then: "I asked you something, Mikey."

"Okay. A statement saying that while we have no official connection with Maggie, we know her to be a person of the utmost probity, etcetera, etcetera."

"Pure waffle," the director replied. "And we know better than most, her probity doesn't exist."

"Okay, then just—we value our past relationship with her and we feel sure that the moment this mistake is explained, blah blah blah."

"More waffle. Besides, the Italian press have already been fed a leak about a mystery jewel."

"Shit."

"Language." Faith listened to the accordion for a moment more, then turned back into the room. "I'm more worried about your attitude than I am about the press. You seem to feel this is some kind of acid test. If we don't rescue Maggie, we're despots, reactionary swine."

"Don't make fun of me," her son responded. "I set a lot of store by honesty in high places."

"Then you're in for a lot of disappointments," Billy told him.

The faint notes of the accordion filtered into the room, a dream accordion with a tone as light as a whisper. Billy Ritz stood up and took Faith's hand.

"Wien, Wien, nur du Allein," he sang, turning her slowly in a stately waltz step. "When I hear this my bones turn to butter." Slowly they wheeled about as he hummed.

"It's so sad," he said then. "We were all so young and now we're scattered across the earth. But what we once had there! *Mein Gott,* such warmth and excitement. Actors and writers and painters and musicians."

In silence they waltzed back and forth, taking small steps. "Billy, you're making me cry."

"We sparked each other. We lived in the same tenements, met at the same coffeehouses, made love to each other's girls. It was a collective art, like a movie company on a set. Together, we made an era."

Breathless now, the little man stopped. "There was a strength in being together. It was a—what do they call it now?—a support system. Ugly phrase. We loved each other. Since then I have been on my own in a very hostile world. Except for you, *Liebchen,* and a handful of other friends, I have been alone."

She kissed his cheek and turned away, brushing off a tear and laughing nervously. "What was it Noel Coward said?"

"The power of cheap music." Billy winked at her.

But she was staring at her son. He could see that she had come to some sort of conclusion, read it in that face that had always been able to communicate without words. "Mom?"

She nodded. "Artists have it tough enough in this life," she told him. "Being a money man, you wouldn't know."

"Mom."

Slowly, as if under hypnosis, her hand went out for the telephone. She dialed the operator. "Get me Associated Press in Rome, please."

"Mom, what the hell are you...?"

"Language," Faith said. "Hello, AP?" She paused.

"Mom."

"This is Her Serene Highness Princess Faith of San Sebastian.

I'm releasing a statement exclusive to you. Can you take this down?"
She waited.

"Please, Mom, what're you saying?"

"Right. The statement reads as follows: We are shocked to learn of the mistaken detention in Rome of Miss Maggie Rose while carrying a paste copy of the famous Gulda emerald. Repeat—paste copy. She was to secure the services of a craftsman to produce a second copy. As we all know, Roman craftsmen are the finest in the world. We trust the authorities will apologize for the inconvenience caused by this honest error on their part. Read that back?" She paused.

"That," Billy Ritz said, "was no waffle."

"Right," Faith told the wire service. "You can confirm by calling me at the regular palace number. I'm sure you have it." She hung up.

"Okay, Mikey," she said. "Now tell me some more about how ugly this prince business is."

· 44 ·

When Prince Michele awoke early Monday morning his room was chilly. A sharp breeze blew in the half-open window. He stumbled out of bed to close it.

Instead, shivering, he stopped short and stared at the odd predawn light. A strange sky glowed in the east over Genoa, not yet truly red nor the more flamboyant colors that would soon appear. Now, at half-past six, a muddy scarlet smeared the horizon, so dark it almost had no name.

Mike shivered violently. The sky was the color of drying blood.

Instead of returning to bed, he began pulling on clothes. He'd had little sleep. The palace phones had begun to ring once the AP dispatch moved. The switchboard was now shut down.

He stared at his toes before pulling on tennis socks. He knew his mother had bravely lied as much for him as for Maggie Rose and for some teary, *gemütlich* sense of being a fellow artist, possibly in the same trouble. And also for Billy, Mike reminded himself. Mom always liked a good audience.

It didn't matter why. It only mattered that her heart was in the right place.

More than you could say for Geni Magari, Mike reminded himself. To think he'd once worshiped the man. Yet here was Magari, like any other cop, breaking the law out of some notion that it promoted the security of San Sebastian. And Billy Ritz calling him "good."

Restless now, Mike yanked on sneakers and pulled a heavy knit sweater over his shirt. He left the palace on foot, jogging for the shingle where the fishing boats lay. At this hour the men would already have returned with their catch, having sorted it into flat wooden boxes, covered the fish with lemon leaves and carted them off to shops and restaurants. The shingle would be deserted, fine for jogging, even better for thinking.

He started at the farthest end of the beach. In the distance, its beam shut down, the Needle stood half hidden in layers of morning mist. Mike's body parted the damp air as he moved along the slippery shale beach. The damp seemed to try to wrap him as if in a shroud.

Fine thoughts, he told himself. But Geni's failures as a human being obsessed him. The man he had once emulated he now considered dangerously flawed. One had to understand why he behaved in this way.

Aging? Mike knew very little about aging, mostly things he'd inferred from what his mother had said. Anyway, Geni was hardly fifteen years older than he was. He wasn't senile. Perhaps it was all too much for a man of simple background? Too much power not to corrupt him?

And didn't all those questions apply equally to Michele Gulda? Or soon would?

He watched a small gray car moving slowly along the inner harbor road in his direction. His heart sank. As it drew nearer he saw that it was a Renault 5-TS with Geni at the wheel. "Excuse me," the secret policeman said. "I was about to use the beach myself. I imagine you'd rather be alone."

"Yes."

At the cold monosyllable, Geni's face went dead. He shifted gears. The little car moved forward. Mike stirred. "You know about my mother's statement?"

The agent nodded wearily. "We have been up all night with the telephone calls. Our official response was the usual 'No comment.'" He eyed the prince sideways, the car still inching faintly forward as if anxious to leave the beach. "It was very loyal of *la Principessa*," he said then. "But it will change nothing." The car moved forward.

"Stop the car!"

Mike was shocked to hear himself shouting. He had never issued that sharp a command in his life.

"This is it, Magari," he raged. "You're going to explain yourself. The frame-up. The death squads. Who the hell do you think you are?"

Geni switched off the engine. He got out and stood beside the auto, as if not wanting to get any closer to the angry young man. "I have given you my word. The killers will be weeded out of the Berets. As for the rest..."

"I'm waiting."

The secret policeman made an odd, futile gesture. Behind him the sky still glowed that unnatural dark red. "The desires of *la Principessa* are plain enough. So are the ambitions of the Mafia for this place. Because we have taught them only gentle lessons all these years, they keep returning with greater force. They wave the papal flag. They very clearly do not stop at murder. If history teaches us anything, it teaches us that anyone, *anyone* can be murdered."

He drew a breath and his faintly lecturing tone seemed to slip a cog, grow more impatient. His olive-black eyes snapped. "So. Who the hell do I think I am? I am trying to teach them that they are not immune. That we can damage valuable property of theirs if they persist in trying to take us over. You once told me"—he glanced around—"here. On this beach. You said both the Church and the Mafia succeeded through fear. But there is more to the world than these two superpowers."

He paused and for a moment seemed to want to break through the impersonal mode of address, as if reaching out from one friend to another. But the habit was too strong. He drew himself back into his lecturer's posture and formal Italian language.

"We live in a world of business interests. Our own land is a business. Instead of wheat or oil," he said, "we sell recreation. If we offered salvation, be sure the Vatican would be on us at once. But it's only material gain we offer, not immortality. So only one superpower covets San Sebastian and we are on full alert."

Overhead the first dawn flight of seabirds swooped and dived against a blood-red sky. They dived into the water, came up with empty beaks. They cried loudly, as if being tortured, "Ai-ai-ai! I ache! I ache!"

"Like everything," Geni Magari said then, "this is a matter of appearances. The Church appears to offer life beyond death. The Mafia appears to offer death for those who oppose it. I want us to *appear* like the 'PERICOLO DI MORTE' sign on a high-tension tower. 'Danger. 6,000 Volts. Keep Off.' That's the only appearance they understand."

They stood silently for a long moment. Then the secret policeman saluted and drove away. The car grew smaller as it headed east toward the bruised and bloody sky.

"Ai-ee!" the gulls screamed.

Mike shuddered.

· 45 ·

In the hills above the harbor, Monday dawned cold. The heights over San Sebastian can get quite chilly in October. For a few minutes, while the sun fires up bright flares of orange and cerise to the east over Genoa, there is a cold wind, the *tramontana*, that blows south across the Alps.

Only the housekeeper and her husband were aware at this early hour, not yet seven, that Her Serene Highness had spent the night here in Prince Florian's ancestral home. She had driven herself up shortly after midnight and now, showered and dressed, she would return to the palace before anyone had awakened.

Faith took a long breath of piney air. It was the start of a beautiful day, no matter what else happened. Florian would probably be furious, at least at first. But she felt sure she could make him see that, since a statement had been necessary, this was the simplest way out. It felt right to her.

Sala Dodici was suddenly filled with people. Maggie had been napping on the long bench. All night she had been awakened by a woman who moaned *"Dove sei, Rinaldo, dove sei?"* mourning for someone she seemed to have no hope of ever seeing again. She and Maggie had seemed to be the last people alive on the planet.

Now it was bedlam here: photographers, the press, uniformed police. It took minutes before Harry Armitage and the recording company lawyer explained matters to her. They had a tearsheet of AP's lead story, carrying the statement issued by Princess Faith.

Maggie stood up and gave them all her number one smile. Thank God for old friends, she thought. Whatever game somebody had been playing with her life, Faith at least hadn't fallen for it. Outside the window she could hear chanting.

"What's going on outside?"

"Fans," Armitage explained. "Real ones. I didn't pay 'em a cent."

He pulled over a chair and helped her stand on it. Behind her the rest of the press began firing questions in several languages. By magic all eight of her trunks now appeared on a trolley, as if Regina Coeli was eager for her to be on her way.

Outside she could see about fifty people. They were chanting but she couldn't hear them over the noise inside the room. She waved to them and a cheer went up that cut through the shouts of the press people. Still standing on the chair, she turned back to the room.

"One at a time, boys," she called. "I always take my men one at a time."

In the emergency room of the Eamon Brennan clinic, the young doctor who had been on duty all night sat sipping an espresso with the senior man who had just come on duty.

There was a twenty-year difference in their ages. Even a night-emergency shift hadn't drained the starch out of the younger man. But the older, hair already graying and thinning, arrived looking washed out in advance of a day's work. His face, even at age forty-five, was harshly cut in lines of fatigue no amount of sleep could erase, no amount of caffeine could lighten.

"Listen," the night man said as he finished his espresso and put down the small cup on its tiny saucer, "you know Giacobbe, the barman who makes the coffee?"

"Giacobbe the spy?" The older man sipped his espresso greedily.

"Asked for the charts for that Froggie who died in Room 9. The sea captain?"

The older man choked on his last swallow of coffee. Coughing, he set the cup down so unsteadily, it rattled the saucer off the table. The smash of breaking crockery made both doctors blink. "I have seen livelier specimens than you," the younger man said, getting to his feet, "in an anatomy course. You look awful."

"Bad night," the day man responded. "What charts did Giacobbe want?"

"Who prescribed what. Medication. The usual."

The older man's face had turned puttyish in color as he sat there staring down at the broken saucer. "What was his reason?"

"Does a Beret have to give reasons?"

The younger man picked up his small leather case, nodded pleasantly and left. Slowly, as if the effort cost him some pain, the day doctor leaned over and picked up the five pieces of broken crockery. He held them in his hand for a long moment, as if trying to remember why he wanted them.

Finally, still not aware of his actions, he got to his feet and wandered over toward the table with the autoclave, where syringes, scalpels, retractors and other gear stewed in a bath of hot steam. He found himself opening the heavy steel top of the autoclave and staring down into it at the four hypodermic syringes. One of them had been used on the Froggie. By him. Did live steam eradicate fingerprints?

A sudden thrust of something sickening mushroomed up inside the doctor's abdomen, as if he had secretly been kicked very hard. He grunted and the broken saucer bits fell to the floor again. And now Giacobbe was snooping around, trying to find out who had done what to the captain in Room 9?

The doctor let the autoclave slam shut. He wheeled and picked up the emergency telephone. He seemed to wait forever once he'd

dialed a number. This was a secure telephone, a direct outside line
that didn't go through the clinic switchboard. Seventeen rings.

Eighteen. Nineteen.

"Yes?"

"Petracca here," the doctor said. He was horrified to hear his
voice shake. "You promised me no problems."

The man at the other end of the line said nothing for a long moment. "Did I?" he asked, then in a dull, heavy voice, "And did you
believe me, Dr. Petracca?"

"Listen, I—"

"No, you listen. We are all impressed with your abilities, Dr.
Petracca. You are getting a second chance to prove them."

"Look here, you—"

"Today."

"Today?" The doctor's voice went up like a train-whistle screech.

"Dr. Petracca, since you believe what I tell you, believe this: After today you will never be bothered again. Isn't that nice?"

There was an insinuating note in the man's voice, as if perhaps
they had once committed some indiscretion together, nothing serious, just holding hands in public or something like that.

"You're telling me..." The doctor's voice seemed to give out.

"I'm telling you that the thing for which you were needed is now
at hand, Dr. Petracca. And once it's done, you are free... forever."

"I couldn't poss—"

"You can," the man said coldly, "and what is more, you will."

The line went dead.

This early in the morning nobody seemed eager yet to drive down
the mountain road into San Sebastian. Faith had the highway to
herself. She shifted into third and sent the sky-blue car around a
corner at forty-five miles per hour. The tires squealed. But she had
everything under control, as always.

It had been a long time since she'd driven this freely and without supervision. There had been a scene in one of Billy's films where
they couldn't use a double except in the longest of shots. She'd had
to take an open car—no, a Jeep—down a tortuous stretch of mountain road much snakier than this one.

Along the way pinches of fireworks went off to simulate someone shooting at her. The Jeep had bucketed wildly from side to side and the whole scene had looked very dangerous. But she'd been driving at only about this speed, or perhaps even more slowly. The camera would speed up the action and later, in the finished movie, the scene would be heart-stopping, especially since it was obviously she doing her own driving.

The smooth, neatly graded road now led down through a long straightaway. She was doing fifty in fourth gear. But another curve was coming up.

Expertly, she downshifted and let the motor's torque slow the Jaguar to forty. Then thirty-five, and she was into another straightaway. The wind blew her hair wildly. She realized she was laughing.

"Deadline: Danger," she said aloud. That had been the title of the film. Something about a female correspondent in a Latin American country where a war broke out. Some fiddle-dee-dee....

"Deadline: Danger," she repeated in a parody of an announcer's doom-ridden voice.

"You in the back," Maggie Rose called. "The cute little fella with the gorgeous mustache. What's your question?"

"Mees Ruz," he began, "can you tal me wh—"

Behind her she could clearly hear chanting outside. Tottering on high heels, she turned around again to look out the window. The crowd had grown, doubled. No traffic was getting through. A star's welcome, finally.

She shifted her weight on the chair and three burly police made a grab to steady it. "Thanks, boys." She started blowing kisses to the crowd outside.

The window seemed to shiver before her face. She saw the hole open up in it, a hole the size of a dime.

That was the last thing she saw. The force of the steel-jacketed .30-caliber slug knocked her back off the chair. At the same time it opened a hole of great size as it left her skull. A sheaf of bluish-pinkish matter exploded. The slug, velocity still lethal, slammed into the RAI television camera and racked it back on its stand.

For a moment no one understood what had happened. Two of

the cops stared down in horror at her corpse, legs awry, sprawled almost headless across the floor.

Then chaos broke out. It was hard to tell—it would always be hard to tell—how much was real and how much had been choreographed. In any case, none of it mattered any more to Maggie Rose.

The sky-blue Jaguar seemed glued to the road rounding a turn at forty miles an hour. The bright morning sun came in at a slant, creating blue sparks in Faith's raven hair.

She hadn't had this much fun in years. But next was the tricky series of switchbacks that always made poor Polly sick to her stomach. She'd have to put on the brakes soon.

She'd have to downshift, brake and steer quite expertly for the next few moments. It wasn't hard, just a bit tricky.

All Brennans were good drivers. Eamon had seen to th—

Her mouth tightened in a thin line. Then she relaxed again. Too lovely a day to think of him. Anyway, she had personally taught both her children to drive well. And perhaps to do other things well too.

Polly was still a little unformed, but Mike was shaping up very nicely, thank you. So that part was fine. That part was lovely.

Here came the sharp curves. They would really test her ability. And, of course, that of the car.

In the blinding white emergency room the day man chewed his nails. He'd always done this, even as a boy. Now that he was in his forties, with fingers that sometimes shook uncontrollably, especially when he hadn't had a fix for twenty-four hours, Dr. Petracca still chewed his nails because it was a way of steadying his hands.

Now and then he glanced at the telephone, or the nurse, studiously working over her time sheets. It was not yet 9 A.M. and there had been no emergency cases to treat. He had had too much time to wonder whether the man on the telephone had been telling him the truth.

Was today actually the day? And, if so, if they'd found a way to land her in the hospital as a patient, moreover as a patient in need of medication, could he do for her as coolly as he had done for some nobody French sailor? And, even more important, would he, Petrac-ca, then be free at last from the hold they had on him?

Probably this afternoon, the doctor told himself. During the lunch hour when some of the sisters were off duty. So, the thing to do was to take a hit around, say, noon. That would steady him down a lot. That would make it as easy as doing the Froggy captain.

The great thing about coke was the way it gave you the skill and sureness to tackle anything.

He sat down at his desk and pretended to read some sheets sent him by a drug company. But then a noise began, a terrifying noise, tearing and ripping and filling the sky with anguish. Dr. Petracca and the nurse jumped to their feet and ran to the outside double doors.

They were in time to see a helicopter settling down in the clinic garden near the Barbara Hodgkins sculptures at the pool. *"Dio mio,"* moaned the nurse.

As they watched, four Gold Berets lifted the canvas stretcher from inside the copter and carried it toward the double doors. Its burden was light. Even at this distance they could see it was a woman with long, tar-black hair. Behind the Berets, Dr. Fonseca trailed, holding a bag of whole blood high overhead as it drip-fed into the woman's arm.

"Attenzione!" he shouted. *"Attenzione!"*

"La Principessa!" the nurse screamed. She broke into great, shak-ing sobs.

Dr. Petracca stood bolted to the spot, unable to move. The fin-gers of his right hand began to twitch as the men laid the stretcher carefully on his operating table.

Princess Faith's eyes opened wide. "Listen," she told Petracca, "I don't know whether I should be stitched up or spanked. Such rotten driving."

Dr. Petracca's glance went to Dr. Fonseca. "She is...?"

"Amazingly good, considering what happened to the car," Fon-seca grunted. "Just a little patching up and a lot of bed rest."

"And keep me away from cars," the Princess added wryly.

In the distance Dr. Petracca could hear sirens. A moment later the palace limo arrived with Prince Florian. "Darling!"

"Wait'll you hear what I did," the Princess told him, "before you start calling me darling. The Jag is totaled."

"But you are...?"

"Amazingly, she is okay," Fonseca said.

Florian burst into tears as he bent over her. Dr. Petracca took a step back. A little patching up and a lot of bed rest.

He glanced down at his fingers and saw them shaking, a strong tremor making them jitter like tree branches in a high wind. He raised his right hand to his face and almost, but not quite, bit his nails.

A little patching up and a lot of bed rest. An injection or two to help her rest.

Dr. Petracca thought of a small shot of coke and how he would feel very soon thereafter. He thought of his own life and how, very soon, he would be free of the shadow over him. Slowly, the hand stopped twitching.

Bed rest. Sedative injection.

In the far corner of the room, beyond where Florian had knelt by the stretcher and was kissing the Princess' hand, behind where she was smiling weakly and stroking his hair, the autoclave sat by itself, a thin wisp of steam hovering over it like a wraith.

"When I think, my dear," Florian was telling her, "what would happen to me if you... What would have happened to San Sebastian! Thank God you're safe."

Yes, Dr. Petracca promised himself. One needle for the coke and one for her air bubble. Or, perhaps, use the same syringe. Why not? In a case like this, hygiene hardly mattered.

· Epilogue ·

So far the truce has lasted six months. Geni Magari is certain they are waiting only until public opinion has gone back to sleep. Meanwhile the killings have not stopped.

There is always a momentum to these great upheavals, especially one that has taken so long to occur. But once it was decided to make no more legitimate offers for casino work, it was simply a matter of getting the Princess inside the clinic. That done, the event kept on rolling.

Geni takes dinner more often now with his parents. He bitterly regrets the depression into which his father has fallen, out of guilt and shame. He has tried to explain that the death would have happened another way, whatever his father had done, but the old man no longer listens.

After the first death, the chain of complicity has been like a list of biblical begats. The smaller fry, of course, go first.

Little Massimo Sgroi was squeezed to death during an unfortunate malfunction of one of the garage's hydraulic lifts. There was hardly anything left to bury. For his fat father, who was only following orders, time ran out when an electric clock fell into the bath with him. There was a lot to bury.

Poor Dr. Petracca went into narcotic shock following the first death. Diagnosed as a schizophrenic paranoid, he was under observation in a mental hospital when, one night, he hanged himself. The cat's-paws taken care of, one would have thought equilibrium had been reached.

But there remained those who understood what had happened, even though none of it could be proved. Scraping together evidence, Geni couldn't find enough to point to any but dead men. You don't take dead men into court. Nor can you interrogate them.

None of his suspicions, of course, has he passed along to Prince Florian. The poor man has sunk terribly low. Each day Jill and Polly place the necessary papers in front of him and he signs without reading. Mike?

Mike has fled "home" to a three-year Ph.D. program at Harvard. It isn't clear when, or if, he'll return. This has embittered the San Sebastiani, who feel rulerless. They are nasty about Polly, too, now that she is showing her pregnancy but no husband. Everything that Faith held together, they feel, is now falling apart.

Geni sits with his parents, watching the late TV news. The phone rings and he picks it up.

A subordinate with a hushed voice tells him that Arturo Giacobbe and Paolo Croce have died in a smashup at the autostrada entrance. A large double-trailer truck shoved their car over a cliff and roared on without stopping. No, no one has a license number.

As Geni pulls on his shoulder holster and jacket, he hears over the TV that the celebrated film director Billy Ritz has died of drowning in his Beverly Hills swimming pool. He was seventy-one years old.

"Where are you going?" Geni's mother asks.

They stare at each other in the half-darkened room, the TV rattling on unheard. There has always been a sort of ESP between Geni and his mother. "Out," he says.

He goes to the window to see if the night is clear or rainy. This high up above the soccer field he can see the palace, darkened in mourning, where Florian sits and, the truce being broken, where there will now come an offer he hasn't the backbone to refuse.

Beyond the palace Geni can see the harbor. A sailing ketch, black as night with indigo sails, is ghosting slowly, slowly into port.

The *Finisterre* has returned.